HEXBREAKER

Other books from Jordan L. Hawk:

Hainted

Whyborne & Griffin:
Widdershins
Threshold
Stormhaven
Necropolis
Bloodline
Hoarfrost
Maelstrom

Spirits:
Restless Spirits
Dangerous Spirits

Hexworld
The 13th Hex (prequel short story)
Hexbreaker

SPECTR
Hunter of Demons
Master of Ghouls
Reaper of Souls
Eater of Lives
Destroyer of Worlds
Summoner of Storms
Mocker of Ravens
Dancer of Death

Short stories:
Heart of the Dragon
After the Fall (in the *Allegories of the Tarot* anthology)
Eidolon (A Whyborne & Griffin short story)
Remnant, written with KJ Charles (A Whyborne & Griffin / Secret Casebook of Simon Feximal story)
Carousel (A Whyborne & Griffin short story)

HEXBREAKER

Hexworld 1

JORDAN L. HAWK

CHAPTER 1

"**BLOODY HELL, WHERE** is Isaac?" Cicero asked. "I'm freezing my arse off out here."

The clock tower atop the Coven showed half past eleven, which made Isaac half an hour late already. With just a week to go until Christmas, winter had set in with a vengeance: the wind whipped through the hair Cicero had so carefully fixed and turned the tip of his nose to ice. If it started snowing, he was giving up on Isaac and going straight back to the barracks. He was *not* getting wet for a man who couldn't be bothered to show up on time.

Even if they had been best friends, once.

"You're not the only one, cat," Rook snapped. The cold had reddened his brown cheeks, and he huddled deep into a thick woolen coat. "Why are we out here with you again?"

"Because Isaac wouldn't have come back here if it wasn't important," Cicero replied.

"So important he went to a party first?" Rook's black eyes flashed with skepticism.

"He said he needed to convince Gerald to come with him—and no, darling, I don't know why," Cicero added, before Rook could ask. "It was just a brief note."

Rook rolled his eyes. "He's probably passed out drunk."

Dominic put a soothing hand to Rook's shoulder. "Why don't you take crow form and sit on my arm? I'll hold you in front of me to block the wind."

"No," Rook grumbled, bumping Dominic affectionately with his shoulder. "I'll suffer with you."

"You mean you can't complain out loud when you're in crow form."

Rook let out a cawing laugh. "That too."

Cicero looked away from witch and familiar, feeling an unaccustomed twist of bitterness in his gut. Isaac wouldn't have suggested meeting here, outside the Metropolitan Witch Police Headquarters, without a damned good reason. Perhaps that's why Isaac was late—he had to nerve himself up to return to the scene of his most painful memory. The place where all his dreams had been wrecked.

The place where he'd smiled at Cicero, years ago—the first person to do so, when Cicero had slunk in through the brass doors, looking for haven. Fur and feathers, he'd been young. Just a scared kitten, really, arching his back at everyone who came too close. Isaac had made him feel welcome. Told him he was safe. That Cicero could stay here until his witch arrived.

Well, his witch was dragging his bloody feet. Too many years had passed, and Chief Ferguson had recently started dropping hints that Cicero had been on the dole long enough. He needed to pay back his debt, pick a witch he thought he could live with, and bond. True, their magic wouldn't be as strong as with *his* witch, the one he'd instinctively recognize when they met. But the MWP wanted to get its money's worth.

And after what had happened with Isaac's witch…

"Damn it," Cicero growled, stamping his feet in an attempt to keep them warm. Maybe Isaac couldn't face coming back here. He might have had a bit too much to drink, trying to gather up his courage, and be lying facedown in Gerald's apartment right now. While Cicero froze his whiskers off like a fool.

The clock high above chimed the quarter hour. Dominic glanced up at it and winced. "Cicero," he said carefully, "we could wait inside."

And make Isaac walk back through those doors alone? Cicero shook his head. "You go on. I'll—"

The clatter of hooves sounded on the nearly deserted street. Cicero turned expectantly, only to see an MWP police wagon instead of a cab as he'd hoped. To his surprise, the wagon pulled to a halt at the curb in front of them, rather than continue around the side to the yard. "Detective Kopecky?" called the young witch at the reins.

Dominic wasn't on duty, but that didn't stop him from trotting down the stairs. "Something I can do for you, MacDougal?"

"Aye—we need a hexman. Figured we wouldn't get one until the morning, but as you're here, sir, maybe you could take a look?" MacDougal didn't wait for an answer, just slid down from the driver's seat and made for the back of the wagon. "A suspicious death—or it might be. Fellow was having a party in his apartment. Witnesses say he took a hex with his absinthe, then lost his mind and attacked his roommate. The roommate shoved him out the window—self defense for certain, you ought to see the bite marks. Everyone swears the dead man was behaving normally until he activated the hex, so I'd be grateful if you'd take a look and make certain it wasn't tampered with."

"Of course," Dominic said. MacDougal swung open the doors to the wagon, revealing a body beneath a sheet. He reached inside and pulled out a square of paper, which he passed to Dominic.

"This is the hex," MacDougal said, but his words seemed oddly far away to Cicero. Feeling as though he were in a dream, Cicero walked to the open doors of the wagon.

A party. A dead man. And Isaac late...

His pulse thundered in his ears as he reached in and flipped back the sheet.

Not Isaac—that was his first thought, the initial rush of relief. But relief gave way to sudden dread, because he did recognize the face of the dead man, even with the bruising and blood from the fall.

"It's Gerald," he said through numb lips. "Gerald Whistler."

The other men fell silent. Then Rook let out a hiss. "What was the address?"

There came the rush of wings, Rook taking to the sky. But as Cicero lowered the sheet once again, he knew in his heart that they were already too late.

"It ain't a fair night for you to be out, Mrs. Zywicki," Tom chided the old woman hanging rather unsteadily on his arm. The sky spit snow, and the wind moaned down the street: sending the lines of wash in the alleyways flapping, blowing a steady stream of coal smoke from chimneys, and turning Tom's nose and ears to ice. He huddled deeper into his heavy blue policeman's coat, grateful for the thick wool.

Cold enough to freeze the balls off a brass monkey, as Tom's Da used to say. The other thing he used to say was to look out for those as needed you, and right now that meant a little old lady who'd had a bit much to drink. Strictly speaking though, helping drunk old ladies make their way home didn't count as walking his beat. If a roundsman caught

Tom, he'd get called in front of the captain.

Well, it wouldn't be the first time, and most likely not the last, neither. "What would you have done, if it had been O'Byrne walking the beat tonight instead of me?" he asked.

"You think I'm drunk," she grumbled.

"Never," he declared, even though her breath set his eyes to watering.

"It's only this cold is no good for my rheumatism," she said. "I took a hex for it before I went out, but it does nothing. Nothing!"

"Did you buy it from a street vendor, then?" he asked, his heart sinking a bit. Half the time, the sort of cheap hex affordable to tenement residents had never even been near a witch. Most likely the "hex" had been nothing but a pretty design on colored paper.

"Some quack," she mumbled, waving her hand dismissively. "On the corner, yes. But he knew my cousin, so I thought, why not?"

Tom glanced over his shoulder, glad the door to Mrs. Zywicki's tenement was near. Maybe if the roundsman caught him, he could claim he was gathering information about a fake hex vendor.

If he did, the captain would just tell him Mrs. Zywicki needed to make her report to the Metropolitan Witch Police instead. The ordinary police force didn't deal with magic related crimes, even if the magic was fake. Which was one of the reasons Tom had felt safe joining their number.

"Here we are," Tom said as they stopped in front of the steps leading up to the tenement where Mrs. Zywicki lived. The wind whistled around the tin cornices, an eerie sound like a distant cry of pain. "Can you make it up the stairs?"

"Yes." She blearily released his arm and patted it. "Thank you, Tom. You are a good boy. Your mother must be proud."

Tom managed to keep his expression neutral. "She's been with the Good Lord since before I left Dublin," he lied. Because he'd never set foot in Dublin, and after everything his family had done...

Well, it didn't seem likely the Good Lord had looked too kindly on any of them.

"Then I'm sure—" Mrs. Zywicki began.

A scream of agony shattered the cold air like glass. Tom's hand went to his nightstick, and he spun away from the tenement, heart pounding. Where had it come from?

Another screech, and now a second voice joined the first. Two women, shrieking as if in terror of their lives.

The shadows of the gaslit street seemed to suddenly become menacing. Tom ran across the uneven pavement, splashing through puddles of half-frozen filth. He put his tin whistle to his lips and blew stridently, but this was the middle of his beat. Would any other patrolmen even hear him?

Residents did—windows opened here and there as the curious stuck their heads out, and a man in a dirt-encrusted coat stumbled out of an alleyway, his eyes wide and worried. "Go to the precinct house and get help!" Tom ordered as he ran past.

There—the screams came from inside Barshtein's Pawn Shop, now tightly locked up for the night. Tom was certain of the lock—he'd tried the door on his first round through the neighborhood, as duty required.

He'd also felt what most couldn't perceive; the faint vibration of an active hex beneath his fingers. Barshtein used an anti-burglary hex on the doors, to keep out thieves. Tom had done his best to ignore the faint buzz through his fingertips, though, just as he always did.

Now, he seized the door and rattled it. Still locked, and the hex in place.

He pulled an unlocking hex from the bag at his waist and pressed it to the door, just above the latch. "Open!" he said—no fancy activation phrases here, not for police work.

The lock clicked, the physical parts disengaged. Tom kicked the door with all his strength, but the hex was strong, and the door remained stubbornly in its frame, held in place by magic.

The cries grew more frantic by the second. He cast about, but there was no sign of any other officers.

He had to wait for help. Or find a way in through a window—assuming Barshtein hadn't laid hexes on the glass.

Or use his talent to break the hexes.

The thought rose unbidden from the murky depths where he'd consigned the past. He couldn't. Hexbreaking was too rare a skill. If anyone found out, they'd want to know why he'd hidden it for all these years.

And what would he say? That it was evil, a curse leading to nothing but misery? That the last time he'd used it, he'd killed his own father?

One of the voices inside the pawn shop fell ominously silent.

Saint Mary, help him—he had to do something. Tom took a deep breath and laid his hand on the lock. God, it had been so long—what if he couldn't do it any more? What if he had no choice but to stand here and wait for reinforcements, while people who depended on him for protection died just a few feet above his head?

He felt the hex beneath his palm. Like a vibration, or the heartbeat of some tiny animal. Closing his eyes, Tom imagined himself laying an invisible hand on the vibration. Stilling it, the heartbeat dying away.

Nothing. No buzz against his palm now. He'd done it, as natural as breathing.

Tom sent the door slamming back against the wall. The shop was dark, the light from the street blotted out by the shades drawn for the night. The shrieks continued from above, but now they were accompanied by a rhythmic thud, as of a body hitting solid wood with great force.

He groped through the shop, striking his knee against the counter and sending over a small glass display. He knew the layout of the store—Mr. Barshtein was the sort who'd offer a copper a cup of water on a hot day, and never complain when the police came around looking for stolen goods. Tom found the door behind the counter; fortunately, this one wasn't locked, and he slipped through. A narrow beam of light showed from the top of a flight of stairs on the other side of the tiny back room.

The stairs groaned as he ran up them. "Police!" he bellowed as he flung open the door.

The smell struck him first, like wet, rusted iron. Red streaked the walls and floor of the parlor. A woman's body lay in front of the stove, unmoving and masked in blood. Tom's gorge rose at the sight of the savage bite marks on her neck, arms, and face.

A man hurled himself against one of the two doors leading from the parlor. His dressing gown was spattered with blood, his face so streaked with gore Tom barely recognized him.

"Stop!" Tom shouted. "Police!"

Barshtein ceased flinging himself against the door. Instead, he turned to face Tom, an inhuman growl rumbling from deep inside his chest. He looked utterly deranged, lips drawn back from bloody teeth, hands twisted into claws. And his eyes…

The whites had gone completely scarlet, as if every vessel in them had burst at once.

The apartment seemed to waver around Tom. The wallpaper faded, became the rough brick of a tenement. Gaslight changed to fire. His brother's teeth snapped at him, no recognition in those bloodshot eyes, while Molly screamed at him to break the hex. And all the while, innocent people burned, their cries like something from the very pits of hell.

Tom swung his nightstick with an inarticulate shout. The heavy locust wood smashed into Barshtein's raised arm. Bone cracked beneath the blow, but Barshtein didn't so much as flinch. Instead, he lunged at Tom. His good hand scrabbled at Tom's throat, as if he meant to throttle him.

This time the nightstick connected with Barshtein's skull. The bloody red eyes rolled back into his head, and he collapsed at Tom's feet.

Tom stood above the unconscious body, chest heaving. This wasn't September 15, 1889; it was December 18, 1897. He was Tom Halloran, not Liam O'Connell.

This wasn't happening. It couldn't be.

Not again.

CHAPTER 2

"SIR?" TOM ASKED from the doorway to the captain's office. "Can I have a minute of your time?"

Captain Donohue leaned back in his chair, puffing on a post-luncheon cigar. Smoke drifted around the small office, curling beneath the green-shaded light on Donohue's desk. "Halloran," he said with an uncharacteristic smile. "What is it you're wanting?"

The smile sent a little shiver of unease through Tom. Ordinarily, he wasn't a favorite of the captain—no surprise there. If a copper didn't take bribes from folks just trying to get by and live their lives, how was the captain to get his due share?

"I just wanted to ask about Mr. Barshtein." He'd wanted to come by the day after the murder, but by bad luck it had been scheduled as his off day. It would have seemed suspicious if he'd come in just to ask about a closed case. "The fellow I arrested the other night."

"All over the papers the last two days," Donohue said with a satisfied grin. "*Lunatic murders wife; innocent maid saved by alert patrolman.* Good work, Halloran. You'll get another medal for this."

Tom managed a faint smile of his own, although inside he felt sick. He didn't deserve a medal. Sure, he'd saved one innocent, but it didn't make up for all the blood on his hands. Especially not if there was some connection...

There couldn't be. The night after the riots, he'd burned the spent hexes, so no one could copy them and make more. Everyone else who'd known about them had died amidst fire and blood.

It had been eight years. And yet, the way Barshtein had acted, as though he felt no pain, felt *nothing* beyond the desire to kill, had taken Tom right back to the night of the so-called Cherry Street Riots in lower Manhattan. Barshtein's eyes had been red, just like Da's, and Danny's and the rest who'd taken those accursed hexes.

Donohue looked at him expectantly. Tom forced his smile wider. "Thank you, sir. I didn't do it for a medal, though."

"Lucky for the maid Barshtein forgot to activate the anti-burglary hex, eh?" Donohue shook his head. "You wouldn't have gotten through in time, otherwise."

Tom's smile grew even more strained. "The Lord works in mysterious ways."

"Aye, that's the truth." Donohue looked up at him. "Anything else, Halloran?"

He ought to leave it alone. Walk away and forget what he'd seen. There couldn't be a connection, not after so long. "I just wanted to ask… what happened? Why did Mr. Barshtein kill his wife and try to kill their maid? The newspapers didn't really say."

"Why? Because he's a madman." Donohue shrugged. "When he woke up, he started trying to attack anyone he laid eyes on. Not speaking a word, mind you, not even when we put him in restraints. I sent him over to the lunatic asylum. Let them deal with him."

Tom bit his lip. If he asked anything more, it might seem suspicious. Donohue obviously considered the case closed. "I was just wondering if the maid said anything had set him off. Like if Barshtein took a hex, for instance."

Donohue frowned. "There was something about an absinthe hex."

"An absinthe hex?" Tom asked blankly.

"Some sort of frippery those bohemian types enjoy," Donohue said with a dismissive wave of his cigar. "They take it with the drink. Makes them hallucinate or some such."

Tom's spirits lifted slightly. Hallucinations sounded bad, but not the same sort of bad as the Cherry Street Riots. "So the hex made him hallucinate, and that's why he attacked his wife?"

But Donohue was shaking his head. "Nothing like that. The absinthe hexes inspire bad poetry, maybe, but that's about it. The MWP sent a hexman around to take a look, and he said there was nothing wrong with it." Donohue frowned. "Why? Barshtein say anything to you before you knocked him out?"

"Nay. Nothing." But he couldn't stop seeing those bloody eyes. Barshtein's face had haunted Tom's dreams, turning alternately into the faces of his brother and father. Accompanied by the shrieks of those in the burning tenement, the thumps as the desperate leapt to their deaths.

"It's just...I have a feeling," Tom said. "Call it copper's instinct. Something ain't right. My gut says there's more to this than just a man losing his wits for no reason."

Donohue stubbed out his cigar and fixed Tom with a speculative look. "You think the MWP's hexman made a mistake?"

Did he? "I don't know. But the way Barshtein acted...I've been a patrolman for eight years. I've seen men so drunk they didn't remember their own names, and I've hauled many a man to Blackwell's Island. But none of them behaved the way he did. The way he didn't cry out when I broke his arm with the nightstick. It weren't natural."

Donohue folded his hands across his belly and regarded Tom for a long moment. Tom tried to return his stare, hoping the captain didn't perceive all the things he'd left out. All the things he hid.

"I wouldn't mind taking those MWP bastards down another notch," Donohue mused. "The lot of them should have been thrown in jail after their former chief tried to kill Commissioner Roosevelt, if you ask me. Bunch of prancing fops." He contemplated Tom for a long moment. "That's it, then. Go down there and light a fire under them."

Donohue surely didn't mean to send him to the Coven, did he? "Sir?"

"What's your duty assignment today, Halloran?"

"I'm on reserve."

"Well, tonight you get to sleep in your own bed. Tell the sergeant I'm reassigning you to the day shift. Take yourself over to the Coven and make them listen."

Tom felt as though the floor had tilted, leaving him off kilter. Why hadn't he anticipated this? "MWP Headquarters? Now?"

"Have you got mud in your ears? Yes, patrolman, now!"

Tom scurried out. The sergeant only grunted when Tom informed him of the altered duty assignment. Within minutes, Tom found himself mounting the steps to the Second Avenue El platform.

It was all happening too fast. Since becoming Tom Halloran, he hadn't set foot south of 42nd Street. Too much risk of someone from the old days recognizing him.

And now he was not only returning to lower Manhattan, but marching straight to MWP headquarters, where a photo of his younger self lay buried in their rogues gallery.

It had been eight years. After eight years, surely no one would recognize him, assuming anyone who might was even still alive, or still in Manhattan. No one would have any cause to connect twenty-six year old Tom Halloran, veteran patrolman, with seventeen-year-old Liam O'Connell, East River tunnel rat.

The train pulled up with a clatter, and Tom stepped on. Noting his uniform, the conductor didn't ask for payment. Tom took a seat and stared out over the city as the train jerked back into motion. Smoke streamed from chimneys in the cold air, forming a haze against the otherwise clear sky. Advertisements flashed on distant buildings, taking advantage of the new hexes which allowed the words to change depending on who was looking at them.

He'd go to the Coven, give his report, and leave. That would satisfy the captain. Donohue didn't really think Tom would get results. He just wanted to irritate the MWP and remind them they weren't the only police in the city, and sending his least-favorite patrolman was the easiest way to do it.

Tom wouldn't spend any more time there than he had to. Unless there really was some link between that long-ago night and Barshtein's sudden homicidal madness...

Probably Tom was overreacting about the whole thing. There was no need to get all riled up. The past would stay where it belonged, quiet as the bones of the dead. He'd go back to pretending he was a good man, a good copper, and not a criminal who should have ended up swinging from the gallows.

"Listen," Rook said, "I know you're upset Gerald is dead. So am I. But people get into fights. They drink too much, do stupid things, and that's just how it is."

"Gerald Whistler fainted at the sight of blood," Cicero shot back. "And you expect me to believe he bit off his roommate's ear before going for the throat? That's featherbrained even for you, crow."

They strode through the halls of the Coven—or rather, Cicero strode, and Rook tagged along behind him. Flapping and squawking as usual, even if he *was* in human form.

The halls of the Metropolitan Witch Police's headquarters were seldom quiet, but with the upcoming merger of the New York and Brooklyn forces, today they bordered on bedlam. Some idiot—probably the ones on the Police Board—had decided the Brooklyn headquarters would be shuttered, and everyone moved into the Coven, no matter the place barely had enough space to begin with. Cicero dodged between two witches carrying boxes, wove through a group of unbonded familiars snarling at each other, and ducked as an owl passed overhead. Being a crow instead of a cat, Rook had more trouble getting through tight spaces, and Cicero had almost a minute of blessed silence before Rook caught back up with him.

"Someone murdered him," Cicero said, before Rook could start up again. "Using magic."

"Would you hold up?" Rook grabbed him by the shoulder. A lock of dark hair flopped over one eye. In a city of Irish, Germans, Italians, Indians, Turks, blacks, Chinese, and Jews, it was impossible to say exactly what blend had given rise to Rook's creamy brown skin and shining dark hair. Rook claimed not to know himself. "There's no evidence magic was involved. None!"

"The hex—"

"Dominic looked over the absinthe hex," Rook interrupted. "It was an unfamiliar brand, but nothing was wrong with it. Not to mention everyone else at the party used the same hex, and none of them became violent."

"And Isaac? He missed our meeting, he's not in any of his usual haunts, and none of the other ferals have seen him since Saturday."

That took the wind out of Rook, at least. "I talked to the roommate myself. Isaac never showed up at the party."

"And you're not worried?"

"Of course I am!" Rook's fingers tightened on Cicero's shoulder. "It's never good when an unbonded familiar suddenly vanishes off the face of the earth. Maybe he was on his way to the party and saw Gerald fall. It spooked him, and he ran."

"Ran where? Besides, he was already late to meet me. He wouldn't have been just arriving at the party when Gerald died."

"Then maybe it's a coincidence." Rook shook his head. "Magic wasn't involved, Cicero. Which means it's a case for the regular police. Ferguson already told Dominic and I to go back to the investigations we were working on before. I know you feel responsible for Isaac, but—"

Cicero jerked away. "You don't know anything." Twitching his coat back into place, he turned his back on Rook. Curse the crow for not listening to him. For not *believing*.

For reminding Cicero that, after everything Isaac had done for him, it was his fault Isaac hadn't been safely within the walls of the MWP.

"Well, Ferguson must have changed his mind," he shot back over his shoulder. "Otherwise, why would he call me to his office to meet about it?"

Rook didn't reply and didn't try to follow. Cicero slithered around a final group of detectives and found himself outside Chief Ferguson's door.

He paused, hand half-lifted to open it. Was his coat in place? Hair perfect?

Pushing open the door, Cicero turned his most charming smile on the room. "Ciao, darlings," he drawled. "I..."

His voice caught in his throat. Ferguson was there, as expected, and Athene perched in owl form beside his desk. But there was someone else, not expected.

He found himself blinking at a human wall of blue uniform, the fabric strained tight around the chest at eye level. He took a step back and looked up.

Judging by his freckles and milky skin, the newcomer was Irish. An old break, no doubt the souvenir from some sordid fight, had left a slight crook in the man's nose. His dark blond hair appeared to have been cut by a blind drunken barber. The heavy boots on his large feet needed polishing, and dirt showed underneath ragged fingernails.

And the world stilled, settled around a single point. A deep instinct set into Cicero's bones, something stupid and blind that didn't care about anything but the flow of magic. That didn't give a damn about the fear suddenly choking his throat.

Because this man—this *ogre*—was his witch.

CHAPTER 3

TOM DIDN'T MEAN to stare, but he couldn't help it. Of course, he'd been staring nonstop since he'd entered the Coven and asked to speak to someone about a dead man and a bad hex. The witch detectives, the familiars popping in and out of animal form, the cacophony of human voices, barks, meows, and caws, was enough to make his head spin.

Not to mention the women. Unlike the regular police force, the Witch Police took anyone with magic and a familiar. He vaguely recalled it had been a point of contention between them and the Police Board headed by Roosevelt, with the commissioner determined to impose requirements of height and strength that would have removed most of the females immediately. The MWP must have won that particular battle —maybe the board had been afraid they'd resort to attempted murder again.

But this newcomer made Tom stare for a different reason altogether. He had olive skin and black hair, carefully oiled and brushed until not a single strand was out of place. Kohl outlined yellow-green eyes, making their brilliant color even more startling. His lips were plump and red, as if asking to be kissed, and the thought sent a curl of desire through Tom's groin.

Judging by the somewhat feminine cut of his coat, wide at the shoulders and tight at the waist, the fellow might not even mind Tom thinking about him that way. His nails were neat, and Tom couldn't help but note how *clean* and orderly he was, like he'd just stepped out of a bath. The idea of that flawless skin glistening with a sheen of water turned that faint ember of desire into a flame.

The man stared back at Tom for a long moment, eyes going wide, lips parting slightly. Then, without warning, his expression closed, like shutters thrown across a window.

"No," he said. Though he looked Italian, his accent sounded mainly English to Tom's untrained ear. Turning his back to Tom, he folded his arms across his chest and stared resolutely at the wall. "No. Absolutely not. I refuse."

Ferguson sighed and rubbed at his temples. The Witch Police Chief seemed harried—and no wonder, with all the people turning into animals and magic and whatnot going on around him. "Cicero…"

"No!" The man—Cicero—shot a quick glance at Tom over his shoulder, then turned immediately back to the wall. "You can't make me."

"Make you what?" Tom asked. Was everyone here barmy?

Cicero didn't reply, merely stared loftily at the wall, as though the rest of them were beneath his notice. If Tom offered that sort of attitude to his captain, let alone the regular police chief, he'd get a sore lip and a quick discharge for his trouble. But Ferguson only appeared vexed.

"Cicero here is an unbonded familiar," he said. "A cat, in case you couldn't guess from the attitude."

"Oi!"

"He feels a man who went insane and tried to kill his roommate was driven by magic rather than madness," Ferguson went on, ignoring the familiar's outraged objection. "Even though there's no evidence. But the event occurred after the fellow ingested an absinthe hex, and his eyes were bloody."

Saint Mary preserve him. "Just like Mr. Barshtein," Tom said.

Cicero half turned. "Wait…who?"

"The man who murdered his wife the other night," Tom said, and waited for comprehension to dawn in Cicero's eyes. It didn't. "You know…the crime on the front page of all the papers two days running?"

"I don't read the newspapers," Cicero said with a sniff. "Terrible for the skin. Wrinkles, darling."

"I…" Tom couldn't think how to respond, so he turned his attention to Ferguson instead. "Good. Then I'll just have someone send over a report and let you, er, gentlemen, get to work." The MWP would figure things out without his help, surely. He could keep his head down and go back to his life, and the past would stay where it belonged.

"Unfortunately, it isn't that simple." Ferguson folded his hands on his desk, gaze going from Tom to Cicero. "We've delved thoroughly into the case. Gerald Whistler went mad at a party, where everyone else took the exact same hex as he did. None of them suffered anything beyond the usual effects of too much alcohol. Our own hexmen thoroughly studied Whistler's hex to make certain it hadn't been altered. It wasn't. There's no evidence of magical interference, so technically there's no reason for the MWP to become involved. And since it seems obvious the roommate acted in self defense, our counterparts at the regular police have decided the death is exactly what it seems—the result of too much drink."

Cicero stiffened. "Isaac—"

"However," Ferguson overrode Cicero's protest, "a second, similar case in a different precinct gives me a bit of leeway. Not enough to launch a full investigation with a team of detectives, particularly since the upcoming merger with the Brooklyn Witch Police has the place in shambles. But enough to poke around a bit. So, assuming I can secure your captain's permission, Halloran, I'd take it as a favor if you and Cicero could collaborate. See what, if anything, you can turn up."

Cicero's hiss was eclipsed by Tom's own indrawn breath. He'd only come here so his conscience could rest easy. He needed to stay as far away from any investigation as possible—not end up involved in it himself. Certainly not with an MWP familiar looking over his shoulder.

But he couldn't say any of that, so he spit out the first objection that sprang to mind. "I ain't a witch."

Ferguson tapped one of the piles of paper on his desk. "True. I had your precinct run over your file, while you were waiting outside. Your scores were abysmal."

No wonder he'd had Tom cool his heels in the hall so long, if he'd sent someone to fetch Tom's file. The scores in it were fake, of course— or rather, they'd belonged to another man, who'd died in an alley not long after stepping off the boat from Dublin. In truth, Tom had never been officially tested by anyone.

But Da always said the O'Connells were known for their witchery, and his own brother had been one. Maybe he would have been too, if life had gone differently.

"That's not possible." Cicero marched to the desk and snatched up the file. Tom held his breath, expecting Ferguson to explode at the impertinence, but the chief only looked mildly amused. Cicero frowned at what he read, then shook his head. "It doesn't matter. Isaac's *life* is at stake."

"Who is Isaac?" Tom asked, even more bewildered than before.

Cicero ignored him. "I need someone with subtlety, with…elegance. Someone who thinks before he acts. Not a patrolman who will just beat a confession out of the first idiot we come across!"

"Hey now." What the devil was wrong with the fellow? Tom might not be the smartest man in New York, but he certainly didn't appreciate being called stupid by a painted-up nancy he'd barely exchanged words with. "I ain't never beat a confession out of anyone in my life, boyo."

Everyone ignored him. Ferguson scowled at Cicero. "Either work with Halloran, or let it go."

"I can do it myself," Cicero shot back.

The owl on the perch behind Ferguson's desk abruptly launched itself into the air. Tom started, but it only glided to the floor—and, in a puff of smoke, turned into a woman dressed in a sensible shirtwaist and divided skirts. She was as golden as the owl, her hair tawny and her eyes a pale brown that bordered on yellow.

"Stop being an idiot, Cicero," she snapped. "You're a familiar of the MWP. We aren't letting you wander off alone to get killed."

Cicero drew himself up, his eyes going to green ice. "Oh, but it's all right if other familiars get killed? Is that it, Athene?"

"Isaac knew the risks when he walked away," Athene said, at the same time Ferguson snapped, "Damn it, Cicero." They exchanged a glance, and Athene went on. "There's no reason to think magic was involved in Whistler's death, and even less to think his sudden attack of mania had anything to do with Isaac at all. Even with what Halloran brought, we'll be on thin ice with the Police Board by sanctioning you to look further into things. So either take our offer or leave it. Either way, we're done here."

Cicero seemed to hesitate for a long moment. He still held Tom's file in his hands, and his long, clean fingers crushed the edges of the paper. "I have to think," he said, shooting a glare at Tom now. "And I can't do it with him *looming* at me."

"What did I do to you?" Tom exclaimed. Cicero ignored him, sweeping past and out the door.

Silence settled briefly over the office, punctured by a series of loud barks from elsewhere in the building. Ferguson sighed and rubbed at his eyes. "Well. My apologies, Halloran. Honestly, I thought Cicero would be eager to help. I don't know what's gotten into him."

"He's a cat," Athene said succinctly. There came a puff of smoke, and she returned to her perch.

Ferguson sat back in his chair. "I know we don't do things the way you're used to," he said, which was a hell of an understatement. "Why don't you take the rest of the day and think it over? Decide if you want to pursue this." He stared broodily at the doorway through which Cicero had vanished. "And believe me, no one here would blame you if you didn't."

Cicero stepped through the door of Techne and took a deep breath. The familiar mélange of absinthe, cigarettes, and coffee filled his lungs and eased the bands that seemed to have constricted his chest ever since he'd stepped into Ferguson's office.

Not to say the café's air was a peaceful one. Customers crowded around tables beneath a painting of the Seven Arts: proclaiming poetry, expounding on philosophy, and arguing politics. Languid young men lounged in chairs sipping absinthe, while artists whose shabby coats bore flecks of paint sketched the faces around them. A group of women worked feverishly on a poster advocating free love and the abolition of marriage.

Thinkers and poets and dancers. His people. And all of them as far away from some Irish ogre with a crooked nose as was humanly possible.

God. Just thinking about the man—Halloran—brought the sting of bile to the back of Cicero's throat. Isaac was out there somewhere, lost in the teeming city, and *this* was the help Ferguson gave? Someone who would use his fists before his brains, assuming he even had any?

Who might use his fists against Cicero, given enough drink. Just like his father and too many of the men who'd followed in his wake. Before the MWP; before Isaac's gentle patience convinced him he didn't have to jump at every shadow.

"Cicero!" called Leona. As usual, she was dressed in a man's suit, her hair tucked up beneath a trilby hat. "Come help us with our signs. We're taking them to the consolidation celebration with us."

On January 1st, New York, Brooklyn, Queens, Staten Island, and the East Bronx would merge into a single, behemoth Greater New York City. Needless to say the New Year's Eve celebration at city hall had been the only topic of conversation for weeks. Cicero found himself unable to summon up any enthusiasm, given the circumstances.

He flicked a hand in Leona's direction. "Not today, darling," he said, keeping his tone light. "My head can't take the arguments at the moment."

"Looking for a bit of hair of the dog, then?" she teased.

He hissed theatrically, although the term made him think of Isaac's mastiff form. Cicero dropped into a chair at the last empty table and waved at Noah, Techne's owner. "Coffee, extra cream, darling," he called.

The coffee appeared with alacrity, just the shade of near-ivory he liked. "I'm glad to see you," Noah said, brushing his hand lightly across the back of Cicero's neck. "I'm busy with this crowd now, but if you'd like to come back after closing…?"

"I'm not sure I'll be in the mood," Cicero admitted. At Noah's questioning look, he said, "Trouble with the MWP. You know how it goes."

Noah didn't, of course, at least not directly. He had witch potential, but—like most of the bohemian crowd—talked endlessly about how magic was an art and shouldn't be degraded by capitalism, and definitely shouldn't be used in service of the police.

Easy for him to say, when he didn't have to worry about being kidnapped off the street and forced to bond.

Still, he was sympathetic, at least. "You deserve better," he told Cicero, squeezing his shoulder. "Just as Isaac did."

Isaac. Cicero couldn't go a minute without being reminded of his failure today, it seemed.

Noah gave him a last pat on the arm and went to attend to the other customers. Relieved to be left alone, Cicero took a sip of his coffee and closed his eyes. He breathed in the scent of hot cream and let the murmur of conversation wash over him like a breeze on a hot day.

"I don't see why you bother having Noah put any coffee in it at all."

Cicero's eyes snapped open, and he glared at the man who had rather presumptuously taken the seat across from him. Of course, Rook was never anything *but* presumptuous. "I don't criticize how you take your coffee, crow."

"Yes, you do." Rook settled back in the chair as if he meant to stay there all day.

Cicero tried not to argue with the truth, unless it was convenient for him to do so, so instead he asked, "Where's Dominic?" Rook and Dominic had been inseparable since bonding two years ago; it was almost strange to see one without the other.

Noah brought Rook a steaming cup of coffee and left again. Rook pushed it to one side and leaned over the table, his black eyes fixed intently on Cicero. "You've been frantic over Isaac, but the moment Ferguson gives you official permission to investigate, you take off like your tail is on fire. I was worried, so I told Dominic to wait at the Coven and flew after you. What's going on?"

Cicero tried to ignore the twist of dread in his stomach. He couldn't do this—couldn't say it out loud. Saying things out loud made them true. "Keep your beak out of it."

"The hell I will." Rook frowned. "Talk to me, Cicero. I know you. Something's wrong, and I mean besides Isaac's disappearance."

Maybe he could put Rook off with some of the truth. "It's the 'help'—and I use the term loosely—Ferguson chose for me." Cicero prodded the file he'd dropped on the table. "Thomas Halloran." He tried to spit out the name, but it flowed a little too well on his tongue.

"What's wrong with him?" Rook asked.

"What isn't?" Cicero ticked off the points on his fingers. "He's a patrolman—no experience in investigation at all. He's...he's rough. Uncultured. Says 'ain't.' His file claims he's as normal as they come, no witch potential at all."

Rook's black brows swooped low over his eyes. "So? Who cares?"

"I do." Cicero swallowed hard, but there was nothing for it. Rook would keep at him until he confessed. "Whatever bloody tests they use in Dublin scored him completely wrong."

"They aren't always accurate." Rook folded his hands in front of him. "So how do you know they're wrong in this case?"

"Because he's my...my witch."

"Your...oh." Rook trailed off uncertainly. "That's...that's good though, isn't it? I know Ferguson was badgering you to choose, so he must be happy about it."

"I didn't *tell* him!" Cicero exclaimed. "And you can't either. This is a disaster!"

Rook reached across the table and put his hand on Cicero's. "Calm down and explain why."

Rook's fingers were warm and firm, his touch kind. Cicero's eyes ached, and he blinked rapidly. "This isn't what I want," he said past a constriction in his throat. "I always thought my witch would be...you know." He gestured vaguely to their surroundings with his free hand. "Artistic. Clever. Bohemian. We'd sip coffee and quote poetry. Argue about art and beauty. Instead he's..." Cicero let his hand fall. "Not like that at all."

God only knew what the ogre had thought of Cicero's clothes, his kohl-lined eyes. Not that Cicero couldn't guess easily enough. Back before the MWP, he'd met up with plenty of men who thought a fist in the face was the only way deal with a fairy. His mother had certainly favored the type, after *papà* died. A string of big, rough brutes who proved their manhood with crude insults and quick blows.

He wasn't going to bond with that sort. No matter what his stupid magic thought about the matter.

Rook let go of Cicero's hand and pulled the file to his side of the table. "At least give Halloran a chance before you decide there's no hope." He studied the papers inside. "Look—he has two medals for saving people from drowning in the East River!"

"Oh good, a witch who can swim," Cicero muttered. "Just what every cat familiar dreams of."

"There aren't any complaints against him," Rook went on.

"Probably the people on his beat are too frightened to speak out."

"His address isn't very good," Rook said. "Not terrible, but you'd expect a copper working that part of town to do better for himself. There must be plenty of opportunity for bribes." His dark eyes flicked up from the file. "Maybe he's honest?"

Cicero crossed his legs and arms. "Why are you determined to find something good about him?"

"I'm just trying to get you to think instead of react." Rook sat back. "Yes, you have to pick a witch soon. But no one is going to force you to bond with Halloran if you don't want to. If Ferguson tried, every familiar in the MWP, including our new friends from Brooklyn, would riot. So there's no reason for you not to at least talk to Halloran about it."

Cicero shot upright. "Fur and feathers, no!"

Rook gaped at him. "What? You were the one who thought I was an idiot for not telling Dominic he was my witch the moment I met him!"

"Well, you were," Cicero replied with a sniff. "But that was different." He let his hands fall to his lap. "Besides, look how well my advice worked out for Isaac."

Rook winced. "You aren't to blame."

"Aren't I?" Cicero shook his head, feeling suddenly tired. Most afternoons, he'd be curled up in the sun right now, napping with the other MWP cats. "You and Dominic were so happy. I thought…well. I was like a stupid child, believing in fairytales. What could go wrong?"

Just everything. Isaac hadn't been entirely certain, but Cicero had pushed him. Told him to be honest. Made him think he'd end up like Rook and Dominic, that he'd find not just a witch but the love of his life.

Isaac had believed him. Gone to his witch. And come back bleeding and bruised, sobbing out his story while Cicero listened in horror. His witch had beaten him, all the while screaming he wouldn't bond with a cocksucking Yid...

He was supposed to have been safe in the MWP's walls. They were all supposed to be safe.

Halloran was built like a brick wall, with fists to match. And he worked for the non-magical police, who everyone knew were just a bunch of corrupt thugs. Cicero didn't want to end up in the hospital like Isaac had.

"You can't tell anyone," Cicero said, leaning across the table and seizing Rook's wrist. "Not even Dominic. Promise me!"

Rook's full lips tightened, but he nodded. "All right. But in turn, you promise you'll at least talk to Halloran?"

It wouldn't change Cicero's mind, but it wasn't as if he had a choice in the matter. "An easy promise to keep, since Ferguson won't let me investigate otherwise," he said, draining his coffee.

His feelings were beside the point. Isaac had been his best friend all the years they were at the MWP together. As Rook had inadvertently reminded him, it was his fault Isaac had gone feral. His fault Isaac had spent the last year working in questionable resorts and dive bars, instead of safe in the MWP barracks.

Cicero could work with Halloran for a few days, if it meant justice for poor Gerald. If it meant some chance to save Isaac. He'd grit his teeth, get through it, then let Halloran go his separate way. With any luck, he'd never set eyes on the man again.

CHAPTER 4

TOM SAT IN the corner of the saloon across the street from his apartment, sipping a five cent beer. Men crowded the long bar, and the clack of billiards sounded from the pool tables near the back. Children rushing the growler for their parents entered with empty pails and left with them full of beer. A few women drifted through, chatting and laughing with the regulars.

He knew them all. This wasn't just his beat, it was his neighborhood. Even after he took the uniform off at the end of the day, they were still his responsibility.

"Look out for those as need you."

Family, Da had meant when he said that. And family included the rest of the gang, even if they weren't blood.

"But what about me?" Tom wanted to shout back through the years. He couldn't afford to get any further involved in Barshtein's death. If there was a connection to that night eight years ago, then the deeper he delved, the more likely he was to find his own secrets exposed. What good would spending the rest of his life in prison do anyone?

Besides, there was probably no link beyond his own paranoia. How could there be? He'd burned the filthy hexes to make sure what happened on Cherry Street could never happen again.

It had been the least he could do, given it was his cursed hexbreaking that had gotten them into the situation to begin with. Some fancy collector from Fifth Avenue had hired the Muskrat gang to steal an old book from some other rich fellow. But the vault it was kept in was sealed with magic as well as locks, and for that they needed a hexbreaker. The Muskrats knew about Tom's—then Liam's—talent, so they'd approached Da, looking for an alliance.

The job had gone perfectly. The hex had been the strongest Tom had ever broken, but he'd managed it. Da had been so proud.

And so greedy.

They should have just handed the book over. Let the Muskrats give it to the collector, taken their share of the profits, and walked away.

But Tom had touched the book, and with his hexbreaker talent sensed the hexes hidden inside the binding. Da had reasoned they must be valuable to be concealed like that.

So he'd looked out for those as needed him, by betraying the Muskrats and stealing the book. Molly had learned some Latin from her time in the convent, and claimed it was some kind of medieval psalter. The hexes were hidden beneath the ancient leather of the cover, the symbols on them drawn in rusty brown ink and looking like nothing modern. Molly thought maybe the monk who'd copied the psalter in the first place had been the one to hide them, because there was a note with the hexes whose writing looked the same as that in the rest of the book. She'd parsed it as best she could—something about being the most terrifying warriors the world had ever known.

Which had sounded damned good to Da. Why not use the hexes to rule the waterfront and reap the profits?

He'd paid for his ambition with his life. And Danny's, and Ma's, and Molly's. And the lives of a tenement full of folk who'd had nothing to do with any of it.

Liam died that night, too, in a way. Family gone, home gone, death and blood on his hands. He'd been nothing but a ghost. Until the night Saint Mary led him to a cold alley not far from Castle Garden and gave Tom Halloran a second chance at life.

The absinthe hex Barshtein took was nothing like the ones they'd found in the book. Those had been made with sharp-edged runes and the images of tangled beasts, knotted together in combat. No one could confuse the two. So, no matter how similar the symptoms, there couldn't be any direct link.

There was no reason for him to go back to the MWP tomorrow. It would be madness to do so. If anyone found out he'd once been Liam O'Connell, he'd spend the rest of his life doing hard time at Sing Sing.

The familiar—Cicero—would probably refuse to work with him

anyway. What the man had against Tom, he'd no idea. Was it because Tom was Irish? Cicero looked Italian, but his accent was English, and Saint Mary knew there was no love lost between them and the Irish. Still, thanks to Tammany Hall, anyone who worked on either police force would be surrounded by Irishmen. And women, given what he'd seen in the MWP.

Cicero might try to investigate on his own, despite Ferguson's objections. Tom snorted at the idea of the fop trying to question a witness, or chase down a suspect. Pity the witch detective who got stuck with a useless creature like him, too flighty even to read the newspapers.

Of course, if Cicero did try to pursue the case alone, he might attract the wrong kind of attention, what with his pretty face and perfect hair, and eyes that glowed like peridots. Ferguson had been right to insist he have some sort of protection. The fellow would probably faint dead away the first time someone raised their voice to him.

Most likely he'd get discouraged and quit within a day. But if he didn't?

"Tom?"

Tom blinked, half surprised to find himself still seated in the saloon, with an empty mug at his elbow. Bill Quigley, wearing his blue uniform, slipped onto the bench across from him.

"Better look out, Bill," Tom said with a nod. "If the roundsman catches you in here, it'll be hell to pay."

"Ah, hang the bastard," Bill said. His nose was red from the cold, and he stripped off his gloves to blow on his fingers. "It's too cold to walk these streets without something to warm the belly, eh?"

"If you say so," Tom said, amused despite himself.

"Oh, aye, I forgot who I was talking to. Saint Tom himself." Bill winked. "And here having a drink with the rest of us mortals."

"Shut your hole," Tom said, but he grinned when he said it. Bill was an all right sort. The closest thing Tom could claim to a friend, really.

The barkeep brought Bill a whiskey. He downed it, made a face, and handed back the glass. "In fact, it's your fault I'm in here," Bill said when the barkeep left. "I figured you hadn't yet heard the news about Barshtein."

"Did he recover his senses?" Tom asked. Maybe the doctors on Blackwell's had been able to help after all.

"Nay." Bill's expression sobered. "He's dead, Tom. His heart gave out, they say."

Tom sat back. "Oh."

"Saves the expense of a trial, anyway." Bill rose to his feet and clapped him on the shoulder. "I'm off before the roundsman comes by —and if I get in any trouble, I'm blaming it on you. Have a drink for me, eh?"

"Sure thing, Bill," Tom murmured.

Dead. Just like Da and Danny. Just like the people screaming as they burned in the tenement fire.

Barshtein had always had a friendly word for Tom, the offer of a cold drink in the summer and a hot one in the winter, whenever Tom had the day beat. And now he was dead. Branded a murderer by the world.

If there was truly a thread binding Barshtein's death with that night on Cherry Street, Barshtein and his wife wouldn't be the last victims. They'd only be the first.

And if Cicero sauntered into the middle of it, alone and unprotected, it wouldn't matter how pretty his eyes were.

"To hell with it," Tom muttered. "I guess I'm in this whether I like it or not."

Tom swallowed back his nervousness as he walked up the marble steps to the Coven. He'd slept poorly, before making his way to the precinct first thing, to inform Captain Donohue of his temporary new duties. Donohue hadn't seemed particularly sorry to see him go.

Now all Tom had to do was convince Cicero to work with him. He rehearsed his arguments as he walked. One: Cicero might know the particulars of Whistler's death, but Tom knew about Barshtein's, and it only made sense to share the information. Two: he'd be better at intimidating anyone who needed a bit of encouragement to tell the truth. Three—

A dark shape swooped in from above. Tom ducked instinctively, as, at the last moment, the crow transformed into a handsome man and landed on the step beside him.

"Sorry about that," said the familiar. His grin gave the lie to the apology, teeth bright in his brown face. Shining black hair framed features whose blending defied Tom to name all the races involved, other than to say the fellow's ancestors hadn't been ones to stick to their own.

"Er, it's fine," Tom said, telling his heart to settle back into its place. Molly spooked him the same way a time or two, back in the day, and laughed herself silly after.

The man held out his hand. "Rook," he said. "Familiar to Detective Dominic Kopecky. I expect you'll meet later."

"Tom Halloran," Tom said automatically as they shook. "I…why do you think that?"

"Because I know why you're here," Rook said. "Speaking of which, you don't want to keep Ferguson waiting." He started off, and somehow Tom found himself scrambling to keep up. "How long have you been a patrolman, Mr. Halloran?"

"Eight years," Tom said automatically.

"And where are you from?"

"Dublin," Tom lied. Wasn't all this in his file? Who *was* this familiar, anyway?

Ah hell. Had something given him away already? Did they suspect he'd been lying from the start? Had someone recognized him, or thought they did, and dug back through the rogues gallery until they found a decade-old photograph?

Should he run, and hope he managed to get out of New York before they locked him away for life?

"Not as much of an accent as I'd expect," Rook remarked.

Tom's heart beat in his throat. "I've been here long enough to lose some of it." He glanced around, but didn't see anyone who seemed like they were closing in to make the arrest while Rook distracted him.

"You Irish are fond of dogs, aren't you?" Rook cocked his head to one side. "Or do you consider yourself more inclined to cats?"

Wait. Maybe this didn't have anything to do with him after all. "Is this about Cicero?"

"Nooo," Rook said, suddenly looking elsewhere. "Nope. No."

That settled it. Everyone in the MWP, familiars and witches alike, were completely off their nut. Did magic drive a man mad, just by its use? Or did they start out that way?

When they reached Ferguson's door, Tom knocked hastily and was relieved when the chief yelled at him to come in. He was less relieved when Rook followed him inside.

As soon as he stepped in, Tom found his gaze drawn to Cicero, who sat in a chair against one wall. Something about the familiar filled the room, made everyone else in it seem oddly pale in comparison. Dark rings showed beneath his yellow-green eyes, as though he hadn't slept well, but his hair was as perfectly in place as before. His coat was a variation on the style he'd worn the day before, its hue a shocking shade of red. He sat neatly, one leg crossed over the other, his manicured hands folded on his knee. When Tom entered, he glanced up—then frowned and shifted his attention to glare at Rook.

Well, at least he wasn't scowling at Tom for once.

"Good morning, Halloran," Ferguson said. "Reporting for duty?"

"Aye, sir. I've cleared it with my captain. And I brought the absinthe hex with me from evidence, for comparison." He cleared his throat awkwardly and turned to face Cicero. "I ain't used to this sort of work, it's true," he said. "But I've thought it over, and there are good reasons for us to work together. One—"

"Yes, yes," Cicero interrupted with an airy wave of his hand. "Save your breath. I've decided you're quite correct." He rose to his feet in a single, lithe motion. "Don't just stand there gawping, crow. Make yourself useful and take us to Dominic."

"Far too much ornamentation," Dominic groused as he bent over the two hexes, examining first one, then the other, through his jeweler's loupe.

The desk Dominic and Rook shared was at one end of the enormous room housing the MWP detectives, near the windows where the cat familiars routinely napped in the afternoon sunlight. Dominic had been a hexman before bonding with Rook, and most of his work since consisted of comparing various hexes and determining their primary components for evidence.

"Is that a bad thing?" Halloran asked, peering over Dominic's shoulder. His eyes, a troubling shade of blue, fixed intently on the hex, and a little line of concentration sprang up between his brows.

"Oh, yes," Dominic said. "Well, no."

Cicero rolled his eyes and glanced at Rook. The two familiars stood back from the desk, Cicero because he had no particular interest in the details of hexes, which were useful in general but dreadfully boring in particular.

And Rook because he was a pain in the arse.

Rook gestured to Halloran, whose bent posture meant his trousers pulled tight across his backside. The crow wagged his eyebrows in what was probably intended to be approval.

Stop it, Cicero mouthed at Rook. Rook substituted obscene motions of his pelvis, so Cicero slapped him lightly on the arm. Halloran glanced back over his shoulder at the sound.

"The sooner you learn to ignore them, the happier you'll be," Dominic said without looking up. "Now, to answer your question more fully…perhaps it will be easiest to show you." He opened a drawer and took out a leather wallet containing his hexman tools, along with two scraps of paper.

As Dominic sketched out a quick pair of hexes, Cicero found his attention wandering back to Halloran. And, yes, Rook wasn't exactly *wrong*. Halloran couldn't fairly be described as the ugliest man in all Manhattan. *If* one liked the big, rough types, at any rate. Given a decent haircut and manicure, and something to wear besides an ill-fitting police uniform, and he *might* be passable. Might.

"Now, which of these unlocking hexes do you think is more powerful?" Dominic asked, shoving the hexes he'd drawn in front of Halloran. "One of these can unlock a simple, standard lock, and the other—with the proper magic behind it, of course—could get you into a bank vault."

Halloran eyed the hexes, then Dominic. "Given what you said before you started scribbling, I'm thinking this one," he said, tapping the simpler of the two.

Dominic's mouth curled into a smile. "And if I hadn't said anything about ornamentation beforehand?"

Halloran laughed ruefully; a low, throaty sound that resonated in Cicero's belly. "Ah, you got me there, friend. I would have figured on the fancy one."

"As most people would," Dominic said, sweeping the hexes away. "And the makers of commercial hexes take advantage of it. They add bright colors and swirls and flourishes, all of which do nothing!"

Rook leaned casually on Dominic's shoulder. "My Dominic prefers things simple," he told Halloran with a wink.

"If that were true, I'd never have bonded with you," Dominic replied fondly.

Cicero looked away. Across the crowded room, a flame-haired witch from Brooklyn gesticulated wildly at Cicero's office mate Greta, a tiny familiar less than half his height. Apparently tired of whatever the witch had to say, she shifted into wolverine form and showed her teeth. He backed off with such haste Cicero nearly smiled.

Rook touched his shoulder lightly, a slight frown of concern on his face. Cicero took a deep breath. It wasn't Rook's fault he and Dominic were perfectly suited as lovers as well as friends. It was the fairytale every familiar wanted to believe in, and the MWP did nothing to dissuade. One day, a familiar would be minding their own business, look up...and there would be their witch. Dashing, charming, strong, funny...whatever the familiar needed them to be.

Rook had found that with Dominic. Found not just a magical bond, but one of love. And Cicero had fancied himself oh-so-wise, having advised Rook to just tell the befuddled hexman that he was a witch, and Rook's witch to boot.

In fact, he'd been an idiot. A child, wanting to believe that the stories were real, and some handsome prince would come along just for him. And now, instead of a prince, he'd ended up with an ogre.

"The hexes that Gerald Whistler and Abraham Barshtein took were over-ornamented," Dominic said, gesturing to them. "And that makes it easier to confirm they were drawn by the same hand."

Halloran straightened. "Then if we find out who drew them…"

But Dominic was shaking his head. "There's nothing wrong with them. They had no effect on the others at the party where Whistler attacked his roommate. Given the proper magic behind them, they should—and apparently do—work as advertised." Dominic read the activation phrase. "*Take Me to the Green Fairy.*"

"So they're some new brand on the market, and it was just a coincidence Whistler and Barshtein both took one," Rook said.

Cicero pressed his lips together, wanting to lash out but uncertain how to do so. Couldn't Rook see? Putting it down to coincidence, with three people dead and Isaac missing?

"If it's a new brand," Halloran said slowly, "Why ain't there a name in the activation phrase? Maybe you don't use commercial hexes much here in the MWP, when you can make your own, but even the hustlers and quacks add their names in. *Dr. Payne's Pain-Away, Takes the Pain Away.* Or *Mr. Smith's Collars Stay Clean Longer.* That sort of thing."

Dominic looked thoughtful. "You have a point."

"Unless this was someone making hexes for their friends," Rook put in. "Someone who normally hexes ice boxes to keep them cold or something, but drew up a few extra outside their normal line of work?"

"Then it's still a connection between them, ain't it?"

Huh. It seemed the ogre might have a brain in there after all. "Halloran's right," Cicero said. The man in question shot him a surprised look, although he could hardly be more shocked than Cicero himself. "Either this is a new brand of hex, which will be out of business in a month because they're terrible at advertising, or someone is privately distributing the things. If it's the latter, then both men must have known the hexmaker, at least indirectly."

"Assuming the hex has anything to do with it," Dominic pointed out, sounding a bit peeved.

Halloran arched a brow. "What's our next move, then?"

"Since we've learned all we can here," Cicero said with a dismissive wave at the desk, "I suppose we'll have to do a bit of walking." He eyed the window with distaste. "At least the rain stopped."

CHAPTER 5

"**MIND TELLING ME** where we're going, then?" Tom called after Cicero.

The familiar had led the way from the Coven and out onto the street. The morning rain that had dampened Tom's coat on the way to the Coven had ceased, leaving behind gloomy, overcast skies. A municipal hexman perched atop a ladder, repainting a faded hex meant to protect a building from fire. Horse-drawn cabs clopped past, and pushcart vendors offered hot noodles or cocoa to passers-by.

Cicero slid through the crowd as easily as if he'd been in cat form, finding gaps too small for Tom to fit through. Before long, he was far ahead.

"Hey!" Tom shouted. "Hold up there!"

The sight of his uniform caused the crowd to part, although he received a share of unfriendly looks as he shoved his way through. Catching up with Cicero beneath the Fifth Avenue El, he grabbed the familiar's arm. "I said hold up!"

Cicero jerked out of his grasp. "Don't manhandle me." Peridot eyes flashed defiantly up at Tom. "I'm not your bloody property."

What the devil was wrong with the fellow? Tom released him and held up his hands. "Sorry. Just don't go ignoring me. We're meant to be working together, ain't we?"

Cicero's lips pressed together in annoyance. Tom had the sudden urge to reach out and run his thumb across them, coax them back to their normal, inviting shape.

Maybe the insanity of the MWP was contagious.

"Yes," Cicero admitted finally. "But we're blocking traffic."

"Then we'll walk, but at least stay with me. And I'd appreciate some answers."

Cicero didn't say anything, but he fell into step beside Tom. Tom chose to take it as an encouraging sign. "Where are we going? And who is Isaac? You keep saying his life is in danger."

They passed a toymaker's shop, the window filled with tin soldiers, dolls, and wooden trains in anticipation of Christmas. One of the dolls blinked unnervingly as Tom passed. *Our hexes give a semblance of life sure to delight any child!* promised the lettering on the window.

Saint Mary, what would they think up next?

"Isaac is my friend," Cicero said at length. His shoulders hunched beneath the heavy coat he'd donned against the cold. "And a feral."

"Which is…?" Tom prompted.

Cicero snorted. "Fur and feathers, you really don't know anything about familiars, do you?"

Tom bit back a protest. Maybe if Cicero thought he was an idiot, it would be easier to keep his old identity a secret. "Never had to before," he replied, which was true enough as it went. Aye, his brother Danny had been a witch, and even had a familiar. But Liam had been the younger brother, and Danny hadn't seen fit to talk about such things with him. He and Molly had been friends, but she hadn't spoken of it either. How they'd met, or bonded, or any of it. Why she'd left the convent, or how she'd come to run with an Irish tunnel gang instead of finding decent work.

She'd loved Danny. Maybe that had been all the reason she needed.

God, how she'd screamed when Danny died in his arms.

"Ferals are unbonded familiars who don't work for the MWP or anyone else," Cicero said. "Isaac used to work for the MWP, but he left. He needed a job, so Gerald helped him find work, a place to live, that sort of thing. I hadn't spoken to him for a while, but he sent me a note, asking me to meet him in front of the Coven. Late at night, because he was going to a party at Gerald Whistler's apartment, and he wanted to convince Gerald to come talk to me as well. Only he never made it to the party, and Gerald went mad and attacked his roommate."

That sounded ominous. "What did Isaac want to talk to you about?"

"He didn't say." Cicero frowned. "I assume the sort of thing he didn't want to put in writing."

"So why ain't the Police Board more concerned about a missing familiar?"

Cicero laughed, but it had a bitter edge. "Concerned about a feral? Darling, the whole *point* is to leave familiars without protection if they don't work for the MWP, or the government, or some businessman with money. That way they can sigh and say, 'See what happens when you try to live your own life away from us? Better play it safe.'" Cicero shook his head. "A familiar can either make the best of it, accept the work, and bond with a witch they'll hopefully at least get along with, or take their chances of being captured and force bonded."

Tom felt queasy. "Force bonded?"

"That's how I know Isaac didn't just take off on a train to New Jersey or some other God-forsaken wasteland." Cicero's eyes darkened to emerald. "He would have told me, sent a telegram, something to make sure I didn't worry. At the least, he would have left word with one of the other ferals we know, like Rook's brother."

"Rook's brother is a feral?"

"He chose freedom over safety." Cicero shrugged. "Then again, it's probably easier to defend yourself when you turn into a horse."

An aching, sick feeling settled at the bottom of Tom's stomach. He'd never wondered about the lives of familiars, just assumed they were like everyone else. But Cicero made it sound dangerous, filled with painful compromises. "Is it common?" he asked, even though he wasn't sure he wanted the answer. "Forcing familiars to bond, I mean. Is it something you have to worry about, or just one of those things that happens once in a while…?"

Cicero gestured at a hardware store on the corner. "'*Our refrigerators are specially hexed to keep food cold longer,*'" he read aloud. "Look around you. How many hexes do you see just on this street? The magic to power them has to come from somewhere. A good witch and familiar team can make a great deal of money. A mediocre pair can still earn in a month more than most men earn in six. If you have witch potential and want a familiar, you could just wait for one to choose you…but after a while, that gets tiresome, and your bank account stays empty. Maybe it would be better just to take what you want instead of waiting for something that might never come."

"And once the bond is formed?"

Cicero stared resolutely at the sidewalk in front of them. "It can't be broken in life. One of the two has to die. Forcing a bond is illegal, but it isn't a capital offense. On the other hand, murder is. Any familiar who killed a witch to get free of an undesired bond would find themselves first in prison, then the electric chair."

Tom's feet slowed to a stop. Cicero took another step or two, then halted as well. "That's horrible," Tom said. "Something needs to be done. Why ain't the reform papers writing about this, instead of worrying about folks drinking beer on Sunday?"

"Because it benefits the men and women in the Fifth Avenue mansions," Cicero said with a roll of his eyes. "Really, darling, don't be so naïve."

Tom knew how the world worked, knew money flowed mostly in one direction and to hell with the poor bastard who ended up with empty pockets at the end of the day. But there was wrong and then there was *wrong*, and this seemed terrible in a way he couldn't articulate.

"It ain't right," Tom repeated, because he didn't know what else to say.

"Many things aren't," Cicero agreed. "But it's not like we can do anything about it. What we *can* do is try to find out what's happened to Isaac."

Tom wanted to argue, but the words stuck in his throat. "You're right." He fell in beside Cicero again. "So what sort of work did Gerald and Isaac do, anyway?"

Cicero stopped in front of a tenement. A sly smile curved his lips, and he shot Tom a wink. "You'll see soon enough. Now let's go up and see if Gerald's roommate is at home."

"Let me do the talking," Cicero instructed as he knocked on the door. Even under his light tap, the cheap wood shook in its frame. The hallway they stood in was dim, illuminated only by whatever feeble light could make its way from a single window at the far end.

The door opened, and a man blinked out at them. He was very pretty, dark haired and dark eyed, his skin a delicate shade of fawn. An ugly bandage swathed his head, covering his mutilated ear. The Oriental-style dressing gown he wore was badly faded and probably third hand, but its remaining color livened the dingy surroundings. "Yes?"

"Good morning, darling. So sorry to wake you this early." Cicero fluttered his eyelashes. An answering smile crept over the other man's face. "I'm Cicero—did Gerald ever mention me?"

"Gerald?" The man lifted his hand involuntarily, as if he meant to touch his missing ear. "I think...perhaps?"

Cicero opened his coat to reveal the familiar's badge pinned to his vest. The man's eyes widened and he nodded. "Oh, yes! The familiar with the MWP. They told me the hex didn't have anything to do with…with what happened." His lip trembled.

"We're still looking into the situation," Cicero said with a nod in Halloran's direction. "Can we come in?"

"Oh! Yes, I'm sorry." He stepped back. "I'm Pascal Esposito—but you probably already knew that."

"Charmed." Cicero shook his hand lightly. "This is Patrolman Halloran. He's here to be decorative."

Halloran made a sputtering noise, which Cicero ignored as he followed Esposito into the squalid little apartment. The single room was on a corner, and so had two windows, one of which was boarded over. Nearly every inch of space was filled by a pair of beds, a table, and a chair. Dresses hung over the ends of the beds, and cosmetics and a small mirror took up much of the table. It wasn't hard to deduce Esposito's line of work.

Bracing himself, Cicero glanced over his shoulder at Halloran, anticipating a sneer of disgust, or perhaps outrage. Would he threaten Esposito?

Halloran's expression was sympathetic. "My condolences on your loss," he said, and was even tactful enough not to specify whether he meant Gerald or the ear.

Well. That was…not what Cicero had expected at all.

"Thank you." Esposito perched on the edge of one bed. Cicero took the other, and Halloran selected the chair. Even seated he was absurdly imposing, the small room seeming to make his shoulders even broader. "Gerald's left me short on the rent. And with this," he gestured to his head again, "I can't work." At least, not anywhere even slightly respectable. "I don't know what I'm going to do."

"Tch. Awful." Cicero folded his hands on his knee. "Now tell me, where was Gerald working last? I hadn't spoken to him for a few months before this terrible business."

He knew, of course, but starting with a few questions he already had the answer to seemed the best approach. Establish the reliability of the witness, as Athene always said.

Esposito picked absently at his fingernails. The cuticles were horribly ragged; no doubt it was a habit. "He tended bar at one of the resorts on Bleecker Street. The Spitting Rooster."

"Subtle," Cicero said, glancing out of the side of his eye at Halloran. A flush showed on Halloran's fair skin, and Cicero couldn't resist the urge to see how far he could make it spread. "Ever heard of it, Halloran?

It's on the roster for *all* the good slumming tours. And those newspapers you're so fond of do like to go on about the depravity and sin of such places, wondering why the police haven't shut them down to make the world safe for decent folk. Personally, I think the reporters must like visiting, since they go there so often to toss off their…articles."

Halloran's blush deepened, but he said, "And did Isaac work there as well, Mr. Esposito?"

Esposito frowned slightly. "Yes. Not behind the bar—he was an, ah, entertainer." He glanced automatically at the dresses.

After he took Cicero's stupid, disastrous advice. "Do you work there?" Cicero asked, because he couldn't think about that right now. About Isaac shivering and shaking, his big brown eyes ringed with bruises.

"No." Esposito shook his head. "The man who owns the resort, Sloane, likes to hire familiars when he can. They say he's one himself."

Now *that* hadn't been in the case file. Cicero leaned forward. "But Gerald wasn't a familiar."

"I said when he can," Esposito snapped waspishly. Maybe there was nothing to the rumor; maybe he'd just been putting a salve on the sting of not being hired.

"Of course, darling, of course," Cicero said, patting Esposito lightly on the knee. "Was Gerald in any sort of trouble?"

"Any threats?" Halloran added. He didn't seem to be doing a very good job of letting Cicero ask all the questions. "Strange visitors?"

Esposito's eyes strayed to the boarded-up window. It must have been the one Gerald had gone out of. A shiver went down Cicero's spine, which had nothing to do with the unheated apartment. "Yes," Esposito said at last. "Or, maybe. I'm not sure. I came home early one day and found Gerald at the table, talking with a stranger. A man. They fell silent the second I opened the door, and the man left immediately. I asked who he was, and Gerald told me it was someone from the Rooster. When I asked his name, Gerald got angry and said it was none of my business." Esposito sniffed. "He normally wasn't that way with me. Rude, I mean."

"And you never saw the man again?" Cicero asked.

"No, but I heard a name, as I was opening the door. Karol."

Without a last name, the information wouldn't do them much good. Halloran shifted forward, the chair creaking dangerously under his solid weight. "I know this is difficult for you," he said gently. "You'd rather put Mr. Whistler's death behind you, I'm sure. But can you tell us one last time exactly what happened?"

Esposito's face took on a yellowish hue, and he seemed to shrink in on himself. "We were having a party. Nothing big—we didn't have the room for it—but a few friends. Gerald had a bottle of absinthe and some hexes. We toasted and took the hexes." He swallowed convulsively, and his voice shook. "Then Gerald…went insane. Threw down his glass and just…attacked me. Like an animal."

He touched the edge of the bandage on his head. "He bit me—clawed at me. I was in shock. Couldn't believe it was happening. Everyone was screaming. Then he got my ear in his teeth, and I realized he meant to kill me." Esposito shuddered. "It was all so confusing, but I knew I didn't want to die. I shoved him, as hard as I could. He fell back and his legs hit the table, and…and he stumbled into the window. The glass broke, and he fell."

"It's all right, darling," Cicero soothed. Halloran produced a handkerchief and silently passed it to Esposito. "It's almost over. Everyone at the party took the same hexes, yes?"

"Yes. And drank from the same bottle." Esposito blew his nose loudly.

"And Isaac wasn't here?"

"No."

"Are there any other details?" Halloran asked. "Anything you can remember at all?"

Esposito swallowed and nodded. "Gerald's eyes. He drank and took the hex, and his eyes turned red. The white parts, I mean."

Halloran looked grim. "Thank you. You've been very helpful," Cicero said. "I think that's all the questions we have."

They started out, but Halloran paused in the doorway. "Mr. Esposito? Don't blame yourself. You did what you had to do to save your life. Ain't nothing for you to feel any guilt over."

Esposito blinked watery eyes. "Thank you. I…yes. Thank you."

Once the apartment door shut behind them, Cicero said, "You were kind to him."

Halloran arched a brow. "Because roughing him up would have been so much more effective?"

"Of course not!" Cicero gestured vaguely at Halloran's muscular arms. "I just assumed—"

Assumed he'd sneer at an obvious fairy like Esposito. Bluster at him, maybe threaten, for no other reason than he could. Ogres like Halloran didn't have to be nice, so they weren't.

"You figure I don't know how to be a decent fellow," Halloran said.

"That I don't care if guilt eats a man alive, when none of what happened was his doing. I know just what you assumed."

The bitterness in his voice took Cicero aback. Before he could think how to respond, Halloran clomped off toward the stairs. Cicero stared after him for a few moments, before his wits caught up with him. "Where are we going?"

"We've learned all that we can about your dead man," Halloran replied. "Now it's time to look into mine."

CHAPTER 6

CICERO REMAINED SILENT as the Sixth Avenue El rattled and clattered its way through the city. Tom supposed he ought to take it as a blessing —the familiar had made his low opinion of Tom clear enough from the start. His shock over Tom's ability to act like a decent human being shouldn't have had any teeth.

Maybe it wouldn't have stung as badly if Cicero hadn't been so damned…Tom groped for the right word, but couldn't find any that fit right. You couldn't help but look at him, no matter who else was in the room. And not even because of the way he dressed or lined those beautiful gemstone eyes of his, though Saint Mary knew that didn't hurt.

He'd done a good job of questioning Esposito, too. Better than Tom would have expected.

So maybe Cicero wasn't the only one who'd jumped to conclusions he oughtn't.

They descended the platform, and Tom led the way to Barshtein's shop. It was the walk of a few blocks, but soon enough Tom felt his shoulders relaxing. Back on familiar ground, and well away from anyone who might recognize him as Liam O'Connell.

"Where've you been, Tom?" Mrs. Zywicki called from the stoop of her tenement.

"Duty reassignment," he told her. "Just temporary, though."

"Thank the Good Lord for that," said Finn Cooper, who had parked his pushcart on the sidewalk in front of the tenement. The dead fish piled within stared glassy-eyed from their bed of snow.

A few others called greetings as they drew closer to the pawn shop. "I've never seen people so glad to see a policeman," Cicero remarked.

Tom glanced warily down at him, but for once Cicero didn't look as though he were secretly laughing at Tom. "This is my neighborhood. I look out for it."

"Apparently." Cicero looked back over his shoulder at Cooper. "A pushcart on the sidewalk. Isn't that illegal?"

Tom snorted. "And who is it hurting? No one in the neighborhood, that's for sure. I arrest him, put him out of business, and then what? He's got no job, and Mrs. Zywicki has to walk all the way to the market to get something to make her dinner. And her with a bad hip and all."

"And I suppose the bribes don't hurt, either," Cicero said.

Tom stopped. Working with Cicero might be his best chance to get to the truth of things, but that didn't mean he had to take abuse from some fop who'd never walked a beat in his life, no matter how pretty he was. "Let's get one thing straight," he said. "You can say I'm a witless fool, act all surprised when it turns out I ain't some—some whatever it is you think of me. But I ain't never taken a bribe, and I ain't never beat up some poor fool just to get an easy confession. This is my neighborhood, and I look out for the people in it, understand?"

Cicero blinked up at him, eyes wide. He moistened his lips, a quick flash of tongue against their softness. "I...yes." He lowered his gaze. "I'm sorry. I've offended you. Unintentionally, even."

"Well, aye," Tom said gruffly. "Intentionally too, I'm sure."

Cicero laughed, a bright sound against the rumble of passing carts. "Yes, but you wouldn't expect me to apologize for those times, would you?"

Tom snorted and started on his way again. "Saint Mary forbid."

"I am sorry, though," Cicero added, scurrying to keep up with Tom's long strides. "Truly."

"Apology accepted."

"Good." Cicero ostentatiously rearranged the hang of his coat over his shoulders. "Now that's settled, where are we going?"

"Here."

Tom's steps slowed as he reached Barshtein's. The pawn shop's sign, displaying the traditional three balls hanging from a bar, swung slowly in the cold breeze. The curtains were pulled tight over the windows, and a small sign indicated the store was closed under police orders.

"Did they have children?" Cicero asked. "The man who lived here, I mean. And his wife."

"Thankfully, no." Tom shuddered. At least there'd be no children left to remember the sight of their father's teeth red with their mother's blood.

Saint Mary, there had been nothing left of Ma's face by the time Tom reached his parents. Nothing but raw meat, and Pa turning to kill, his eyes bloody and nothing sane left behind them.

The light brush of Cicero's fingers on his wrist brought him back to the present. "Halloran? Are you all right?"

Tom swallowed. Halloran. Right. He was Thomas Halloran, whose sainted mother had died in Dublin long ago. Whose family still lived there, happy and full of love. Who wasn't a hexbreaker and had never laid eyes on those damned hexes. "I'm fine."

"I did read the newspaper reports," Cicero said in a subdued tone. "Eventually. Returning here, after seeing what happened...it can't be easy for you."

Tom gratefully seized on the excuse. "This is a quiet beat," he said, reaching for the door. "I ain't used to such sights, it's true."

"I can't imagine anyone is used to seeing a man tear out his wife's throat with his teeth," Cicero said with a shudder. "And least, I certainly hope not."

Tom tried the latch. Locked, but no hex on it, thank heavens. He took an unlocking hex from his pouch and applied it. A moment later, they stepped into the dusty confines of the shop.

Only a little light filtered through the drawn curtains, but he found himself reluctant to open them. They weren't doing anything illicit, but Tom didn't feel like answering questions if anyone spotted them. Cicero lit the gaslights, then looked around. "What a mess."

Tom's heart sank at the destruction. The cabinets had been wrenched open and all but the cheapest baubles removed. Those lay scattered about on the floor: a bracelet of glass beads, a wind-up tin soldier, and a banjo made from a cigar box. Barshtein had sometimes bought items of little worth, if he knew the seller needed the money badly enough.

Cicero strolled through the shop with his hands on his hips. "Now that your fellow boys in blue have taken everything of value—all of it was evidence, I'm sure—what's left for us?"

Shame heated Tom's cheeks. No wonder people like Cicero had such a bad opinion of the police, with the men helping themselves to whatever they wanted. "None of this would likely have been useful to us anyway," Tom said, instead of trying to find an excuse that didn't exist. "We should look for…I don't know. Ledgers, private letters." He turned his face to the ceiling with a grimace. "Which he probably kept in the apartment upstairs."

They climbed the stairs with heavy feet. Thank Mary it was winter, because even in the cold the place reeked of spilled blood and fluids. The gore-soaked rug had been shoved to one side, but otherwise the place was just as it had been the night of the murder.

"Dear heavens." Cicero's olive complexion took on a distinctly greenish hue, and his hand fluttered above his chest. "This is horrible."

"Aye." Tom pulled his gaze from the dried blood spattered on the wall. "Let's see what we can find."

A stack of paper lay on the table. "The maid said he was sitting there, writing." Tom pointed to an overturned chair. "He had her bring the bottle of absinthe. He kept the hex in a drawer."

"Just the one?"

"Aye. I think he'd taken up drinking the stuff not long ago. Maybe he wanted to see if he liked it."

"Hmm." Cicero moved to the table, stepping lightly. The floor didn't so much as creak beneath his feet. His yellow-green eyes sharpened, as did his expression, all languidness replaced by concentration. He reminded Tom of a stalking cat, pacing the floor and listening for mice in the walls. "I don't mean to disparage your neighborhood, but it seems more of a whiskey sort of place."

"I would have thought the same," Tom admitted. He moved to a bookshelf, peering at the titles.

Cicero joined him. Tom was painfully aware of just how close the familiar stood, and felt an almost irrational sense of disappointment when he turned all his attention on the books, without so much as a glance at Tom. So close, Tom could smell Cicero's hair oil, combined with some cedar scent he couldn't quite place.

"Oscar Wilde," Cicero read. "Now there's a fine Irish witch for you."

"If you say so. I never heard of the fellow," Tom said. "Was Barshtein part of your set, then?"

Cicero arched a brow. "My set, darling? Whatever do you mean by that?"

"You know." Tom stared at the titles, none of which were remotely familiar. "Bohemians."

"Oh, is *that* what I am," Cicero drawled.

Tom sighed in frustration and turned away. "Never mind."

"No, no." Cicero caught him by the elbow. "Certainly it's *one* of the things I am. Believe it or not, we don't all know each other. There are a number of different cafés and restaurants throughout Manhattan that attract the...artistic sorts, shall we say."

Tom tried to imagine Cicero painting or playing the piano. "Are you? An artist, I mean."

Cicero's mouth curled into a slow smile. "Perhaps. Although they say familiars make the best muses."

Tom had the sudden, unbidden image of Cicero posing for a painter. Stretched out languid and boneless on a couch in some dingy apartment, his hair artfully disheveled, his clothing arranged to reveal smooth skin, or perhaps gone altogether...

"I'm going to try to find his household ledger," Tom said hurriedly. "You keep looking at...this..."

Tom found the ledger tucked into a drawer. While he perused it, Cicero continued to prowl the apartment. "Barshtein was trying his hand at poetry," the familiar said as he shuffled through the papers on the table. "He wasn't very good, mind you, but so few are. I wonder if he was beginning to find his life as a pawn broker a bit confining?"

"Possible." Tom tapped the ledger. "Look at this entry. It's from a few weeks ago, but I recognize the name."

Cicero joined him, leaning in close to read Barshtein's cramped handwriting. "I don't."

Instead of explaining, Tom asked, "What did you say about slumming tours?"

"In regards to the Rooster?"

"Aye. You said it was popular?"

"If one would call it that." Cicero frowned slightly. "People don't feel they've gotten their money's worth unless they've been shocked by fairies. Though I would have thought Barshtein could have found plenty of them in a neighborhood like this."

"The neighborhood his wife and customers live in?" Tom countered.

"You make an excellent point. Why?"

Tom ran his finger over the name. "Barshtein might have had other business with him, but the fellow listed here runs slumming tours."

They made their way to a 24-hour restaurant not far from the Coven, the sort frequented by coppers and criminals alike. Tables crowded close together, their tops covered in cheap checkered cloth. The air reeked of boiled cabbage and onions.

"I'm told the corned beef is good," Cicero said with a delicate shudder.

Tom settled into the seat across from him. "What, you think I like corned beef just because I'm Irish?"

"Don't you?"

"Aye," he admitted. "Still."

The mirth faded slightly from Cicero's face. "You're right. I've made entirely too many assumptions about you already."

Before Tom could say anything, the waiter appeared. Cicero ordered coffee and a fish sandwich. Tom went for the corned beef and coffee. "And extra cream, if you would," he called after the waiter.

"From Dublin, are you?" Cicero asked while they waited on their food.

Lord knew this wasn't a conversation he wanted to have. He needed to divert it quickly. "Aye. But what about you? You look Italian, but you sound English."

Cicero smiled slyly. "The two things most guaranteed not to endear me to your heart. Or are you not an Irish heretic?"

"I follow the pope in Belfast, if that's what you mean. Not that I've been to confession in a while, mind you." Not in eight years, because lying to the people around him was one thing, but lying to a priest was another. "You don't have to tell me if you don't like. I figure we're all New Yorkers now, and it don't matter much where we started out."

"My parents moved to London long before I was born," Cicero said with a graceful shrug. "My father had a little grocery in Clerkenwell. I spent most of my formative years there, until the place burned to the ground. My uncle was about to move his family to New York from some awful backwater in Italy, and suggested we all go together to make our fortunes. We ended up in the tenements, where my father promptly died from typhus."

Did Cicero still speak to his remaining family? His distant tone made Tom suspect the answer would be no, but it was too personal a question to ask a man he'd just met. "I've noticed you familiars don't use last names," he said instead. "Is it just tradition, or...?"

A shadow crossed Cicero's expressive face. "Mainly tradition," he said. "Like a woman taking her husband's last name. In the old days, our witch would give us a new name altogether, once we bonded."

"Like a pet?" Tom asked, revolted.

A sort of mocking smile twisted Cicero's mouth. "Exactly like a pet, darling," he said, but the lightness of his voice seemed to hide something much darker beneath. "Or a slave. Or even a servant, I suppose—I've heard of rich folk who call all their housemaids Jane, so as not to bother learning a new name every time one leaves and another takes her place."

Molly had come with her own name, Tom knew that much at least. For all the bad Danny had done, at least he'd not treated his familiar like a possession. "That don't seem right."

"Well, the practice has largely been given up." Cicero shrugged. "Still, the tradition of relinquishing our surnames persists. I think the MWP encourages it so we see the force as our family."

"You ought to call me Tom, then. Especially as we're to be working together."

"Perhaps I will." Cicero's sly grin returned. "Thomas."

Tom snorted. "Why do I get the feeling nothing is ever easy with you?"

"Because that would be boring."

The coffee arrived, along with a small pot of cream. Tom added a splash to his coffee, then pushed the rest of the pot across the table to Cicero.

Cicero looked down at it, then back up. "For me?"

"I thought you might like it."

"What, you think I like cream just because I'm a cat?"

"Don't you?" Tom countered.

Cicero laughed. "Yes. Still." He lifted the pot to his lips and dipped his tongue in.

Their eyes met. Cicero slowly curled his tongue, the cream white against his lips. Blood rushed to Tom's groin, and he glanced away hastily. The restaurant was doing a good business, and he let his gaze drift over the other customers, focusing on them instead of the thoughts Cicero had put into his head.

One of the men clearing his plate of corned beef seemed familiar. Someone Tom had seen on his beat?

"Your food, sirs," said the waiter.

Tom tucked into his corned beef. Cicero took a dainty bite of his fish. "So, it seems Barshtein may have taken a slum tour recently," Cicero said, "and the tour might have stopped at the Rooster."

"A lot of 'seems' and 'mights' I admit," Tom remarked. "I could track down the fellow who does the tours and beat the truth out of him, if you'd like."

Cicero rolled his eyes. "I apologized once already."

"Only for the times you didn't mean to insult me."

Cicero threw his napkin across the table at Tom. "We need some way to get inside the Rooster. If it is the source of whatever caused Barshtein and Gerald to go mad, we have to find out."

"Take the tour ourselves?" Tom suggested.

Oh hell—Tom knew where he'd seen the man sitting across the restaurant before. He took a second look, heart beating in his throat. The years had put on their wear and tear, which was why Tom hadn't recognized him immediately. Once-brown hair had gone gray, and deep lines carved the man's weathered skin. His blue eyes seemed to have sunk back into his skull, as if they no longer wished to see the cruelty of the world. But the shape of the jaw, the arch of cheekbone, the old scar bisecting his hairline, brought his name to the surface of Tom's mind.

Horton Phelps. The leader of the old Muskrat gang. The very man Da betrayed to get his hands on those damned hexes.

CHAPTER 7

TOM FELT HIS heart stutter in his chest.

Phelps. Here. Of all the damnable luck.

Phelps hadn't glanced in his direction. And if he did, most likely he'd only notice the police uniform, and not take a close look at Tom's face. Even so, Tom desperately wished he could put on his helmet in the restaurant without looking either rude or insane, and drawing unwanted attention to himself.

"No," Cicero said. "If we took a tour, we'd only see the main rooms. The public areas."

It took Tom a moment to recall what they were even talking about. The slum tours. Right. "That's all Barshtein saw. Probably."

"Perhaps." Cicero tapped his fork lightly against his plate. "But let's assume he'd developed an interest in the bohemian set, as you put it. I've never been to the Rooster myself, but I know people who have. My friend Noah, for one. It was he who suggested Isaac talk to Gerald about finding work there in the first place."

Tom shifted in his chair and tried to glance casually across the room. One of the waiters blocked his view of Phelps, so he couldn't tell if the man was looking his way or not.

"Barshtein might have gone back once the tour introduced him to the place," Cicero went on, "both to meet with those he felt a kinship with, and to indulge certain desires in a neighborhood well away from his wife, as you suggested."

"More 'ifs' and 'mights,'" Tom said distractedly.

Cicero shrugged. "The Rooster is the only potential connection we have between Barshtein, Gerald, and Isaac. And we'll have better luck discovering the truth if we can go behind the scenes, as it were. How good are you at acting?"

Tom started, dropping his fork. "Um…I'm…all right, I suppose," he lied frantically. "Never had the need." Except for the entirety of his adult life.

Cicero sighed and put a hand dramatically to his forehead. "We're doomed. Maybe you can just play stupid."

Tom leaned over and hunted for the fork, which had made a loud clatter on the tile floor. When he sat back up, he found Phelps staring at him.

Their eyes met, and time slowed to a crawl. The look of recognition dawning on Phelps's face was clear for him to read.

Saint Mary, he should never have come south of 42nd Street, not for anything.

"Pay attention, Thomas," Cicero said, snapping his fingers in Tom's direction. "I have a plan."

The corned beef felt like it wanted to return the way it had come. Tom swallowed hard. "Tell me."

"If we worked at the Rooster, we'd have a much better chance at finding out what, if anything, is going on there." Cicero leaned forward and dropped his voice conspiratorially. "Now, I'll have no problem getting hired, but no one is going to pay you to look pretty and sit on their lap. And the gentlemen at this resort aren't looking for the *other* sort of treatment."

Tom's brain spun, torn between panic over Phelps and Cicero's words. "Wait. Your plan involves sitting on men's laps?"

"Don't be silly, darling. I have far too much talent for that." Cicero took another sip of the cream. "I'll be on the stage."

What on earth did the fellow mean to do? "You seem awfully confident."

"Of course I am." Cicero winked at him. "I'm an artist."

Either Cicero's confidence was completely warranted or wildly misplaced. Either way, there was nothing Tom could do about it. "You said some of the bohemians go to the Rooster. Won't they recognize you? It ain't a secret that you work for the MWP, is it?"

Cicero's lips pursed thoughtfully. "I could pretend to leave. Have a public row and quit dramatically. It would mean sneaking back into the

Coven every day, but that won't be a problem. Most people can't tell one black cat from another."

This plan seemed more ill-thought-out by the moment. And Tom could barely keep himself from checking to see if Phelps was still staring. "Why would they believe you quit?"

Cicero sipped his cream, his eyes distant. "Because I don't have much time left to choose a witch."

Tom was beginning to suspect he hadn't paid enough attention to familiars. With no feral colony in his precinct, he hadn't given them much thought. Now his ignorance was making him feel like he'd been walking around with his eyes deliberately closed. "What do you mean?"

"I mean the MWP doesn't let familiars live on the dole forever," Cicero snapped. "It's a police force, not a charity. Eventually, we have to bond with someone so the MWP can get some real use out of us, even if we haven't found our witch."

"What does that mean, exactly?" Tom asked. "'Your' witch?"

"A familiar can bond with any witch. But there's always one whose magic is the most...compatible, let's say. Together they'll make better hexes, stronger magic." Cicero studied the pot of cream as though it held the answers to life inside it. "We recognize him or her on an instinctual level. It doesn't always work out."

"Just because the magic is compatible, the rest maybe ain't?" Tom guessed.

Surprised flickered over Cicero's face. "Indeed. But the point is, whether we find our witch or not, we have to decide eventually. My time is getting short, and everyone at the MWP knows it."

"Oh." It made sense, in a way, but it didn't sit right with Tom. It didn't sound like familiars had any safe alternatives, so they had to bond with someone for life by a certain date, even if they weren't sure it would work out?

"I'll pretend Chief Ferguson gave me an ultimatum," Cicero went on, "and I quit because I'm not letting anyone tell me what to do."

"At least that part's believable enough," Tom muttered. "What about me?"

Cicero eyed Tom as he finished off the rest of the cream. "Gerald was a bartender. I wonder if they're still short a hand? Can you mix cocktails?"

"I could learn, I suppose. But what if they've already hired someone?"

"Rook can teach you," Cicero said with airy confidence. "And I imagine the proprietor likes to keep a few brawny sorts around, in case anyone has too much to drink and gets rowdy. Or tries to make off without paying the fellows in the upstairs rooms. That might do for you, if we can't get you hired otherwise."

Tom tried to think of some other possibility, but his mind kept circling back to Phelps. He risked a glance…and discovered only an empty chair.

"I've no better ideas," he said. "All right. I'll come by the Coven in the morning."

"I'll make my dramatic debut this afternoon, I think," Cicero said

"Good." Tom tossed enough money to cover the bill and tip on the table and rose to his feet. "Then I'll see you tomorrow."

Cicero frowned at his hurried departure, but didn't remark on it. "Ciao, Thomas. Thanks for the cream."

Tom left the restaurant, half-expecting Phelps to ambush him on the way out. But there was no sign of the man, either inside or on the crowded street. Tom cast about for several minutes, before admitting it was hopeless.

Phelps had recognized him as Liam O'Connell. Whether a man who'd once headed a gang would go to the police, or take matters into his own hands, Tom didn't know. But as he turned his steps toward home, he couldn't shake the feeling he'd see Phelps again soon.

Cicero burst through the doors of Techne. "That's it!" he proclaimed at the top of his lungs. "I'm done with the MWP. Finished!"

All eyes turned to him. He made certain he was dramatically framed by the door, head flung back, eyes closed. The only thing spoiling the moment was that it had started raining after he stormed away from his fake argument with Rook on the front steps of the Coven. *That* had almost been enough to get him to turn around, but he soldiered on for Isaac's sake. Now his hair was wet, and his coat damp, and if he'd known the case would require this sort of sacrifice he might have reconsidered the whole thing.

"Good!" called Leona from her usual table. "To hell with the coppers! Just another part of a corrupt system designed to—"

Cicero ignored the rest of her words to focus on Noah, who rushed over to him. "You poor thing!" Noah exclaimed, grabbing his hands. "And you're wet—come upstairs, immediately."

Cicero let Noah lead him up the back stair to the apartment above the café. He'd been there many times before, of course. Noah was handsome and not at all bad between the sheets. Or on the pillows, or the couch, or wherever they ended up.

He let Noah fuss over him a bit, drying his hair and wrapping him in a warm blanket. "What happened?" Noah asked, once he'd made Cicero comfortable.

"It was awful, darling." Cicero leaned against Noah's shoulder, doing his best to look miserable. "Chief Ferguson called me into his office. He said that, since I hadn't chosen a witch for myself, he'd do it for me." He shuddered dramatically. "The man he picked..."

He trailed off, the words sticking in his throat. He'd meant to describe Tom, but now that the moment had come, it felt wrong. Not that he'd ever bond with the fellow—that was out of the question. But Tom hadn't proved quite the ogre Cicero had assumed. Casting him as such didn't seem fair, somehow.

Fortunately, Noah didn't need any description. "The devil!" he bristled. "How dare he! What about the other familiars? Did they stand up for you?"

Cicero dabbed at his eyes. "I thought Rook would. Instead, he accused me of having no loyalty, no honor!"

That part they'd shouted at each other on the steps, in full view of any reporters and passers-by. Rook had probably enjoyed his side of the mock fight, but it had left Cicero feeling queasy.

Because there was a grain of truth to all of this. Ferguson would never force Cicero to bond with someone he hated. But the ultimatum would come, and it wouldn't be long.

Time was running out. He had to choose, and do it soon.

Noah clasped his hands and drew him close. "Bond with me."

Oh.

He should have expected this. Noah frequently bragged about his witch potential, and they were friends and sometimes lovers. And yet, somehow the possibility had never occurred to Cicero until now.

Noah wouldn't be a bad witch. His paintings might not be the most inspired, but he appreciated the arts and the finer things in life. They had a great deal in common, and if the idea of bonding with Noah didn't set his heart to racing...well, wasn't it time to abandon that dream for good anyway, now that his stupid magic had decided a rough Irishman was its match?

And if it felt like settling, obviously that was the best he could expect from life. He couldn't fall back on the excuse of waiting for his witch any more. Time to take a hard look at his options and make a choice.

Time to grow up and stop believing in fairytales.

If he chose Noah, he'd have to leave the MWP. Noah would never agree to work for the police. And since he was the witch in the relationship, his opinion would be respected. No one would presume to pressure him to work at the MWP just because they'd invested in Cicero.

Cicero didn't want to leave. Not really. His life with them wasn't perfect, but they'd given him shelter when he most needed it. And, the assassination attempt against Roosevelt notwithstanding, they did try to do some good in the world.

"Not this moment, of course," Noah said hastily, perhaps reading something in Cicero's expression. "There are some other things I need to attend to first. I'd want to do something to mark the occasion, after all. Just say yes, and I'll start planning right away."

At least the case gave him an excuse to put off the inevitable a little while longer. "I need time to think," Cicero said truthfully. "I'm sorry, Noah."

"Of course," Noah soothed. "You've had a terrible shock. Take your time. I'll be here when you're ready. At least say you'll stay with me in the meantime."

His kindness threatened to bring more tears to Cicero's eyes. Which was stupid. "I have a friend to stay with—another feral—for a little while at least," he lied. "But I need a job. You were so kind to Isaac, I thought you might be able to help me as well?"

"Of course." Noah stroked the side of Cicero's face. "Anything for you. The way you dance, you'll be working at the Rooster by tomorrow night."

"You're hired."

Cicero kept a smile of triumph from his face as he stepped down off the stage of The Spitting Rooster. The main room was underground, just below street level, and accessed by a narrow stair from the front. At one end was the stage, complete with faded velvet curtain. A piano stood by the stage, and a bar ran the length of the nearest wall. Curtained alcoves occupied the opposite wall, and a stair in the back led up to the ground floor. No doubt the private rooms were up there.

Tables filled most of the remaining space. A few men moved among them, sweeping the floor and straightening up for the evening. They'd all stopped to watch Cicero's audition.

"Thank you," Cicero said, crossing to where the Rooster's owner sat at the bar. Sloane was a big man, his hair worn long and an enormous mustache concealing most of his mouth. His small, flat eyes stayed on Cicero, and a little shiver ran down his spine. Sloane was a familiar all right. Some sort of predatory reptile, most likely.

"I'll find someone who can play the right music—the piano isn't going to work." Sloane settled back in his chair. "You start tonight. By tomorrow, we'll have every chair in the house filled."

"Of course we will, darling," Cicero replied. "I have some thoughts on that. A tease with a slow build up."

A smile cracked the part of Sloane's mouth visible under the mustache. "I like the way you think. You were wasted at the MWP."

"Oh, Noah mentioned that?" Cicero made sure to look shame-faced. "I never wanted…but they paid, and…"

"We all do what we have to do," Sloane said grandly. "But play your cards right, and you can make better pay here."

So long as he didn't mind fucking for money. Considering he'd joined the MWP to get away from that life, Cicero doubted he would have remained here even if his defection had been real.

"I'd rather work for another familiar any day," he said. "I've never met one who owned his own business before."

And that was when he felt it.

A little prick, like a hypodermic needle, slipping under the skin of his chest. There and gone so fast it would be unnoticeable to most. But Cicero recognized the hex meant to reveal whether a familiar was bonded or not.

He'd felt it before, in those dark days before he'd gone to the MWP. It had sent him running down an alley, heart racing, terror icing his veins as footsteps pounded after him. And he'd felt it a few times since…but on those occasions, he'd simply parted his coat to display his MWP badge, and the caster had slunk away.

Now he fought to keep the fear off his face. Probably one of Sloane's men had used the hex, just to make sure of his story. After all, the MWP always worked in bonded teams; this would be the easiest way for Sloane to make sure he wasn't lying about having left the force.

Maybe it was a good thing Ferguson had refused to put a detective team onto the investigation.

Sloane's smile widened, but it was a cold, slow thing that showed too many teeth. "Indeed. Most of our kind take on a more…subservient role. It's unfortunate."

Steps sounded on the wooden floor, and Cicero turned quickly. The newcomer was a large man, almost as big as Tom. He wore a heavy coat and a tall hat. Cauliflower ears protruded from beneath the brim, and he looked as though his nose had been broken more than once. "This is Joe Kearney," Sloane said. "My witch."

"Pleased to meet you," Cicero lied, holding out his hand. He was almost positive Kearney had been the one to use the hex a moment ago.

Kearney seemed less than pleased to meet Cicero. The hand he extended was covered with a fingerless glove, hex signs burned into the leather. "I'm in charge of security," he said.

Meaning the hexed gloves probably let him punch with more than human force. Cicero fluttered his eyelashes playfully. "I feel safer already."

Kearney shot him a look of disgust and tromped away. An odd attitude for a fellow who worked at a resort like this. Not to mention that his own familiar apparently employed him.

Everything about the situation put Cicero's hackles up. From the hex, to Kearney, to Sloane's reptilian smile.

Fur and feathers, what if Tom didn't manage to get hired? Because the idea of working here alone, with no one at his back, made Cicero's skin crawl with fear. For the first time, he was grateful Tom was large and intimidating.

"Ignore him," Sloane said. "You'll be dealing with me." He held out his hand, his skin cool against Cicero's "Welcome to the Rooster."

CHAPTER 8

OF COURSE THE SPITTING ROOSTER had hired a replacement bartender already—Tom had thought the idea insanely far-fetched, but clung to the hope that this type of resort was somehow different than a regular saloon full of thirsty customers.

What they lacked, however, was someone with a strong arm to turn the crank on the ice crushing machine and bring up the heaviest crates of booze from the basement. The new bartender was a thin wisp of a fellow by the name of Ludolf Ho: half Dutch, half Chinese, and pure New Yorker going by the fast way he talked.

"You'll sweep up when it's needed," Ho explained as they set up for the night. "I make the cocktails, but you can pull the beer. And if someone gets rowdy at the bar, you can stop the trouble without Mr. Kearney having to leave his post at the door."

Kearney had taken a shine to Tom right away. "Just what we need," he'd said, clapping Tom on the shoulder. "Another good Irish lad to keep the place running."

By ten o'clock, the tables at The Spitting Rooster were half full, which didn't strike Tom as bad for the Tuesday before Christmas. So far, the most exciting thing that had happened was Ho sending him into the cellar for another crate of whiskey. The Rooster's entertainment consisted of men in makeup and dresses, singing or dancing on the stage. When not performing, they circulated among the customers, sitting at tables so they could be bought drinks at outrageous prices, or else disappearing into the curtained alcoves. Or up the stairs, in a few cases.

The latest act bustled off the stage and the curtain fell. There came some desultory clapping, but only about half the customers, if that, seemed to pay attention at any given time. The rest either chatted amongst themselves, or with the rouged men sitting at their tables. The piano player slid off his bench and came to the bar. A small, dark man carrying a flute of some kind took his place near the stage. Sloane stepped in front of the curtain and the murmur of talk died down. Not the usual way of doing things, then.

"We've something very special for you tonight, gents," Sloane said, rubbing his hands together. "You've all heard of Little Egypt, that wonderful lass who brought the hoochie coochie to our fair shores." He gave an exaggerated wink. "And who apparently dances in at least ten dives a night here in New York alone, plus another dozen in Chicago."

There came a ripple of laughter. Sloane grinned. "Given her busy schedule, as gentlemen we couldn't ask her to visit us here at the Rooster. No, we have something better for you lads. Forget Little Egypt, as I present to you…Cicero."

He stepped aside, and the curtain pulled back.

Cicero stood alone on the stage, his arms held above his head, bent at the elbows. His black hair gleamed in the lights, and his eyes, more heavily lined than usual, were incandescent. A thin veil hid the lower part of his face. Diaphanous pants rode dangerously low on his hips and brushed the tops of his bare feet. Above, he wore only a tiny beaded vest, too small to close in the front. It left the skin of his flat belly exposed, along with his lower back and most of his chest. All of which had been shaved completely free of hair and oiled until he gleamed.

The audience fell silent, including the other entertainers. A few moans came from behind the curtains, but otherwise everyone was fixated on the sight.

Including Tom. His throat tightened, and his prick stirred. Had he thought Cicero pretty before? The man was ungodly handsome, all dusky skin and black hair, and those eyes like peridots that burned with an inner light all their own.

Then the music started, and Cicero began to dance.

He moved with all the effortless grace of a cat, a ripple of motion flowing from his hands, down his arms, undulating across his belly and hips. His feet barely adjusted to match, tiny steps, even as his upper body arched and swayed. The vest pulled back as his arms shifted, revealing the flash of exposed gold where a slender ring pierced each nipple.

Tom needed to look away, to watch the crowd. They were here on police work, no matter the pretense. But he couldn't tear his eyes from the spectacle.

At the same time, he didn't know quite where to rest his gaze—the smooth expanse of Cicero's flat belly, or his rolling hips, or his sinful eyes. Cicero turned his back on the crowd, his rear shaking and twitching in the most indecent display Tom had ever beheld. And he shouldn't be staring at Cicero like that, they were working together for heaven's sake, but he was as hard as he'd ever been in his life.

The music came to an end. Cicero stood poised for a long moment, his body perfectly still, allowing the room one last look at him. Then the curtain fell.

The crowd went wild—clapping and stomping, shouting for an encore. A number of the other performers leapt to their feet and made for the backstage. One or two of the customers seemed likely to try to join them, but Kearney had taken up position in front of the stage and glared them down.

Tom felt stupefied as he tore his eyes away from the curtain. Ho blinked dazedly, a bottle of whiskey in his hand, as if he'd forgotten what he was doing with it. Aware of Tom's gaze, Ho grinned and poured a drink. "Care to run this back to him? My compliments."

Tom nodded. "Um. Aye. Right," he managed past the tightness in his throat. He needed to calm down, to remember where he was and why. But it wasn't easy, when all he could see was Cicero's lithe body, moving in a way that promised things Tom had barely even let himself imagine before.

"Make sure he knows it's from me," Ho stressed as he handed over the glass. "Tell him he can drink free, if he wants to come to the bar."

"I will," Tom said, taking the whiskey. He ought to be grateful for the chance to talk to Cicero without raising suspicion, but he couldn't help but feel a twinge of…what?

Not jealousy; that would be insane.

The area backstage consisted of a short hall with a series of dressing rooms off it. When Tom stepped into the hall, he found it crowded by the other workers. Sloane's voice cut through their excited babble. "Back to work. Take advantage of the state the crowd is in, eh?"

There came a general muttering. "But you will show us, won't you, Cicero?" one entertainer called in a falsetto voice as they began to troop back to the main room.

"Of course, darling. We'll do an act," Cicero replied from inside the dressing room.

Sloane lingered in the hall. "I've got five offers—three for the alcoves, two for upstairs," he said to Cicero.

Cold water dripped into Tom's chest, battling with the heat there. They were here to investigate Whistler and Barshtein's sudden madness and Isaac's disappearance—Cicero wouldn't actually do anything more than dance, would he? Certainly he wouldn't go upstairs with some man, let him peel off those gauzy pants, run hands over that muscular torso, and explore the rings set in flat, brown nipples...

Cicero laughed. "A few nights from now and you'll have triple that—and triple the price."

Sloane grinned. "Indeed. I'll give them your regrets."

Tom stepped into one of the empty dressing rooms and waited behind the door while Sloane passed. He wasn't entirely certain whether his mission from Ho would meet with the proprietor's approval, and there seemed no reason to risk the chance to speak to Cicero.

Once Sloane was gone, Tom slipped back out and went to the dressing room Cicero shared. The small space was crowded with wigs and dresses. Cicero leaned over a table, touching up the kohl around his eyes in a mirror. The thin fabric of the pants draped over his backside in a way that didn't leave much to the imagination, and Tom felt himself getting hard again. Not that he'd fully deflated since the moment Cicero had stepped out on that damned stage.

"Oh, there you are," Cicero said as Tom shut the door behind him. "Any luck yet?"

"Nay." He knew he should say something else, anything, but he couldn't stop staring. "Ho—the bartender—sent this for you."

Cicero snorted. "An admirer. Leave it on the table."

Tom put down the whiskey. He ought to ask Cicero about his plans for the investigation, now that they'd managed to find a way into the inner workings of the Rooster. But his brain seemed stuck in molasses, unable to move forward from the sight of Cicero's undulating hips, his petit backside both concealed and revealed by his costume. The flash of those nipple rings against olive skin.

Their eyes met in the mirror. Surprise flickered across Cicero's face, then shifted into something else. Something heated.

He put the kohl down and slowly, deliberately straightened and turned to face Tom. The gaslight gleamed off the little rings in his nipples, each set with a tiny hex charm. Cicero very deliberately ran his gaze down Tom's form, and Tom felt it like the touch of a hand. To his shock, he could see the growing outline of Cicero's cock against the thin fabric of his hoochie coochie pants.

This wasn't real. Was it?

Things happened, in the precinct barracks. On reserve nights, the men were expected to sleep there, in case of a riot. The cots were close together, and they were all men, and men had needs. He and Bill had tossed each other off on the nights they both ended up on reserve. But that wasn't...like this, whatever this was. That was in the dark, an impersonal touch, and not to be spoken of ever.

"What did you think of my performance, Thomas?" Cicero asked, sauntering slowly closer.

"It was..." Obscene? Scandalous?

"What?" Cicero was close now, too close, almost touching. Tom needed to only lift his hand by a few inches to cup Cicero's hip. "Cat got your tongue?"

Tom tried to laugh, but it came out more of a groan. Cicero's smile sizzled with heat, and he leaned in, his lips a hair's breadth from Tom's ear. "Ever had it French?"

Tom's prick twitched against the confines of his pants. A hand was one thing, but a mouth? He knew whores charged double for that, but he'd never been able to bring himself to pay for sex. "N-Nay," he managed to say.

Cicero's hands found the buttons of Tom's trousers. His fingers skated lightly over the bulge of Tom's prick, teasing through the fabric. "Do you want it?" he whispered as he popped each button free.

Maybe Cicero was a fairy of the other sort, the kind Ma had told endless stories about. Because Tom surely felt as though he were under a spell. "Aye." Be polite, that was how one treated with the Folk. "Please."

Cicero's plump lips curled in a hungry smile that held an edge of wildness. "Now there's a word I haven't heard often." His hand slid beneath Tom's unbuttoned trousers, clever fingers wrapping around Tom's painfully hard cock and pulling him free. For a moment, the touch was so intense, Tom thought he might be just as happy pumping into Cicero's hand.

Then Cicero went to his knees.

Tom opened his mouth to say...he didn't even know what. Tell him to stop. Beg him to continue. But his brain seemed to have seized up, like an engine with no oil, and nothing came out.

Cicero shot him a smoldering look. He held Tom's prick in one hand, at the level of his face. It was filthy and tantalizing, and the most arousing thing Tom had ever seen.

Until Cicero leaned forward and ran a long, slow lick along the underside.

His hips jerked, and he barely managed to keep in a cry. Cicero grinned, clearly enjoying having this power over Tom. He licked again, lingering on the tip this time, lapping precome from the slit. "Mmm," he purred. "So close already. Let's see how you like this."

Then he wrapped his lips around Tom's cock and slid his mouth all the way down its length.

Tom turned his shout into a choked sound. Cicero's tongue and lips worked him, cheeks hollowing as he sucked. By all the saints, this was nothing like the touch of a rough hand in the dark. This was everything *but* impersonal, and Tom slid his fingers into Cicero's hair, unable to help himself.

Cicero's hands drifted up Tom's thighs, and he felt a sudden, agonized pang of regret that his trousers kept that touch from his skin. The other man's hands cupped his arse, urging him forward, and Tom let his hips move tentatively. Cicero pulled back, his tongue curling around the flared head in a way that made Tom's knees weak.

"You can fuck my mouth, if you'd like," he said.

Then he dove back down, and Holy Familiar of Christ, had he really offered what Tom thought? His hands were tight on Tom's buttocks, head bobbing determinedly, and Tom thrust forward to meet him. Cicero moaned encouragement, although how he could even breathe with Tom's prick shoved down his throat, Tom surely didn't know.

His fingers curled involuntarily in Cicero's hair, and his hips moved in a rougher version of Cicero's undulating dance. Cicero looked up at him, his peridot eyes hot and sinful, while Tom's prick slid wetly over his red lips. And oh God, he was doing something with his throat, some vibration that felt like a purr, and Tom's balls tightened.

"Going to come," he managed to say, and tried to push Cicero away. But Cicero would have none of it, his mouth hot and wet and insistent. Tom barely suppressed a cry, shooting hard, and Cicero swallowed it all down, throat working a second spasm from Tom's prick.

Cicero sat back on his heels. His plump lips were red and slick, and parted just a bit. Still dazed, Tom reached out and ran tender fingers over his cheek.

Cicero jerked away. He stood up quickly and turned to the mirror. "You'd best get back to work, before Kearney notices you're gone."

"I..." Had Tom done something wrong? How had the man gone

from sucking his cock to ordering him away so quickly? "Thank you." It sounded stupid, but he didn't know what else to say. "That was…"

"Incredible, yes." Cicero flicked a dismissive hand in his direction. "Now go. I've work of my own to do, remember?"

He might sound indifferent, but the rigid outline of his cock told another story. "What should I do?" Tom asked, feeling utterly off balance. It wasn't a question he'd ever had to ask before. A friend gave you a hand in the dark, and you did the same.

But the way Cicero had looked at him, so hungry. Wanting *him*, it felt like, though what a fellow like Cicero would want with Tom, he couldn't imagine.

"Go back to the bar." Cicero picked up the whiskey and downed it in a single gulp. "Horrid," he said with a shudder. "Take this back to Ho and tell him thanks from me. Keep an eye on the crowd."

"I…aye." Tom knew when he was being dismissed—and rightfully so. They weren't here for pleasure, after all.

But even so, he couldn't help but feel a bit lost as he walked alone back to the front of the building.

Chapter 9

Cicero stood very still, listening to Tom's retreating footsteps. His cock ached, and he wanted...

Nothing sane. Fur and feathers, that had been downright stupid. Things were complicated enough without adding sex to the equation. But he'd been caught off guard at the sight of Tom in something other than his police uniform. He wore no coat, his sleeves rolled up to reveal pale, freckled forearms, corded with muscle. He'd even done something different with his hair, making it look less a disaster. The fit of his vest showed off his barrel chest, and without a coat to conceal them, his muscular thighs were a temptation Cicero could have done without.

And the way Tom had looked at him, like Cicero were a steak dinner and Tom a starving man...

He could still taste Tom in his mouth, despite the bad whiskey.

He'd half-expected a blow, or at least a rough shove, once Tom came in his throat. Cicero had sucked enough cocks in his time to be resigned to the fact that some men felt the need to prove their masculinity with their fists. Instead, Tom had run his fingers over his cheek, so tender, like the caress of a lover.

Which they weren't. And wouldn't be. This had been a terrible mistake, and it certainly wouldn't happen again.

Bloody hell, he'd completely forgotten to tell Tom about his misgivings concerning Sloane and Kearney, let alone the hex aimed at him earlier. What was wrong with him, acting like a youth so distracted by sex he couldn't think of anything else? If Rook found out, he'd never let Cicero hear the end of it.

So. Time to stop thinking about Tom Bloody Halloran, and start thinking about what they'd come here to do in the first place.

Cicero slipped out of the dressing room and into the hall. It was deserted, but still he waited a moment, listening intently. The muted sound of the badly tuned piano drifted from the front room, accompanied by the rhythmic creaking of beds overhead.

He shifted to the balls of his bare feet and padded silently down the hall to the closed door at the end. It swung open at his touch and he slipped through. Beyond was a small, unlit room cluttered with what appeared to be props used in the stage acts: couches, swings, a hobby horse, and other assorted paraphernalia. Two closed doors let out from the room, one directly across from him, the other to his left. The first probably led to the short hallway connecting the side door, cellar stair, and front room. The other must lead to an interior chamber. Light showed from beneath it.

Cicero closed the door soundlessly behind him and shifted into cat form.

Instantly, the room brightened; he could make out every detail of the worn fabric, the flaking paint on the hobby horse, the silk flowers twined around the swings. The smell of mice tantalized, mingled with the scents of the various people who had traipsed through. Sloane, Kearney, others he didn't recognize.

He spared a moment to give his shoulder a quick lick, smoothing down the fur. Satisfied, he slunk across the room to the door on the left. A dry, dusty scent clung around it, and he opened his mouth to better sift through the smells. A reptile had been here—Sloane?

The creak of a chair alerted him someone was inside. He froze, every sense straining. The chair squealed again, this time followed by footsteps approaching the door.

Cicero darted across the floor and beneath a couch. The cushions reeked of sex and sweat, and of the mice that had used the stuffing for their nest. Cicero went to his belly, eyes narrowed to slits so no reflection would betray him.

Sloane stepped out of the room, then shut and locked the door. Placing his hand on the latch, he said, "Werner's alarms: so you can put your mind at ease."

Cicero's ears pricked up. It was clearly the activation phrase for an alarm hex. He remained beneath the couch as Sloane passed by. The door to the outer hall opened and shut.

Once he was certain Sloane wasn't coming back, Cicero eeled out from under the couch. He paused to clean the dust from his whiskers, pondering as he did so.

An alarm hex might not be out of place in a pawn shop or a pricy saloon like Hoffman House, where swells drank themselves senseless. But in a tawdry resort like the Rooster?

There was something in that room Sloane didn't want anyone else to see.

Which meant they needed to find a way inside.

Tom's nerves were in a right twist by the time he reached the Coven the next afternoon.

He'd slept late, having been up most of the night. In part that had been because of the hours he put in at the Rooster, and in part because he'd lain awake in bed after returning to his apartment. His mind circled back again and again to the feeling of Cicero's lips, the expression in his eyes, as he'd sucked on Tom's cock. When he had finally waked, it had been to find himself almost painfully hard. He'd tried to keep his mind clear when he stroked himself, but then the image of Cicero's mouth on him had returned, and he spent in an instant.

Tom found Cicero quickly enough, at Kopecky and Rook's desk. As Tom approached, Rook spotted him. The dark skinned man grinned broadly and give Cicero a nudge.

The devil? Cicero wouldn't have said anything to Rook, would he?

Cicero glanced up, and a small frown creased his forehead, quickly gone. He turned back to Kopecky as if Tom were barely an acquaintance, let alone a man whose spend he'd swallowed only the night before. Then again, what had Tom expected?

A smile at least. That would have been nice.

"Good morning, Halloran," Rook said. He was smiling, at any rate.

Kopecky looked up from the hex he was busy drawing. "Oh, hello, Halloran," he said, sounding a bit distracted.

"It's Tom," Tom said. Maybe he was only working with the MWP temporarily, but these were Cicero's friends. Even if Cicero didn't seem too friendly this morning.

"Dominic," Kopecky replied, and went back to his drawing.

"Rook," Rook said with a wink. Cicero huffed softly.

Was Cicero angry at him for some reason? He tried to catch the familiar's eye, but Cicero remained fixed on whatever hex Dominic was creating. "So, er, what…?" Tom asked, gesturing to the paper.

"A locking hex," Rook said.

"Oh. And we need one because…?"

Cicero heaved an irritated sigh. "Because I did a bit of poking around last night. There's a room in the back—Sloane's office, I'd guess—with an alarm hex on it. I'd like to find out what he's hiding that's so important. But I'd also prefer he not realize anyone has been inside, which means we need a hex not only to unlock the door, but to relock it once we're done." He shifted uncomfortably. "And there's something I didn't tell you yesterday."

He related the information about Sloane and Kearney—and that they'd hexed Cicero to make sure he wasn't bonded. "What?" Tom exclaimed. "Why didn't you mention this last night?"

A faint flush spread over Cicero's cheeks. "I was distracted."

Huh. So maybe he wasn't as indifferent to what they'd done as he pretended.

Dominic let out a long-suffering sigh. Rook leveled a knowing look at Cicero. "It's a good thing Ferguson insisted on someone else going with you, then, isn't it?"

"I can take care of myself," Cicero snapped back.

"You are the most stubborn—"

Dominic cleared his throat loudly. "I'm done," he said, thrusting the paper at Cicero.

Cicero snatched it from Dominic's hand. "Come on," he shot at Tom, and stalked past him.

Tom glanced at the two detectives, hoping for some enlightenment. Rook only shook his head, an annoyed expression on his face. Dominic offered Tom a commiserating smile. "Some familiars take more… work…than others," he said. "Believe me, I know."

Rook let out an outraged squawk. Deciding that was his cue to leave, Tom hastened to catch up with Cicero.

They traversed a maze of narrow corridors, threading deeper into the heart of the vast building. Eventually Cicero threw open a small door, revealing an incredibly cramped office with two desks and two chairs jammed inside. A pale woman sat at one of the desks, staring dejectedly at the pile of paper in front of her.

"Are you any good at figures, Ro?" she asked.

"Don't call me that, Greta," he said. "And I'm a dancer, not a mathematician. Go ask Dominic for help."

She peered up at Tom. "And who the devil are you?"

He blinked. "Um. Tom? Halloran?"

Cicero waved at Greta. "Don't mind her. Wolverine, don't you know. Now why don't you clear out, Greta darling? I need to talk to Tom alone."

Greta bared her teeth at Cicero. "Cats. Always think they're better than the rest of us."

"I'd noticed," Tom said without thinking.

Greta laughed. "I like you," she said, sliding out of her chair. The top of her head barely came to his chest. "Whatever business you've got with Ro, don't let him push you around. And if he tries to pull the I'm-an-aloof-cat act, snap his suspenders."

"Oi!" Cicero glared fiercely at her. Greta laughed again and departed, closing the door behind her.

"Fur and feathers," Cicero muttered, dropping into the chair opposite the one Greta had vacated. "I swear, I'm counting the seconds until she finds her witch and leaves me alone."

"Or you find yours," Tom said.

The look Cicero gave him could have flayed skin. "Shall we discuss our case?"

"In a minute." Tom hesitated, wondering if he should take Greta's chair. Or maybe standing would be better for this. "What did I do to make you so angry?"

Cicero's lips parted, but he didn't say anything. A look Tom couldn't interpret flashed over his face...then he seemed to deflate slightly. "Nothing."

"Don't say that, when it's clear you're mad." Tom felt as though he groped in the dark. Was Cicero angry because he hadn't reciprocated in the dressing room? "Is it...about last night? What happened? You all but shoved me out the door, otherwise—"

"Last night?" Cicero asked. "What on earth do you mean?"

Tom felt the blood creeping into his face. "You know."

"What, when I sucked your cock?" Cicero spoke the words like they meant nothing. Like he'd done it a thousand times before. "Of course not. I haven't given it a moment's thought."

Sickness settled in Tom's belly. He'd thought Cicero wanted a connection, when their eyes had met last night. But maybe it had all been just an act.

"I have." The words scraped coming out, but Tom wouldn't lie. Not about this. "I ain't in the habit of...that sort of thing."

Cicero shrugged, a graceful ripple that distantly recalled the dance he'd performed. "You were in a strange place, exposed to new experiences," he said matter-of-factly. "It's only natural to react otherwise than one ordinarily would. Nothing to worry about. It doesn't mean a thing. Tonight will be entirely different."

Tom wanted to argue. Instead, he took a deep breath and forced himself to relax. "I see."

"Now," Cicero said, turning his attention to the paper piled on what was presumably his desk, "I spoke to some of the other entertainers at the Rooster last night. Apparently Isaac had some regulars. I haven't gotten any names yet—I didn't want to seem too suspicious on the first night. And, as I said, I want to get a look at Sloane's office." He drummed his fingers on the desk. "The problem is how we're to get past the alarm hex. I heard Sloane use the activation phrase, but we need to be able to deactivate it to get inside. If the company has an office in Manhattan, we might be able to talk them into giving over the more common phrases used, and hope Sloane didn't have his customized."

Tom hesitated. Cicero's cool demeanor didn't invite confidences, but what choice did he have? If Sloane wasn't involved with whatever had happened to Barshtein and Whistler, it seemed likely he was tangled up in something nasty. "Can you keep a secret?"

Cicero's expression instantly grew wary. "When I need to. Why?"

"Because I have something to tell you, and you can't share it with anyone else." Tom swallowed against a throat gone suddenly dry. "Promise me."

"That sounds ominous."

"I have a way to get us past the alarm hex."

"All right," Cicero said, though he didn't sound at all happy about it. "What is it?"

It was as close to a promise as Tom was going to get. "I'm a hexbreaker."

It shouldn't have been so simple to say it aloud after all this time. But there it was. Hanging in the air.

Cicero gaped at him. "A…that's incredibly rare. Why wasn't it in your file?"

"Because it's a secret." Tom rolled his eyes. "Why do you think I asked you not to tell anyone?"

"A secret? Why?" Cicero looked at him as though he'd lost his mind. "I'd think the police would kill to have a hexbreaker employed. You could be earning twice your salary, easily! Or forget them and come work for the MWP. Whatever your old precinct is paying you, I'm sure

Ferguson would double it."

How could he explain it wasn't a gift, but a bloody curse? If he hadn't been a hexbreaker, the Muskrats would have had no use for an alliance with his family's gang. Da would never have known about the hexes in the psalter. Tom's parents would still be alive, and Danny, and all the rest.

But he couldn't say any of that. "Promise me you won't tell anyone else."

"All right, all right." Cicero looked uneasy, but let the issue go. "It certainly simplifies matters for us, at any rate. I'll see you tonight—let's say between my second and third performance?"

"Aye. I'll be there."

"Well, if there's nothing else, I have a report to write for Ferguson." Cicero began to shuffle the papers on his desk.

Knowing himself dismissed, Tom turned away without speaking further and let himself back out into the corridor. Once the door shut behind him, he paused, leaning against the wall.

As if he didn't have enough potential problems with Phelps, now someone else knew he was a hexbreaker. Knew something that could tie him back to Liam O'Connell.

And it was a man who sucked his cock, then acted like he hated him.

Surely though, if Cicero meant what he said, if he'd truly been unaffected by what they'd done, he wouldn't have been so angry. Wouldn't have avoided Tom's eyes there in the office, when he said it was just a mistake.

No, Tom's first instinct had been right. There had been more to last night than just a quick act, without meaning.

If only he could get Cicero to admit to it. And for that...well. Tom had a few ideas of his own.

The cooler air of the dressing room was a welcome relief against Cicero's heated skin. His style of dance might not be as obviously strenuous as something like the can-can, but it was enough to set him to sweating, even without the crowd of bodies adding to the heat.

He smirked at his reflection as he checked the mirror, adding a bit of rouge to his cheeks. It hadn't taken long for word of his previous performance to spread. The Rooster was absolutely packed tonight, with hundreds of bodies jammed into the main room, and most of them there to see him. After his first performance of the evening, he'd received over a dozen offers to take him into one of the rooms or alcoves. After the second, there had been more, and this time some of the sums named had been far in excess of what he earned in a week at the MWP.

When this had started, he hadn't intended to actually take any of the offers up. Now he wasn't so certain. The money was good, and it wasn't as though it hurt anyone, or interfered in the actual investigation. And maybe it would get his mind off Tom.

Had Tom watched him again, as keenly as last night? Had he been aroused? He was due any moment, assuming he could get away...

No. Last night had been a mistake, and he'd already told Tom as much. Tonight, Cicero would be on his best behavior.

As if summoned by his thought, Tom stepped inside. Cicero stayed focused on his reflection as Tom shut the door behind him. "They're wild for you out there." Tom set a whiskey aside. "I told Ho how much you appreciated the drink last night, so he couldn't wait to send me back with another."

Cicero set aside the rouge. "How cruel of you, darling, getting his hopes up like that."

"It ain't just his hopes that are up," Tom said dryly. He moved closer, the floor creaking beneath his weight. In the mirror, Cicero could see he had his sleeves rolled up again, the flex of muscle as he moved. What would he look like without a shirt at all? Given the golden hair furring his forearms, he'd probably have a nice thatch on his chest. What would it feel like to run his fingers through it?

Cicero's traitorous cock swelled against the thin fabric of his pants. Blast it, he had to stop thinking about Tom like this. Nothing more was going to happen between them. It couldn't.

Rook swore that sex between a familiar and his witch was like nothing else in the world, even if they weren't bonded yet. But Rook said a lot of things just to hear himself talk.

Tom was very close to him now. "It looks like he's not the only one," he murmured in a low, husky voice. Did he refer to the bulge in Cicero's pants, or his own?

Cicero had to say something. To stop this. "I'm not getting on my knees for you again." But his voice shook with lust, betraying him.

"Wasn't going to ask you to," Tom murmured, his breath hot on the back of Cicero's neck. He slid a strong arm around Cicero's waist, pulling him against his solid body. His other hand cupped Cicero through his pants, fingers curling around the outline of his cock, tugging gently.

An unwilling gasp escaped Cicero. He straightened, meaning to pull away, but the hand on his prick was palming him more firmly now, and he couldn't help but press into it. Tom's other hand drifted from around Cicero's waist, trailing a line of fire over the bare skin of his belly. Tom pushed the costume's small vest aside, exposing Cicero's nipples. His fingers explored one of the rings, then tugged gently.

A bolt of pleasure shot from nipple to groin. Cicero gasped again, more loudly this time, his back arching into Tom's broad chest. Tom's lips brushed Cicero's ear, and he whispered, "What are the hexes for?"

"They enhance—ah!" Another tug all but undid him, combined with the teasing pressure of Tom's hand through the gauzy cloth of his pants. "Pl-pleasure."

"Good," Tom whispered. Then he shoved down the front of Cicero's trousers, exposing his cock to the air.

Tom might not have done it in French fashion before, but he obviously was no newcomer to working with his hands. His callused fingers stroked Cicero's cock like an expert. Cicero swallowed a moan as Tom tugged on him, gathering the liquid at the tip and using it to slick his palm as he slid it back down to the base.

"F-fuck," Cicero stammered. Tom's fingers curled around him, a firm tunnel, and Cicero thrust into it helplessly. Tom's own erection pressed against his arse like an iron bar, and he ground back against it. Tom grunted, stroking Cicero more rapidly now, and pinched one nipple around the ring.

"Show me you like this," he growled in Cicero's ear. "I want you to. I want to make you come."

Sparks flared behind Cicero's eyes, and he couldn't suppress a mewling cry as he shot. Tom let go of his nipple and wrapped an arm around Cicero's waist again, keeping him on his feet. His other hand kept moving, milking Cicero's cock, until he made a small noise when it became too sensitive.

Fur and feathers. So much for not doing this again.

There was a long moment of silence, penetrated only by the sound of music from the front, and of sex from above. Cicero sagged bonelessly against Tom's solid bulk, striving to catch his breath.

Tom lifted his fingers, coated with Cicero's spunk, and licked them. "Cats ain't the only ones who like cream," he teased. "You were right about one thing, though. Tonight *was* different."

Cicero wasn't sure if he wanted to curse Tom or himself. He'd expected…well. Not this, obviously. Mainly that Tom would be more interested in his own pleasure, one of those men who liked to have his cock sucked but had no interest in returning the favor in any form.

"Don't sound so smug," Cicero said, but the involuntary grin on his mouth gave the lie to the words.

Tom smiled back. "Going to have to earn it with you, ain't I? That's all right. I'm willing to put in the work." He released Cicero and stepped away. "But for now, we've got a different sort of work to do. So put yourself to rights, and let's get to it."

CHAPTER 10

TOM COULDN'T HELP but feel rather pleased with himself as he followed Cicero down the hall. Cicero might have knocked him off balance last night and earlier today, but Tom figured he'd paid him back in full just now. He'd stripped away Cicero's usual quick tongue, reducing him to stammering and gasping, and the sound he'd made when he came...

Tom's prick stiffened again, and he struggled to force his thoughts away from the feel of the slender body in his arms. He could still smell Cicero's sweat on his skin and taste his spunk on his lips.

He'd never done *that* before, despite his bold words to Cicero. Tugging another fellow's prick in the darkened barracks was one thing, but licking up the spend would have gotten him a beating. He'd wanted to, though. And now that he had, he wondered what it would be like to get it direct from the source, so to speak.

Cicero opened the door at the end of the hall and slipped through. Tom did his best to follow, but he was bulkier and had to open it wider. It was utterly dark on the other side, so he left the door cracked. The thin finger of light revealed stored furniture and other props for the stage. Moving silent as a ghost, Cicero crossed to one of the doors and took out the hexes Dominic had prepared. "How long will it take you to break the alarm hex?" he whispered.

Tom joined him at the door. As soon as he touched the latch, he felt the telltale vibration of magic, like a tiny, quivering heartbeat. One brush of power, and it stopped. "Done."

Cicero arched a brow. "Impressive," he murmured. He placed the unlocking hex against the door. "Oh for…"

"What's wrong?"

Cicero sighed. "Rook thinks he's funny. Next time, I'm going to the general hexmen instead of Dominic." Clearing his throat, he read the activation phrase. "'Rook is always right, and I should listen to his advice.'"

The lock clicked open.

"Right about what?" Tom asked as Cicero opened the door.

"Never mind," Cicero replied sharply. "We have more important things to worry about at the moment."

Sloane's office was surprisingly tidy. A desk took up much of the space, and a liquor cabinet a good bit of what was left over. Shelves lined the walls, and a safe squatted near the door. A calendar hung on the wall facing the desk.

"Look," Tom said, pointing at the calendar. "New Year's Eve is circled in red."

"Maybe Sloane is expecting it to be a busy day?" Cicero suggested with a shrug. "Come on—let's go through his papers. And put everything back exactly as you found it."

There wasn't a great deal to see…but what there was sent a chill up Tom's back. A set of bloodletting tools, which had no business outside of a doctor's toolkit. A stack of unused hexes meant to determine whether a familiar was bonded.

Absinthe hexes, which looked precisely like the ones Barshtein and Gerald had used.

"Bloody hell," Cicero whispered. "Take one of each—you have more places to hide them at the moment." The corner of his mouth curled up, and he gave his hips a little shake, so the gauzy pants swirled around his ankles. "One thing this outfit lacks is pockets."

While Tom did so, Cicero snatched a ledger off Sloane's desk. "What have we here?" he murmured. "Look. Sloane has made several large payouts to 'the benefit of mankind.'"

Tom peered over Cicero's shoulder. "How very generous of him."

"Uncharacteristically so, I'd say," Cicero agreed. "I—"

The sound of one of the doors opening in the other room cut off his words.

Tom exchanged a look of horror with Cicero. "I'll get the funds from my safe," Sloane said, his voice muffled by the door.

Tom cast about frantically. The office was tiny—Cicero might be able to hide in cat form, but Tom?

"Under the desk," Cicero hissed. "I'll set the alarm! Go!"

He didn't have much choice. Tom pushed the chair back as silently as he could and crammed himself into the small area beneath the desk. His knees jabbed into his chin, and the chair could only be pulled in so far. If Sloane came anywhere near this side of the room, he'd be spotted in an instant.

"Your support is appreciated," said an unfamiliar voice with a strong Polish accent. Cicero murmured something unintelligible nearby—the activation phrase for the alarm, no doubt.

Keys jingled. "Anything for the cause," Sloane said from just outside the door.

Tom shut his eyes and strained his ears as the door opened. Footsteps entered the room, and Tom waited for the inevitable cry of outrage.

If they were caught in here…getting fired would be the least of their worries. Given the presence of the absinthe hexes, it seemed likely Sloane was involved in something that had already sent at least three people to their deaths. He surely wouldn't hesitate to add two more to the list.

Or one. Sloane and Kearney knew Cicero was unbonded. Would they kill him, or give him to a witch for force bonding?

Could that be what had happened to the missing Isaac?

There came a muffled thump, then a low series of clicks. Understanding dawned when there came the groan of hinges—Sloane must have unlocked the safe near the door.

A muscle in Tom's awkwardly bent legs threatened to cramp.

He held his breath, silently willing the pain to go away. Instead it continued to build. But he couldn't shift his position to relieve it, not without giving himself away.

If the worst happened, he'd fight, hard as he could. With any luck, he could create enough mayhem that Cicero at least could get away. He wouldn't let the cat end up practically enslaved to some witch, not if it was in his power to prevent it.

There came a rustling noise from the direction of the safe. Then the door thunked shut, followed by the sound of Sloane setting the lock. The whisper of clothing followed, and Tom imagined Sloane rising to his feet.

Saint Mary Magdalene, Holy Family of Christ, keep him from looking in the direction of the desk…

Footsteps retreated toward the door. "Here it is," Sloane said, and the office door shut behind him, muffling the last words.

Tom rolled out from under the desk, straightening his leg. The cramping muscle eased, and he breathed a sigh of relief.

He stood up, in time to see Cicero crawl out from under the liquor cabinet in cat form. The cat was solid black and shining, not a single white hair anywhere Tom could see, and his eyes were the same yellow-green of his human form.

At the moment, he was also covered in dust and cobwebs. He let out three short sneezes, a tiny delicate sound that made Tom's heart melt. He'd never heard kitty sneezes before.

Cicero shifted back into human form and glared at Tom. "Don't you dare say I'm cute," he warned, apparently having interpreted Tom's expression correctly. "Look here."

He reached beneath the cabinet and pulled out a necklace with a broken chain. On it was a silver charm in the shape of a hand. "This belonged to Isaac."

Cold settled in Tom's gut. "Could he have simply lost it?" he asked without much hope.

"No. His mother gave it to him when he joined the MWP." Cicero shook his head. "He would have torn this place apart to find it the moment he knew it was gone."

"Damn it."

"I want to follow Sloane and this other fellow." Cicero stepped toward the door. "Doing it as a cat will be easiest."

Tom grabbed his arm. "I'm going with you."

Cicero hissed. "You can't! Your big feet make too much noise. I can follow them on my own."

"And if they catch you?" Tom tightened his grip, unwilling to let Cicero go. "Sloane was behind Isaac's disappearance. I won't let the same thing happen to you."

Cicero's lips parted. For a moment, he seemed to hesitate. Then his jaw firmed, as if he'd come to a decision.

"You have witch potential," Cicero said, the words all but blurring together, as if he wanted to get them out as quickly as possible. "I know the tests said otherwise, but they were wrong."

The cold spread from Tom's gut to encompass his spine. How the devil could Cicero know that? Maybe familiars could sense it somehow? But if so, then why the tests?

"That means I can—can do something to let you see through my eyes," Cicero went on. "You wouldn't be with me physically, but you'd know if I got into trouble and needed rescue. Would that be enough?"

"Some sort of hex?" Tom asked, confused.

"No. It doesn't matter now—there's no time." Cicero tugged against his hold. "Decide."

"Aye. What you suggested—let's do it."

Cicero took a deep breath. "Then go down on your knees and close your eyes."

Tom obeyed. He heard Cicero's slow exhale—then felt the softness of lips against the fragile skin of his right eyelid.

Cicero's hand caressed the side of his face. "Let me in, Thomas," he whispered, then kissed the other eyelid.

The fine hairs on Tom's skin stood straight up, as if he'd been exposed to a lightning strike. Sparks flashed in the darkness behind his closed eyes. Strangely, the taste of blood filled his mouth, then was gone again.

Tom's heart raced, and he felt Cicero, bending over him. Breath on Tom's cheek. And he couldn't keep himself from tipping his head back and finding Cicero's lips with his own.

For a moment, Cicero didn't respond, his mouth still against Tom's. Then suddenly he was kissing back, tongue darting against Tom's lips. Tom parted them tentatively, and Cicero slipped in, exploring his mouth, then daring Tom to do the same in return.

Kissing was something else that never happened in the darkness of the barracks. Bill would have punched him in the mouth if he'd ever thought to try—which he hadn't. But this…Tom felt drunk on it, desperately hard and wanting more. He wanted to shove Cicero down on the carpet under him, keep kissing while they tugged on each other, sucking tongues like cocks.

Cicero tore free, breathing harshly. "Sloane," he said.

Shame killed Tom's desire as surely as being dunked in icy water. They were meant to be working. Instead, here they were, acting like a pair of fools with no brain between the two of them.

Cicero pressed the locking hex into Tom's hand. "Put things to right, go back out to the bar, and try to pretend nothing is out of the ordinary."

"But how do I see out of your eyes?" Tom asked. *Something* had happened when Cicero kissed his eyelids, but he still wasn't sure what.

"As soon as I'm in cat form, you'll be able to." Cicero eased the door open. "Just close your eyes, and you'll be with me."

Then the man was gone, and a sleek shape darted out the door and vanished into the shadows.

* * *

Cicero ran fast and low to the ground, pausing every few feet to look and listen. He could *feel* Tom with him, as though the witch peered over his shoulder, and the sensation was decidedly unsettling.

Fur and feathers, what had he done?

There were two steps to bonding. The second was for the witch to draw magic from the familiar, but that was only possible after the witch had first looked out of the familiar's eyes.

It didn't mean anything. No need to panic. Yes, he'd taken the first step toward bonding with Tom, but it was hardly an irrevocable one. And the circumstances had demanded it.

Tom's refusal to let him go with no protection should have raised his hackles, but after finding Isaac's broken necklace—not to mention the absinthe and familiar hexes—he'd been grateful for it. Cicero wanted to save Isaac; he had no desire at all to join him. Wherever Isaac was at the moment, Cicero couldn't believe it would be pleasant.

Fortunately, Sloane or his companion had left the door open to the outer hall, indicating the direction they'd gone in. If they'd lost him because Cicero wasted time kissing Tom…

That had been unexpected. He hadn't imagined Tom as the kissing type, were he to be entirely truthful. But then Tom had tipped his head back, lips tentative at first, then firming, the connection Cicero's magic had forged burning in their blood all the while.

God, what a mess this was turning into.

Cicero padded to the hall and peered out carefully. It was deserted, but voices came from the direction of the cellar. He slunk down the corridor, belly almost on the floor, ears pricked forward and every whisker quivering. The voices became clearer, and his muscles tightened. Slow now. Slow and careful, because if he was caught…

At least Tom knew where he was. Tom would come running.

And probably end up dead himself.

Cicero focused on the little spot of warmth that had ignited behind his heart, when he'd kissed Tom's eyelids and used his magic. *"If they catch me, go to the MWP,"* he thought at it. *"Don't try to save me yourself, or we'll both end up in danger. Sloane probably won't just kill me out of hand."*

Probably.

He felt Tom's shock, distantly, through the partial bond. *"Cicero? Is that you?"*

"Do you usually hear voices in your head? Of course it's me."

"Be careful."

Cicero didn't dignify that with an answer. The door to the cellar hadn't quite latched, and he nudged it open a crack with his head. Thank heavens the hinges didn't squeal. He slithered through the narrow gap and found himself at the top of a flight of rickety stairs. The only light came from a single gas jet, but that was more than enough for him to make out details in this form.

The cellar contained a row of large kegs, accompanied by crates of liquor and glassware. A stack of wooden boxes had been shoved to one side, revealing a low doorway.

What was Sloane involved in? Some sort of tunnel gang?

Sloane and the other man stood by the door leading out of the cellar. "Thank you for doing your part for the cause," the stranger said, hefting a satchel.

"Sloane took the satchel out of the safe," Cicero told Tom, who likely wouldn't have seen it from beneath the desk.

Sloane nodded. "Just make sure Mr. Janowski knows to hold up his end of the deal."

The other fellow didn't seem happy. "Karol will come through," he snapped. "As will we all."

"I'm sure you will." Sloane started to turn away, then stopped. "I want the rest of those hexes at least two days before."

He made for the stairs.

Oh hell.

Cicero bolted out the cracked door with all the speed he could summon.

"What was that?" the stranger called.

Damn it. Curse the bloody luck.

Sloane's voice grew fainter as Cicero put distance between them. "A rat," he said…but was that doubt in his voice?

Would Sloane be able to smell him?

He could feel Tom's worry, like a scratch at the back of his mind. *"I don't think he saw me,"* Cicero said, hoping to convince them both. *"A black cat in the shadows, and his eyes would have been blinded from the gaslight. And there are a lot of rats here—I can smell them."*

"I hope you're right."

Cicero reached the dressing room without being seen. Once there, he shifted back into human form. The sense of Tom watching from over his shoulder vanished, since it only worked when the familiar was in animal shape.

Cicero leaned against the chair, fighting to get his breathing back under control. If Sloane realized it was him…

But there was no sound of pursuit. No angry shouts. Just the ordinary noises of the resort on a busy night.

And now they had a name. Karol was Karol Janowski. Surely it would make finding him easier.

Sloane was waiting on more hexes—but which ones? The absinthe hexes, or something else?

And was it Isaac's magic that would power them?

Cicero closed his eyes, remembering the broken chain, the abandoned necklace. He'd have to get it back from Tom, carry it with him when he could. So he could give it back to Isaac as soon as they found him.

"Don't worry, darling," he whispered to the empty air. "I'm coming for you. Just hold on a little longer."

Tom ached with weariness when he climbed the steps back to his apartment an hour before dawn.

It seemed they'd been lucky after all. Neither Sloane nor Kearney had acted as if they suspected anything, and Cicero's final performance of the night had come and gone without incident. He'd dithered about after, chatting with the other performers, then met Tom once his shift finished.

Tom had handed over the hexes and necklace, once they were far enough away from the Rooster. "So what did you think about tonight, Thomas?" Cicero asked, tucking the hexes away in his coat. The necklace went into a separate pocket.

What part did he mean? The kiss? Looking through his eyes?

"I thought it started well enough," Tom said.

"I certainly can't argue with that assessment." Cicero shot him a sly look from beneath his lashes. "I do love a man who works with his hands, you know."

Tom snorted. "You love to hear the sound of your own voice, you mean."

"Because I'm so terribly interesting, darling." Cicero tossed his head. "I meant the other sort of magic, though."

Tom considered. "If I hadn't been so worried for you, it would have been amazing," he said at last. "You really see the world different when you're a cat, don't you? Not much in the way of color, I mean, but it seemed so clear. Scared me half to death, thinking Sloane would be able to see you easy, before I realized you were actually in the shadows and the cellar just looked bright."

"Sorry for the shock." Cicero paused, then glanced up again. "Well. I'll see you in the morning, then."

The desire to kiss him again seized Tom, so overwhelming it stole his breath. Maybe the look on his face betrayed him, because Cicero's eyes widened ever so slightly, and his lips parted.

But they were on the street, and it wasn't possible. Cicero's mouth twisted into a wry smile, and he gave Tom a little wave. Then he was gone, a black cat lost in the night almost as fast as Tom could blink.

It was insane to spend too much time thinking about Cicero, Tom told himself as he walked up to his apartment. God willing, they'd find the evidence needed to expose Sloane, stop whatever he was involved in, and locate the missing Isaac. Then Tom would return to his beat, and Cicero would find his witch, and they'd never see each other again.

The thought left loneliness in its wake. He'd miss the familiar's sharp smiles and teasing humor. The way he held himself, so perfect and poised —until something softer would show through unexpectedly.

The way he'd come apart in Tom's hands earlier tonight, gasping and writhing, all that poise surrendered at least for a moment.

The memory roused him as he unlocked his door. He'd think about it again, as soon as he fell into bed, put his hand to his prick, and imagined —

The opening door sent something scuttling across the floor. Tom bent down and retrieved a folded piece of paper. Someone must have shoved it under his door. He lit the gaslight, shut the door, and unfolded the paper.

In large, blocky letters it read: I KNOW WHO YOU REALLY ARE.

CHAPTER 11

"I DON'T THINK I've ever seen you do this much work," Greta said the next day. She sat back in her chair, feet propped on a box of catnip she'd shamelessly stolen from one of the Brooklyn familiars.

Cicero glanced up in annoyance. He'd staggered out of bed at an indecent hour, so he could spend the morning sorting through the MWP rogues gallery. He'd checked back three years with no luck. Karol Janowski didn't appear anywhere in their list of known criminals, or in any easily accessible file. The sheer tedium of the work made him want to curl up and take a nap, and let someone else do it for him.

Except there wasn't anyone else, certainly not so close to the Greater New York consolidation. Those who didn't have cases of their own were busy planning security for the gun salute at the Battery. The regular police would have men at the celebration and along the parade route, but heaven forbid they coordinate their forces.

Most of the witches would sneer at the idea of working with the ordinary police. Corrupt thugs all, according to their way of thinking.

And, yes, maybe Cicero had thought the same way just a few days ago, before Tom Halloran barged into his life and disrupted everything.

"I'm trying to find Isaac," Cicero told Greta. "And stop anyone else from getting killed, thank you very much."

Greta cocked a pale eyebrow at him. "Are you any closer than when you began?"

"Yes." Dominic had confirmed that the hexes from Sloane's office were drawn by the same hand as those used by Gerald and Barshtein. The necklace at least proved something bad had happened to Isaac in Sloane's office. Well, proved to Cicero—Ferguson would never accept such flimsy evidence as finding a necklace in a place Isaac was already known to be employed.

Tom had believed. Instantly. Just as he hadn't questioned when Cicero asked him to close his eyes.

They had to find out what was in those tunnels behind the secret door. Could Isaac be down there, held captive against his will? Or had Sloane and his cronies used the tunnels to spirit him away elsewhere? And what hexes was Sloane waiting on—and why? He seemed to have plenty of absinthe hexes...not to mention the foul ones to find out if a familiar was bonded or not.

Sloane was a familiar himself. The idea he might be capturing unbonded familiars and selling them to unscrupulous witches turned Cicero's stomach.

Oh God, Isaac. He'd been so patient when Cicero first came to the MWP. He'd ignored the wary hisses, never remarked on how Cicero flinched back whenever anyone came too close. Just taught him what he needed to know about life in the barracks, answered questions, and generally *been* there. A constant, warm support, giving Cicero the time and space he'd needed to relax. To realize he was safe.

Bad enough Isaac had been beaten half to death by the man who should have been his witch. But if some brute had force-bonded him...

"We're at least trying to find him, which is more than I can say for anyone else," Cicero went on, not bothering to hide his increasingly bad mood.

Greta held up her hands. "Don't hiss at me, cat. I just asked a question." She propped her elbows on her desk. "How are things with the patrolman? What's his name again?"

"Thomas Halloran. And they're fine." More than fine, really. Cicero had spent far too much time tossing and turning in bed last night, unable to get Tom out of his mind. Not just the feel of his hand on Cicero's cock, which admittedly he'd thought about quite a bit. Or even the kiss.

"*...it would have been wonderful,*" he'd said, with open admiration in his voice. As if Cicero had let him glimpse something truly magical.

Well, he had, of course. If they didn't do it again, the partial bond would fade in time. And if Cicero did it with another witch before then, the tenuous connection with Tom would break in an instant.

Not that it mattered. He certainly wasn't going to actually bond with

Tom Halloran.

Right?

Somehow, the idea that had seemed so unthinkable just days ago didn't seem half so repulsive now. Tom was…sturdy. Solid. Not at all given to theatrics or explosions of temper.

But why had he lied—or at least hidden the truth—about being a hexbreaker? The talent was too rare not to put to use, not without a damned good reason.

There came a light knock on the half-open door. Tom stood there, dressed in his blue uniform once again.

"Hello, Halloran," Greta said with a toothy grin. "Nice to see you." She rose to her feet and indicated her chair. "I'll take the excuse to leave. Watch out, the cat's got his fur all ruffled this morning."

Once she left, Tom maneuvered his wide frame inside and shut the door. "Is something wrong?" he asked cautiously.

"No. I'm just tired. And frustrated." Cicero gestured to the pile on his desk. "I looked through the rogues gallery and didn't spot either the fellow we saw with Sloane last night, or anyone named Karol Janowski."

Tom shifted uncomfortably. "How…how far did you look back?"

"Three years." Cicero rubbed at his eyes. "Do you think I should have gone farther?"

"Nay! Nay, three years should be fine." Tom sat down in Greta's chair; it creaked beneath his weight. "I wonder if we won't have more luck with the rogues gallery over at police headquarters. The other police headquarters, I mean."

"I wondered why you wore your uniform. Good thinking." Cicero paused. "May I ask you something?"

Tom's expression grew guarded. "What?"

"You and I both know you could parlay your hexbreaking talent into something with better pay and less work than walking a beat. I haven't told anyone, but why keep it such a secret?"

Tom's shoulders hunched slightly, pulling at the wool of his ill-fitting coat. "It's just that…when people know you can destroy most hexes with a touch…some of them want to use you for it. Unsavory types, I mean."

"Yes, yes." Cicero waved dismissively. "But it isn't like *you'd* ever agree to crack a bank vault, or steal a valuable painting, or whatever sorts of things people get up to."

The chair creaked again as Tom shifted uncomfortably. His eyes were downcast, focused on his hands rather than Cicero. "Of course I wouldn't. But it don't stop them from asking. And some folks make it hard to say no."

"Oh." Realization dawned. "Is that why you left Ireland? Blackmail? Someone trying to get you to use your hexbreaking to do something illegal? Were you poncing a fellow you shouldn't have been?"

Tom's fair cheeks turned pink. "Um, aye. His family, they wanted him for the priesthood. I couldn't give in to blackmail, but at the same time I couldn't let him get in trouble for what we'd both done. So I left and swore I'd never tell anyone else what I could do. And I didn't. Until you."

Whatever annoyance Cicero had harbored drained away. No wonder Tom didn't want anyone to find out. "A lost home and a lost love, due to honor. How poetically tragic," he mused. "I am sorry, though, truly. I swear I won't tell anyone else your secret. I still think you're a bit mad not to take advantage—you might very well be the only hexbreaker in New York—but I won't tell."

Tom finally looked up. "Thank you."

Cicero should have left it there, but the devil had his tongue. "Still mourning your lost love then, Thomas?" he asked lightly, as though it didn't matter. And of course it didn't—how could it? It was nothing to him if Tom imagined some other fellow's mouth on his cock, or a different body pressed against his.

"Nay." Tom leaned forward, his blue eyes intent on Cicero. "It wasn't like it is with you."

Cicero stilled. An odd sort of anticipation curled through his gut, and he couldn't seem to keep his heart down where it belonged. "And what is it like with me?"

Tom stretched across the desks and slipped his hand around the back of Cicero's neck. "You know damned well what it's like," he said in a low growl that sent a bolt of heat straight to Cicero's groin.

Tom's mouth was hard on his, demanding. Cicero parted his lips, sucked on Tom's tongue when it slipped inside. Tom let out a muffled groan of desire that made Cicero want to sweep everything off the desk and spread himself out for the man then and there. Tom's hand around the back of his neck was firm, holding him in place while Tom thoroughly explored his mouth. Cicero gave as good as he got, until he could feel Tom's teeth through the press of their lips.

The kiss turned gentler, then ended with a series of soft little pecks. Cicero nipped Tom's lower lip, then leaned back with a sigh as Tom's hand slipped away. Tom's lips were swollen, his face flushed, his eyes dark with desire. Cicero licked his own lips, and Tom's gaze fixed on the sweep of tongue.

"You are..." Cicero trailed off and shook his head. "A temptation. A surprise, unlooked for." He met Tom's gaze. "What did you mean last night, when you said you were willing to put in the work?"

Tom smiled, and the expression did silly things to Cicero's heart. "You ain't like anyone I've ever met. And I don't mean because of the way you dress or the way you dance, or any of that." Tom shrugged awkwardly. "I'm no good with words, but I want to get to know you better. I want to try giving it to you French. Other things."

Cicero's cock stirred and he arched a brow. "Other things?"

"Things I've not done before." Tom kissed him again, softly. "Like this. You probably think I'm a fool."

"No more a fool than I," Cicero said, which was something of an understatement. "Seeing as I want that too."

Fur and feathers, this was insane. Tom Halloran was big, and rough, and didn't even know who the bloody hell Oscar Wilde was. They had nothing in common. Nothing to bind them together, except for Cicero's stupid magic.

Except he couldn't stop thinking about the way Tom smiled. About his kindness. About the feel of his hand, of his lips.

"But later," Cicero said, as much to himself as to Tom. "For now, let's visit the fine fellows at police headquarters and see if they can help us. I do appreciate a man in uniform, after all."

Tom was a fool.

Phelps had left that note for him last night; he was certain of it. Which meant the bastard had followed Tom home the other day, after spotting him in the restaurant. Maybe followed him otherwise.

His shoulders itched as he led the way down the street to police headquarters, certain there were eyes on him. Phelps wanted revenge, that seemed clear enough. He knew who Tom had been, and he knew who he was now.

Knew he had something to lose.

What if Phelps wanted to blackmail him, like the fellow in the story he'd made up for Cicero? Saint Mary, he'd had a turn there, when Cicero asked why he didn't want anyone to know of his hexbreaking. If the familiar hadn't offered him a spark of inspiration, he would have been in trouble. As it stood, he wasn't sure if he should be proud or shamed he'd concocted a plausible story so quick.

Certainly he couldn't count on it happening again. The only smart thing to do would be to cut Cicero out of his life, not get more involved with him. He'd meant to do it earlier, remain aloof, maybe even suggest they keep things professional. But he couldn't stand the possibility Cicero might think him pining for some fellow who didn't even exist, and kissing Cicero as some kind of poor second best.

He'd never known anyone like Cicero, not in his whole life. And he didn't want to go back to that, to not knowing, even if every ounce of common sense said he ought to.

Thank all the saints Cicero had only checked back three years in the MWP rogues gallery. The O'Connells had been witch-blooded, and between him and Danny, they'd ended up being pursued by the magical police rather than the ordinary.

Then again, for all Tom knew, the photos of the O'Connell gang might have been removed after the Cherry Street Riots. Most of them were dead, and with any luck Liam O'Connell was considered among the casualties, even if no body had ever been found. Maybe his picture was in a box somewhere, gathering dust.

Well, at least they were going to the regular police now, who kept their own rogues gallery. Because God forbid the two forces work together instead of bickering like a pair of dogs, each jealously guarding their own yard. At least it worked in Tom's favor this time.

Today Cicero wore a heavy wool coat against the cold, but left it unbuttoned to display a red tie and striped vest. He seemed to flow along the sidewalk, sliding between knots of pedestrians, his hips sinuous. Beside him, Tom felt like a clumsy ogre, stomping along in his boots, his feet and shoulders too big and bulky.

Still, he doubted any officer at headquarters would jump to do the bidding of someone who looked and dressed like Cicero. "Let me do the talking," Tom said as they approached.

Cicero glanced up at him with a sly smile. "Worried about the rivalry between the witch police and the regular police, darling?"

"Something like that."

Cicero snorted. "All right. I'll let you big men with your big sticks have at it. You don't mind if I watch?"

Tom found himself torn between laughter and shock. "Could you have said that without making it sound utterly filthy?"

"Me?" Cicero replied. One of the uniformed men they passed on the steps outside stared at them. His expression changed to outrage when Cicero winked at him.

"Stop that!" Tom said, grabbing Cicero's arm and hastening him to the door. "You're going to end up with a nightstick somewhere you don't want it. And I know how that sounded, so there's no need for *you* to add anything."

"I've no idea what you mean," Cicero said innocently. "You do have the most dirty mind, Thomas."

Thank heavens, Cicero settled down once they were inside. True to his word, he remained in the background while Tom explained what they wanted, coming forward only to show his badge to the officer on duty.

It took far less time than Tom expected to find their quarry. "Karol Janowski," Cicero said as they poured over the photo in the rogues gallery. "A known anarchist, arrested for assaulting the owner of a factory where he worked."

"Aye." Tom stared at the picture, committing it to memory. "So why is Sloane, a businessman if I've ever seen one, working with anarchists?"

Cicero turned away, his expression troubled. "I don't know. But I have the feeling if we can find the answer, we'll find Isaac."

Cicero came to a halt just inside the doors of police headquarters. An ugly mix of snow and rain had started to spit from the sky outside. "On second thought, perhaps we should stay here."

Tom caught his arm and guided him out. "In or out. You can't just stand in the open door, letting the cold in."

"Beast." Cicero pulled his arm free and hunched his shoulders, trying to make himself as small as possible. Puddles of slush were already collecting on the sidewalk, and he wove back and forth to avoid them.

"Anarchists," Tom mused. "Do you think your friend Whistler was mixed up with them? Is that what Isaac wanted him to talk to you about?"

"Possibly." Cicero flinched as a particularly large snowflake struck him in the face. "I don't know."

"No offense, but no one at the Rooster seems like the type to be throwing bombs and shooting people. Not the dancers, anyway—Kearney and Sloane are another matter."

"It isn't all bomb throwing," Cicero replied testily. "Not everyone in the movement is violent, you know."

Tom's gait stuttered. "You're a sympathizer, then?"

"I wouldn't say that." Cicero shrugged. "I know some people with anarchist leanings from Techne."

"Techne?"

"A bohemian café. One I spend my free time in, if you must know."

Cicero wasn't certain why he felt he needed to defend his choices. "You should come some time. You might enjoy it."

Tom appeared dubious, but didn't comment. "What do you know about the anarchists, then?"

A man dressed in a black woolen coat and top hat stood on a busy corner, a mite box in his hands and a sign for the Charity Organization Society beside him. "A donation for the poor this holiday season?" he called to passers-by.

"The anarchists want to put an end to poverty," Cicero said with a nod in the man's direction. "Most of them are good people—and I don't mean just the bohemian set, but the working men and women. They want fair wages, job security, so no man who works his fingers to the bone has to worry about whether his family will have enough coal to keep from freezing. But more—they want equality for everyone: women, blacks, Poles, familiars. Some of them believe in free love, including the right to marry or not for anyone, whether they're of different races or the same sex. Votes for women and familiars."

Tom nodded slowly. "I see the appeal."

"Of course, it will never happen." Cicero glowered at a Christmas display in a window. A tin Santa waved monotonously, though whether driven by magic or winding, he couldn't tell at this distance. "They're all living in a dream world. But Gerald always was a dreamer. Isaac, too."

"Why did Isaac leave the MWP?" Tom asked, quietly enough Cicero could have pretended not to hear him over the cabs clattering past.

"He met his witch," Cicero said, and hoped Tom would leave it at that. Jump to some mistaken conclusion, perhaps.

Tom frowned. "I don't understand. Did the fellow—woman?—not want to work for the MWP?"

Damn it. But perhaps it would be better if Tom knew. If he understood how badly wrong everything could go. "Oh no, he did want to work for the MWP. He'd tested very high for witch potential, so he came by looking for a job. He was a big, tough fellow—a real man's man, as they say." Cicero was careful not to look at Tom. "He seemed friendly, outgoing. Good record. A good man. Isaac was smitten."

Traffic had momentarily cleared, so he ran across the street, avoiding the deepest puddles. Snow fell more thickly now, clinging to his coat and trousers. And his shoes were a disaster, despite the care he'd taken.

He slowed on the other side, letting Tom catch up. "Why do I get the feeling things didn't go as planned?" Tom asked.

"Isaac wasn't certain how to approach him. How to tell him." Cicero swallowed against the guilt tightening his throat. "Rook hadn't been sure either, with Dominic. Rook and I shared an office back then, so I told him to stop being a feather brain and just *tell* Dominic. Of course Rook had to make everything far more complicated than it needed to be, and almost got the three of us killed in the process. But it all worked out in the end, so I...I pushed Isaac when I shouldn't have. I thought I was doing him a favor."

The cold air stung his nose as he drew a deep breath. "Isaac got his witch alone and told him. The next time I saw Isaac...he ended up in the hospital for three days. The stronzo couldn't stand the idea of bonding with a Jewish fairy, so he beat Isaac bloody."

Tom swore under his breath. "I hope he got what was coming to him."

Cicero shrugged. "Ferguson threw him out. Blacklisted him, for all the good it might do." He tipped his head back and stared at the uncaring gray sky. "We were supposed to be safe. That was what the MWP promised us. What Isaac believed. What we all believed. He couldn't come back, after that. Not to the very halls where he'd almost died, thinking nothing bad could happen to him inside the Coven's walls. It broke something inside him, and I...I couldn't help. Well of course I couldn't; it was all my fault to start with."

"To blazes with that," Tom said shortly. "It was the fault of the bastard who thought he needed to hurt someone else to feel better about himself."

Cicero glanced up in surprise, saw Tom's brows drawn together in a glower. Tom caught his look, then shrugged. "I've met the type, plenty of times. The biggest braggers at the bar, usually, who can't wait to talk about how many men they've licked in a fight. Glad to let their fists fly— at least, against anyone smaller. Cowards the lot of them."

"Yes," Cicero agreed, and tried not to sound as surprised as he felt. Maybe taking Tom to meet the crowd at Techne wasn't such a bad idea after all.

The Coven lay before them. Cicero darted up the marble steps. "Thank God," he exclaimed as they entered the building. He shook himself hard, flinging as much water from his coat and trousers as possible, then pulled off his hat and waved it at arm's length. "I'm not leaving again until it's as dry out there as it is in here."

"We have to go to the Rooster tonight," Tom reminded him.

"Isaac had better appreciate this," Cicero muttered. He led the way back to his office. "The real question is, why is Sloane involved with anarchists? I think we can assume those mysterious payments 'for the benefit of mankind' were going to Janowski."

Tom ducked as an owl glided unconcernedly down the hall. "He seems too practical to be caught up in dreams of revolution, I'll give you that. What do these anarchists think about saloons open on Sunday and reforms and the like?"

"They're all for letting a man drink or fornicate as he wants." Cicero smiled wryly. "I see your point, though. The reformers have probably already gotten wind Sloane has a man performing the hoochie coochie on his stage. I imagine they're waiting to shut the Rooster down until after New Year's, so the new consolidated government can take the credit and make a statement against depravity."

"New Year's." Tom met his gaze. "New Year's Eve was circled on Sloane's calendar. And he said he needed hexes 'a couple of days before.' Before New Year's, maybe?"

"We're missing something." Cicero paused outside his office. "Some piece of information that will make sense of all this. We need to get into those tunnels."

"Agreed." Tom leaned against the wall. "We'll do it tonight. Be sure to slip into something more than your hoochie coochie outfit first."

Cicero grinned. "But if we do come across violent anarchists, how else am I to distract them while you knock them over the head?"

Tom snorted. "I'm sure they'd be distracted, all right. I'd best go change out of my uniform. Tonight?"

Cicero nodded and held out his hand. Tom's palm was warm against his as they shook, and Cicero gave his fingers a little extra squeeze before letting go. "Tonight."

CHAPTER 12

"CICERO!" NOAH CALLED from behind the counter at Techne. "Come in; come in!"

"Ciao, darling," Cicero called back, his gaze quickly passing over the café. He'd hoped to find Leona here, but there was no sign of her amidst the customers scattered around the tables. Of everyone Cicero knew, she was most likely to have an idea as to any anarchist leanings Gerald might have had. Leona openly subscribed to anarchist newspapers, had attended more than one lecture by Emma Goldman, and never hesitated to debate politics with any and all comers. Personally, Cicero found her exhausting, but at the moment he would have happily debated anything she liked if it might give him some insight.

Noah waved him over, so Cicero allowed himself to be diverted. "Have you seen Leona?"

"Not in the last day or two," Noah said with a small frown. "Why?"

Could Leona possibly be involved with any of this? Cicero didn't want to believe it...but she had known both Gerald and Isaac. If she knew Janowski as well...

"I thought of something clever for one of her protest signs," Cicero replied lightly. "Ah well. Her loss."

Noah glanced around to see if any customers needed him. "Come into the back with me for a moment."

As soon as they were alone, Noah caught Cicero's hands in both of his. "I've been so worried about you."

Noah's hands were as soft as his own. When they'd fucked in the past, there had been no rough calluses to pull on tender skin. And after, Noah had read poetry while Cicero lounged in a borrowed silk robe, drinking absinthe and whiling away the afternoon in a soft haze.

It all felt like a soft haze, suddenly—his life before Gerald's death and Isaac's disappearance. After the mess he'd made of Isaac's life, it was easier to wrap himself in a cocoon of music and banal poetry, the sort that challenged just enough to seem daring without actually making him think or feel. Until Isaac vanished, and he realized he'd managed to let down his friend a second time.

And then he walked into a room with Tom Halloran in it, and everything changed again.

"I'm fine," he said, squeezing Noah's hands before gently pulling away. "Truly."

The worried line between Noah's brow eased slightly. "I hear you're quite the hit over at the Rooster." A sultry smile tugged at his lips. "Maybe I'll come and see you." He ran a finger along the line of Cicero's jaw. "I hear they have rooms upstairs. Not that we couldn't just fuck here, but wouldn't it feel naughty?"

"Terribly," Cicero lied, even as he shifted back from Noah's touch. "I'm afraid I can't stay."

Noah frowned. "Is something wrong?"

"No, of course not. Just tired." Cicero managed a wan smile.

Noah moved closer, reclaiming the space Cicero had put between them. "You've been working too hard. I know you said you needed time, but surely you've come to realize displaying yourself for the vulgar masses is no life for an artist like yourself. Move in with me now, so I can take care of you. I'll make the arrangements, and we'll bond in a few days."

It shouldn't have come as a shock—they'd discussed it, hadn't they? Fur and feathers, Cicero had even given the thought serious consideration. So why did it feel so wrong now?

"I can't," Cicero said. "Not—not yet. I'm sorry, Noah. It's nothing to do with you."

Noah folded his arms over his chest. "I know you said you needed time, but—"

"And I meant it." Cicero stepped decisively back. "Just give me until after New Year's, all right?" Surely he would have come to his senses by then, and either agree to the bond with Noah, or find a suitable witch at the MWP.

Except the very thought made him feel as though something withered and died deep inside.

Noah's scowl vanished instantly. "I was going to suggest after New Year's—a new city, a new year, and a new life for us. See—we think just alike." He put his hands on Cicero's shoulders. "I understand if you want to wait to move in. But do say you'll come to the Christmas party I'm going to have upstairs." His smile turned conspiratorial. "I have a surprise present in store. Everyone will be there."

Everyone probably included Leona. Cicero managed a smile. "Of course, darling. I wouldn't miss it for the world."

Tom spent the evening on edge. The Rooster was once again crowded with customers, and Ho had kept him working the ice crank. The bartender seemed put out with him—was it because Tom had taken so long coming back from delivering Cicero's drink last night? Maybe Ho suspected what they'd been up to—at least, the part that involved Tom's hand shoved down the front of Cicero's pants.

So long as no one suspected the rest. Sloane must have believed the movement he'd glimpsed last night had been nothing more than a rat, because Cicero had already danced twice without giving Tom any subtle signals to indicate anything had gone wrong. Which meant they still had a chance at getting into the tunnels tonight, if they timed things carefully.

If Ho thought Tom had been gone for too long last night, he'd be furious tonight. There was an unpleasantly high chance that he'd go to Sloane or Kearney once Tom disappeared on him. And if they went into the basement, they'd see the crates had been moved to expose the tunnel door.

Which meant Tom and Cicero had exactly one chance to do this. And that they'd best find another exit.

Of the latter, Tom was confident. He'd grown up in the tunnels near the waterfront, first watching Da and Danny disappear into them, then joining in on their raids on the docks. He might not know this set of tunnels, but he felt confident he could navigate them with less trouble than most.

In the best case, they'd go down, find the place deserted but full of evidence they could take back to Ferguson, and slip out through a basement or manhole.

If the crowd hadn't peaked yet, it surely would soon. Cicero didn't have another performance for an hour. Now was the time.

Tom took a deep breath and stepped away from the ice machine.

"Halloran!" Kearney called.

Tom froze. "Aye, boss?" he asked, hoping he sounded casual.

Kearney jerked his head toward a shadowed corner of the room. "Sloane wants to talk to you."

Tom's heart thudded against his ribs. Did Sloane suspect after all?

He tried to keep his gait slow and his stance easy as he walked across the room, threading in between tables. Men in sack suits and frock coats rubbed shoulders, as did a few women wearing trousers themselves. He caught some appreciative looks, which he ignored.

Sloane sat alone at the farthest table, sipping whiskey and playing solitaire. Tom slid into the seat across from him, surreptitiously wiping his palms against his trousers. Kearney took up position behind Sloane, glowering at Tom. "Evening, Mr. Sloane," Tom said with all the politeness he could muster.

"Drink?" Sloane asked, picking up the half-filled whiskey bottle. Tom nodded, and Sloane poured them each a measure of amber liquid.

"Tomorrow is Christmas Eve." Sloane lifted his glass. "A time of contemplation. Of family." He swirled the glass thoughtfully. "Will you be attending mass?"

"Aye," Tom said automatically. Then he wondered if it was the answer he should have given. Didn't anarchists seek the downfall of the church as well as the government?

Sloane only nodded. "And where will you be receiving the Eucharist?"

Sweat crept down Tom's back. Why the devil was Sloane asking him these things? "The Cathedral of the Holy Familiar."

"Like a good Irish lad," Kearney remarked. His hands were folded in front of him, as if to display his hexed gloves.

Sloane watched him with flat, cold eyes. A reptile familiar, Cicero had said, and Tom could well believe it. "What did you say you did before you came to work at our fine establishment?"

"Tended bar here and there. Mostly over on 11th Street." Given the sheer number of saloons operating there, it had seemed the safest answer when he and Rook invented a back story for him.

It didn't feel safe now. Nothing did.

"I see." Sloane replenished his whiskey. He didn't offer any more to Tom. "You've been spending time with our newest sensation."

Tom's mouth went dry. "Sir?"

"Cicero." Sloane savored his drink. "You've visited his dressing room."

"Mr. Ho asked me to take him a whiskey, sir." Ordinarily he wouldn't have informed on another man, but if it meant diverting Sloane's suspicion, he'd do it happily.

"I see." Sloane leaned back in his chair. "Just remember, I hired you to serve drinks. Not to stick it to some wop whore."

Tom's hands curled beneath the table. He imagined himself punching Sloane's sneering mouth, then shaking him until the bastard apologized.

But if he did, he'd only find himself on the receiving end of a beating. And maybe worse, if Sloane suspected more was going on than a bit of cock sucking. Cicero certainly wouldn't thank him for wrecking their investigation.

"Aye, sir," he said steadily.

"I'm glad we had this little chat." Sloane waved him off. "Back to the bar."

Tom nodded and rose to his feet. He took a step away, when Sloane called, "Oh, and Halloran?"

Tom stopped. "Aye?"

Sloane's grin showed too many teeth. "Merry Christmas."

Cicero huddled on a doorstep in cat form, hoping his fur would prove better at keeping the wind out. The sky had spit out a mixture of rain and snow earlier in the evening, and the sidewalk was unpleasantly damp under his paws. He'd been watching the side door of the Rooster for half an hour since leaving, waiting for Tom to appear.

Just as he'd waited in the dressing room earlier. When Tom hadn't joined him, he'd started to worry. Did Sloane suspect? Or had Tom, in some fit of misguided chivalry, decided to go into the tunnels alone?

But when he'd gone out to dance, there Tom had been, in his ordinary post behind the bar. Unlike most nights, though, he hadn't so much as glanced at Cicero the entire time.

Something had gone wrong.

It was four in the morning, and the last of the customers booted out the door. Most of the other staff had already left, as had the other entertainers. So where was Tom?

The side door swung open, and a bulky shape appeared. Cicero's tail perked up with relief. Tom walked along quickly, hands stuffed in his pockets, head down against the wind. Cicero fell in behind him, trotting along until they were out of sight of the Rooster. As soon as he could, he ducked into an alley and took human form again.

"And where the bloody hell have you been?" he demanded.

Tom jumped, both hands coming up in a fighting stance. Then he spotted Cicero and lowered them. "Good Lord, don't do that! You'll give a man apoplexy." He hurried over to the alley.

"Give *you* apoplexy? What about *me?*" Cicero folded his arms over his chest. "I waited half the night for you. Do you know how worried I was when you didn't come? I saw you when I danced, but you didn't even look at me. So I waited on the street for you, freezing my whiskers off, and it took you for bloody ever to leave. And the sidewalk is wet, Thomas. *Wet.*"

"I'm sorry," Tom said. He reached out and took Cicero's hand in his own, rubbing it for warmth. "Sloane talked to me. Someone—probably Ho—noticed I spend a little too much time with you after performances." Tom's mouth flattened. "Sloane said...he called you..."

Cicero could well guess. "At least tell me you pretended to agree with him."

Tom didn't look at all happy. "I didn't punch him in the face as he deserved."

"At least you had more sense than to try to defend my honor. Not that I have any to defend."

"That ain't true." Tom's hands tightened on his, tugging him closer. "Don't say things like that."

"I..." But Cicero didn't know what to say, for once. He'd heard enough cruel things in his life that repeating them had become a kind of joke. Because somehow it was less painful if he said the words first, instead of hoping they wouldn't be said at all, and then being disappointed.

Tom pulled him closer, in the stinking darkness of the alley, so their legs pressed together. "I'm sorry. I should have been more careful. Now they'll be watching us both."

"We both should have been more careful," Cicero admitted. He sighed and leaned against Tom, felt those warm arms slide around him. "The good news is, if Sloane hasn't fired you, he probably doesn't think you're doing anything more than trying to get...well, what you actually got."

Tom's chest rippled with a laugh under his cheek. Cicero breathed deep, smelling cigarette smoke and sweat from the Rooster, underlain by wet wool. What would Tom's skin smell like with nothing at all between them? "I hope you're right."

"I am." Cicero leaned back slightly to look up at Tom's face. "Sloane has absolutely no motive to keep you on otherwise. Unlike me, of course, who has made him a tidy pile of money."

Tom nodded. It was hard to read his expression in the darkness—Cicero's human eyes were a little better than ordinary, but nothing compared to his cat ones. But Tom seemed pensive, so Cicero went up on tiptoe and kissed him.

Tom's mouth was shockingly warm after the cold air. His arms shifted, and Cicero murmured encouragement when he cupped a hand around Cicero's arse, urging him closer.

Cicero wanted...he didn't know what. Or rather, he knew exactly what. He could beg Tom to fuck him right here, up against the wall. But what had Tom said, about things he hadn't done before?

Their lips parted, and Cicero took a reluctant step back. "We'll work something out," he said, his voice trembling just slightly. "The Rooster will be closed for the next two days. Do you think we might have a chance of sneaking in?"

"Possibly." Tom shoved his hands in his pockets. "At least Sloane doesn't seem to live there, far as I can tell. We'd have to be careful of any guards, or make sure he wasn't in the office for some reason, but it could work."

"Especially since you can get us past the alarm hexes," Cicero added. "All right, then. Shall we try tomorrow?"

Tom shook his head. "Lots of people work a half day on Christmas Eve. Sloane might decide to be one of them, even if the resort is closed to customers. Safer to go on Christmas, I'd say."

Cicero didn't want to put it off...but he knew Tom was right. "All right. I'll see you Christmas, then."

Tom nodded...then stepped forward and gave Cicero a quick kiss. "Merry Christmas, Cicero."

"Ciao, darling." Cicero watched him walk away, hands in his pockets. When Tom was out of sight, he slipped back into cat form and scurried through the alleys and over the roofs, making for the familiar barracks at the MWP.

But he had the feeling that, tired as he was, it would be a long time before sleep found him.

CHAPTER 13

CHRISTMAS EVE, AND Tom sat alone in his apartment, wondering if he ought to venture out to find dinner. The rain and snow had moved off, but the cold had deepened, making him reluctant to stray too far from the stove. The smells of cooking food permeated the tenement, a blend of boiled cabbage, pork, and potatoes. The faint sound of carolers drifted from the street outside, and for the first time in years he found himself humming along.

What was Cicero doing today? Did the familiars celebrate Christmas—or perhaps some of them did, and the rest went elsewhere, or joined in for the food? What was life in the familiar barracks like anyway? From what Cicero had hinted, it was preferable to what he'd left behind to join the MWP.

Tom hadn't thought to miss the familiar as much as he did. They'd only been apart for a few hours, and yet their meeting tomorrow night seemed achingly far away.

There came a knock on his door. Tom frowned—he wasn't expecting any visitors. Was one of his neighbors having some sort of trouble?

He opened the door to reveal Cicero on the other side. The familiar's olive skin was flushed from the cold, and he wore his absurd scarlet overcoat and a thick black scarf. In one arm he cradled a bottle of wine, and in the other a covered basket from which the smell of hot garlic drifted, strong enough to make Tom's eyes water. "Ciao, bello."

"Cicero?" he asked, like a fool.

Cicero flashed him a grin. "In the fur, darling. Mind if I come in?"

Tom stepped back hastily. "Sorry—come in." He shut the door after Cicero swanned past. "I was just thinking about you, actually."

Cicero put down his burdens on Tom's small table and slipped his coat from his shoulders. As always, he was perfectly poised and dressed, his hair oiled and his suit coat and vest immaculate. A spring of mistletoe stuck jauntily from his buttonhole. "Thinking about little old me?" He glanced coyly over his shoulder. "And what were you thinking? Was it naughty?"

"Wondering what you were doing, actually." Tom crossed the room. "I figured you'd be spending the day with the other familiars, not bringing me dinner. And how did you know where I live?"

"As to why I'm here, it's because I find you far more interesting." Cicero removed a number of paper packages from the basket. "As for how, I found your address in your file." He paused, eyes suddenly vulnerable. "You don't mind, do you?"

"Of course I don't." Tom crossed the room and touched Cicero's cheek lightly. It felt smooth beneath his fingers; Cicero must have shaved before coming over. Cicero leaned into the touch, rubbing his cheek against Tom's palm. "I'm always glad to see you."

"Naturally." Cicero looked around the apartment curiously. "Very orderly. Not much in the way of art or ornamentation. You and Dominic ought to get on like a house on fire."

Tom had never stopped to consider what his apartment would look like to someone else. He'd never *had* anyone else here, which was a depressing enough thought on its own. The two rooms had the requisite furniture, enough to meet his needs, store his clothing, and little else. No photographs of loved ones, or postcards pinned to the wall to give it a bit of color. No personality, because some part of him had always thought of this life—this identity—as temporary.

Funny how he'd never realized that before.

Cicero nodded at the paper containers. "I hope you like Chinese food."

"Well enough." He'd eaten plenty when he'd been younger and closer to Chinatown. "Though it smells a bit more spicy than I'm used to."

"Mmmm, I love a bit of spice." Somehow, Cicero managed to make the simple statement sound utterly filthy. He opened the packages to reveal a buffet of noodles, chopped vegetables, and pork. "Now, pour us some wine, won't you?"

They ate slowly, Tom because Cicero insisted on teaching him how to use chopsticks, and Cicero because he fussed over each dish, plucking out whatever interested him and leaving the rest. "I don't know how anyone uses these things," Tom groused as the noodles slid off the bamboo sticks yet again. His fingers felt even more thick and clumsy than usual.

Cicero fished out one of the little hot peppers—Tom had tried a tiny bite and nearly found his tongue on fire—and popped it whole into his mouth. "Practice," he said. "As much as I like to pretend I do everything perfectly on the first try, I'll admit—this once—it took me a while to get right."

Tom grinned. "What, you ain't infallible? Let me mark today on my calendar."

"Very funny." Cicero took a sip of his wine.

"Who taught you?" Tom asked. "And for that matter, where'd you learn the hoochie coochie? London?"

"One of the Chinese familiars taught me how to eat in a civilized fashion, instead of stabbing everything like a barbarian." Cicero rolled his eyes. "I tried to remind her I'm a cat. Claws and teeth. Stabbing things is what I *do.*"

Tom snorted. "Aye. A murderous soul lurks behind your—"

"Don't say cute." Cicero pointed at him threateningly with the chopsticks. "In my cat form, I am elegant, graceful, beautiful, and enigmatic."

"Your human form, too."

Cicero's lips curled into a smile, and he batted his lashes. "My, my, Thomas. You do talk sweet."

Tom flushed. "And you talk nonsense."

The familiar flung his head back and laughed. "I do, don't I? To answer your question, I picked up *Oryantal Dans* from a lovely Turkish lad here in New York city. Men who dance are referred to as *zenne*. I kept up with it after we parted ways, because I enjoy it. And I assumed it would be a good way to get extra cash, should I ever need to."

Cicero spoke so easily of "getting extra cash." And his friend Isaac hadn't only been performing on the stage at the Rooster. Had Cicero done such things himself, before joining the MWP? Bedded men for the promise of money, or a hot meal?

"It's a good thing you did," Tom said, forcing his mind away from such thoughts. It was none of his business.

"Quite." Cicero sucked on one of the chopsticks, but in a distracted manner. Even so, the gesture sent a rush of blood south to Tom's groin. "Do you miss your family?"

The unexpected question took Tom aback. "Aye," he said, because it was true. "My brother especially."

He was on dangerous ground now...but he wanted to give Cicero the truth. Or at least, as much of it as he safely could. "Danny was a good bit older than me, but none of the babies between us survived more than a couple of months. Maybe he felt he needed to look out for me especially after that, I don't know."

And Tom had repaid Danny by killing him.

Maybe it had been a mercy. Danny's bloody eyes staring into his had held no sanity, and ragged chunks of flesh were caught in his teeth. *"Break the hex,"* Molly screamed in his memory. *"Break it, Liam!"*

So he did. And Danny had dropped dead at his feet, like a puppet with its strings cut.

The warmth of Cicero's hand on his brought Tom back to the present. "What happened to him?" Cicero asked gently.

"He died." Tom fixed his gaze on the chopsticks dangling loosely in his fingers. "It was an accident." Because the lie was the best he could do right now, with Cicero regarding him with such tender concern.

"I'm sorry."

"So am I." Tom turned his hand over, palm up, and twined his fingers with Cicero's. "I'm glad you came by today."

Cicero smiled. "Me too. You won't believe how insufferably boring Christmas is in the barracks."

"Tell me about it."

Cicero did, his commentary giving events a color they no doubt lacked on their own. Tom laughed at the right places, and soon enough his gloom slipped away.

They finished the wine, and Tom retrieved some relatively decent whiskey from his cabinet. He sat with his chin propped on his hand, listening to Cicero talk—and watching him, since his gestures and expressions were as much a part of the conversation as his words. He was so different from anyone Tom had met before. So...bright? But that wasn't the right word. Colorful, maybe. But that didn't quite fit either.

He'd known, somehow, that Tom would be alone today. Just as Tom had been every Christmas since the Cherry Street Riots. Oh, he worked hard to get to know the people on his beat, the ones living in his tenement, because this was his home now.

But none of them knew him. They couldn't, especially not at first, when memory of the so-called riots was fresh. He went out of his way to be friendly, cheerful, the sort of fellow who would buy you a round at the saloon, ask about your children, and lend a sympathetic shoulder when called upon. But whenever anyone tried to ask about his life, he gave the most superficial answer and directed the conversation back to them.

And it worked, mainly because people generally found themselves to be the most fascinating topic around. And after the first few terrifying months, the certainty that he'd be recognized, or say something incriminating, faded. His life became routine. Safe, in a way.

Before becoming Tom Halloran, he'd had neither safety nor routine. The change had been unexpectedly welcome, a relief of sorts, not to have to wonder whether there would be money for a roof over his head, or whether he'd be shot by police or angry waterfront guards, or beaten bloody by another tunnel gang. Except that respite had come at the cost of his entire family and everyone else he'd ever cared about. So he tried not to think too hard, just focused on surviving from one day to the next.

That's what his life had become—not living, just surviving. Going through the motions, one day to the next, marking off the steps between cradle and grave in meaningless repetition.

Cicero didn't live that way. Cicero was alive, gloriously so. And he made Tom feel alive, too.

"Penny for your thoughts?" Cicero asked.

"They ain't worth that much," Tom said ruefully. "Just listening to you, mostly."

Cicero laughed. "I do ramble, don't I? Thank goodness I'm so very fascinating."

"Exactly what I was going to say."

"Mmhmm," Cicero murmured skeptically. He put his hand on Tom's again, thumb lightly swiping across the backs of Tom's fingers. "Perhaps we can find something else to do besides talk for a while."

Tom's breath caught, and his skin heated. "Aye. That would be good, too."

Cicero slid out of his chair and onto Tom's lap. Their hardening pricks rubbed together through their trousers as he wriggled into position. The chair creaked warningly beneath them, but Tom found it impossible to care. Cicero's mouth tasted of wine and the fading remnants of the peppers, and he kissed Tom as though his very life depended on it.

"Christ," Tom gasped when they broke apart. His blood pounded in his ears, and a little rush of pleasure shot through him with every shift of

Cicero's hips. He grabbed Cicero's arse, meaning to still him, but found himself kneading the firm flesh instead.

"What do you want, darling?" Cicero murmured in his ear. "Do you want me to suck you again?"

Oh God, he did. But he wanted other things, too, and mainly not for this to be over too soon. "Can I try it on you?"

Cicero leaned back with a delighted grin. "Of course. Where do you want me? Right here?"

"Bed," Tom blurted, then felt his face heat. "If that's all right with you."

"More than." Cicero traced a finger along the line of Tom's jaw, down over his throat, to the top of his collar. "What do you think about getting naked and fucking me?"

"I think you're going to make me come right here if you keep talking like that." Tom tightened his grip on Cicero's arse. "Aye, I want to. But...I ain't...I've tossed a fellow or two off before, sure. But never... you know."

"Never given a man a proper ride?" Cicero's smile grew lecherous. "We'll certainly have to correct that, now won't we?" He leaned back and snagged something from the basket. "I came prepared," he said, dangling a bottle of oil in front of Tom.

Tom couldn't help but laugh. "You came over here to wine and dine me, in hopes of getting me in bed?"

Cicero snorted. "In hopes of? Please, Thomas, don't insult my abilities of seduction. The wine and dinner were because I enjoy your company as well as your cock."

"I'm flattered," Tom said, but in truth he was. He caught the back of Cicero's neck and pulled him down for another kiss. When they parted, he murmured, "Bed, then?"

Cicero slithered off his lap. Tom took his hand and led him to the apartment's only other room. He'd bought the largest bed he could afford, since most didn't give his frame enough space to sleep comfortably, and now found himself grateful for it.

"I'm extraordinarily glad you don't have to share your apartment," Cicero remarked.

Tom shrugged. "Without a wife and children to support, a policeman's salary goes a bit further."

Cicero stopped beside the bed and slowly stripped his coat off, before draping it over the back of a chair. "Would you care to watch me undress?"

Tom swallowed against the thickness in his throat. "Aye."

Cicero made it into a teasing game, removing one cufflink at a time. The vest came off, followed by socks. His fingers lingered on each button as he opened his shirt, the white cloth luminous against his dusky skin. Tom watched the progress hungrily, his balls tightening at the flash of the gold rings in Cicero's nipples.

"You're beautiful," he grated out when Cicero let the shirt fall to the floor. "Every damn inch of you."

Cicero smiled slyly, twined his hands over his head, and did one of the little rippling movements that undulated his hips and drew Tom's attention to his flat belly. God, he'd been wanting to kiss that spot ever since the first moment he'd seen Cicero dance.

So why was he waiting like a fool?

He went down on his knees and pressed his lips to the space just below Cicero's belly button. Cicero's skin tasted of salt and smelled faintly of cedar. The trousers rode much higher than the pants he danced in, blocking Tom's access. So he popped the first button and licked at the exposed skin. Then did the same with the next.

Cicero's breath thickened, and he ran his fingers through Tom's hair. "Keep going. Please."

Tom undid the last button, hooked his fingers in the waistband, and pulled down trousers and drawers all in one motion. Cicero's prick sprang free, tapping Tom on the cheek, as though asking for attention.

Attention he had every intention of giving it.

He caught it by the base, then looked up at Cicero. Cicero was watching him in turn, lips red and parted, his eyes dark with desire. "What should I do?"

"Start with a lick." Cicero's voice trembled. His thighs trembled too, beneath Tom's hands, and Tom found himself absurdly pleased that he'd managed to shake Cicero's composure. "See what you think. It's all right if you don't—"

The words cut off in a strangled gasp as Tom ran his tongue in one long sweep from base to head. Cicero's prick tasted musky and salty. Liquid beaded at the tip, and Tom lapped that off. More salt, and something a little bitter, a diluted version of the spunk Tom had licked off his hand the other night.

He slipped his lips tentatively around the head, then down further. Cicero moaned and curled his fingers in Tom's hair. Tom hadn't realized quite how good it would feel to have a cock in his mouth, tasting Cicero's desire and feeling the little, repressed twitches of his hips as he fought not to thrust deeper.

Tom bobbed his head, as Cicero had done to him, although he didn't go as deep. Next time, he'd try it, but for now he wrapped his hand around the base of Cicero's shaft and pumped him at the same time as he sucked. Clearly the other man didn't have any objections to the method, given the sounds he was making.

"Enough," Cicero gasped finally, pushing Tom back. "I don't want this to end too soon. Especially since I'm the only one naked so far."

"It was good, then?"

"Wonderful," Cicero bent to kiss him, clearly not minding the taste of himself in Tom's mouth. "Sometime soon, I'll let you keep going until I come. But right now, I want you to give me a good ride."

CHAPTER 14

CICERO RETREATED TO the bed, sinking down on it in a marvelous sprawl of arms and legs and slender, muscular torso. Tom rose to his feet and fumbled off his clothing, torn between the need to feel Cicero's skin against his own, and his worry that maybe Cicero wanted someone who looked a bit more like himself, and a bit less like a brick wall.

But Cicero had come here of his own volition, when he could have gone anywhere else in the city. He watched Tom undress through hooded eyes, the tip of his tongue darting out to touch his lips. "You're quite the sight," he purred.

"Do you like?" Tom asked hopefully.

Cicero indicated his erection and cocked a brow. "That is normally what this sort of reaction means, you know. But yes, if you must hear it. As much as I'm enjoying observing your glory, though, I'd much rather *feel* it."

Tom slipped into bed beside him, and Cicero immediately wound his body around Tom's. And oh God, it was better than he'd dreamed, the press of hot skin against his own, the shift of muscle beneath his hands, the hard jut of Cicero's cock touching his with nothing to separate them. He groaned from sheer pleasure, and Cicero laughed softly. "If you think this feels good, just wait."

"You'll be the death of me," Tom mumbled against his lips. Then the words turned into a gasp as Cicero pinched one of his nipples. It felt as though the little nub of flesh had a direct connection to his balls, pleasure shooting through him until he arched against Cicero's lithe body.

Cicero followed his fingers up with his mouth, teeth scraping lightly against the sensitive skin. Christ, no wonder men came to clubs like the Rooster, desperate for this sort of contact, even if they had to pay for it. He slid his hand up the bare expanse of Cicero's chest and found one of the nipple rings, tugging on it until Cicero writhed and whimpered.

Gripping Cicero's hips, he rolled onto his back and pulled Cicero on top of him, so he could reach the other nipple with his mouth. Cicero's cock left a slick trail on Tom's belly, and his hips rocked as Tom sucked hard. "Fuck, that's good," he mumbled. "Would feel good even without the hexes, but—unh..." he dissolved into wordlessness as Tom used his teeth.

After a minute or so, Cicero pulled away. Tom lay under him, the blood singing beneath his skin, his prick aching for attention. Cicero's pupils reduced his irises to thin yellow rings, and his lips were red and wet and inviting. "I want you. I want you to fuck me with that big cock of yours until I beg for more."

Tom nodded dumbly. "Aye. Please."

Cicero grinned and rolled off of him. "How do you want it?" he asked as he picked up the oil. "Facing away or towards?"

Tom hadn't realized there were options. "We can do that? Facing, I mean?"

"Certainly." Cicero grabbed a pillow and stuffed it under his hips as he lay down. "The pillow will help with the angle, and make it easier on my back." He licked his lips. "Now watch."

He poured the oil over his fingers, then drew up his legs, exposing everything to Tom's gaze. One long finger slowly circled the puckered ring of his arse, then eased in. "Mmm." He arched a little as he worked the finger into himself. "Feels good."

Tom's heart pounded against his ribs, and he was harder than he'd ever been in his life.

Cicero writhed on the bed as he added a second finger. "Ahh. Yes. Watch, Thomas. See me opening myself up for you?"

"Aye," he managed. Anything more was utterly beyond his powers of speech.

"You want to put your cock here, don't you?" Cicero teased. "Slide it in and out, just like I'm sliding my fingers."

The sight and words alone were almost enough to have him spurting. "Oh, God, aye."

"Then be a dear and use the oil on your cock." Cicero withdrew his fingers and grinned wickedly. "And do be thorough—I want every last inch of you in me.

Tom's hands shook as he slicked himself generously, and he almost dropped the bottle. He took up position between Cicero's uplifted legs, guiding his cock to press the tip against Cicero's passage. "Nice and slow, darling," Cicero murmured. "Rock back and forth a bit, until you're past any resistance."

Tom's throat was too tight to speak, so he only nodded and pressed forward carefully. Cicero's body parted for him, and a startled sound of pleasure escaped him. There was a little resistance, as Cicero had warned, but he eased forward and back a few times in succession. Then something relaxed, and he was in.

"That's it," Cicero moaned. "Now the rest."

Heat and tightness engulfed Tom's length as he pushed in, Cicero's body gripping his, as if urging him deeper. The pleasure was intense, different than the feel of a hand, even of Cicero's clever mouth. "God," Tom swore.

Cicero's eyes were wild, and he gripped Tom's shoulder with one hand, the other on his own prick. "Does it feel good?"

"Better than good. You?"

Cicero grinned broadly. "Incredible. Kiss me."

Tom bent over, and Cicero arched up, until their mouths met. He felt himself slipping deeper, until his balls slapped against Cicero's skin. "Yes," Cicero gasped against his lips. "Yes, yes, yes, fuck me, *ride* me."

Cicero let go of him, head falling back. Tom shifted his stance slightly —and Cicero nearly came off the bed, back arching and mouth parting. "There—there—that spot—"

Tom gripped Cicero's hips and rode him, every thrust dragging a mewl of sheer pleasure forth. And, Christ, it was incredible, watching Cicero so undone, speared on his cock and helpless with ecstasy. He felt dizzy with pleasure and power, that he could do this, make someone like Cicero come apart this way. "Say it's good," he begged.

"Bloody hell, Thomas," Cicero's face contorted, teeth flashing between parted lips. "You don't know how good. Us, like this, *together*. Tell me you feel it too, that it's not just me."

"I feel it," Tom said, because how could he *not*? The way they moved in time, Cicero's ankles locked down behind his back, thighs flexing as he met Tom's thrusts. There was something primal in this, a magic older than hexes, older than witches and familiars, older than humankind.

"I can't hold out any more." Cicero reached for his prick again, but

Tom was there first, wrapping one big hand around it. Those luminous yellow-green eyes widened, and then Cicero let out a laugh of sheer delight, sprawling back into the sheets. Just taking everything Tom gave him, luxuriating in it, and the sight turned Tom's blood to flame. Tom felt his sack tighten—and then Cicero let out a shout, come shooting out of his prick and onto his chest, his body clenching around Tom's.

It wrung an answering cry from Tom. He drove in deep, loosing jet after jet into the wet heat of Cicero's body, until his balls almost hurt from the force of it.

He let go, bracing himself so as not to simply topple over. His head swam, senses saturated. The little room smelled of their mingled sweat and come, and Cicero made a soft thrumming sound of contentment, almost like a purr.

"Oh," Tom said, when he could talk again. "Oh, hell. That was..."

Cicero wriggled, and Tom gently freed himself. "It was, wasn't it?" Cicero asked.

Then he laughed, and Tom found himself laughing too, just for the joy of it. He wrapped his arms around Cicero and they rocked back and forth in the bed, chuckling like a pair of fools.

Eventually their mirth died away. Cicero rested his head on Tom's shoulder, absently running his long, clever fingers through the curly hair on Tom's chest.

"When do you have to be back at the barracks?" Tom asked.

Cicero's hand stilled. "I don't, actually. It's not as if there's a curfew. So long as they have some idea of where we are, we can do what we like."

"And where did you tell them you were going?"

"Here, silly." Cicero propped himself up to see Tom's face. "Why would I lie?"

"They think we're working on the case, then?"

"No one is that naïve," Cicero said with another laugh. "I told Greta I was coming to see you, and she made some horrible joke about plum pudding that I'll spare you the pain of hearing." The look on his face became guarded. "You aren't ashamed, are you?"

"Of course not!" Tom tightened his arm around Cicero's waist. "It's just...the idea of other people knowing what we're up to..."

"Oh." Cicero looked as if he hadn't even considered the matter. "I'm terribly sorry, darling. After years in the barracks, knowing each other's business, most of us familiars tend not to think twice about it. Look at it this way—if I went back right now, half the familiars there would smell you on me and know what we were up to without my having to say a word."

The part of Tom that had spent years carefully hiding everything he didn't want anyone else to see was appalled. "Holy Familiar of Christ."

"Blaspheming, and on Christmas Eve." Cicero pressed a kiss to Tom's cheek. "No one will think twice. Most of them won't even think once. No one *cares*, Thomas. As wonderful and fascinating as all of this has been to us, it's not of much interest to anyone else. And if you're concerned what they'll think of you, then don't be. For whatever reason, more familiars prefer their own sex in bed than not."

It required some adjustment in his own thinking. But hadn't he told Cicero he'd put in the work? "So," he said slowly, "if you stay the night, when you walk in the barracks tomorrow, everyone will know you've come straight from my bed?"

As spent as he was, the thought was surprisingly arousing. A sly grin crept over Cicero's lips. "You like that idea, don't you?" He leaned over and planted a kiss just at the corner of Tom's mouth. "And yes, tesoro. I will."

"Will what?"

"Stay the night."

"Good," Tom said, drawing him in for a proper kiss. "Because I need some more practice with my French."

Don't tell them you're a police officer," Cicero said as he stepped daintily along the icy sidewalk beside Tom. "I'm still pretending to be on the outs with the MWP, and you're still just a bartender at the Rooster I've struck up a friendship with."

Tom barely restrained a roll of the eyes. "I know. You don't have to remind me."

Cicero had indeed stayed the night, then spent a lazy Christmas morning drinking coffee and lounging about while Tom made them pancakes atop the little coal fired stove. Before returning to the familiar barracks, though, he'd asked if Tom would like to come to a party with him.

"Just a little something Noah—the owner of Techne—is throwing," he'd said.

"You want to talk to the anarchists before we try to get into the tunnels tonight?" Tom guessed.

Cicero let out a little huff. "No, darling, I want to go to a party with my friends. Yes, Leona will be there, and yes, I will take the chance to speak with her." He shrugged. "If you don't want to come, you don't have to. I can meet you back here around, say, ten o'clock? I just thought you might like to meet them."

Tom's chest warmed. Cicero wanted him to meet his friends, which made Tom think he meant for whatever it was they had to continue. "Of course I'll come."

Now they traipsed down Greene Street, Cicero dressed at his most outrageous. Short of his dancing costume, at any rate. The kohl was thick around his eyes, and Tom was almost certain his lips and cheeks owed their redness to something other than the cold.

"I'm terribly sorry, darling," Cicero said. "Nerves, you know."

A group of men loitering on the street stared at them. Tom glared back, glad for his size. "Nerves? What...oh."

"I'm almost afraid to ask what the 'oh' was for."

Tom shrugged. "You're worried they'll look down on you for bringing the likes of me along."

Cicero let out a little hiss. "Don't be absurd. Quite the opposite. I'm worried you won't like them."

"Why shouldn't I?" Tom asked, bewildered.

"To begin with you're..." Cicero considered him a moment. "Steady. Not easily upset. Whereas they're *artists,* which means everything must be terribly dramatic at all times."

Tom snorted, breath puffing steam in the cold. "I don't see why you'd worry about that. After all, I like you well enough, don't I?"

"I'm wounded to the quick." Cicero fluttered his eyes and put a hand to his chest in mock affront. "Oh, look, here we are."

The café was dark, its curtains drawn, but Cicero led the way down an alley and around the back. "Cicero!" called a woman from the fire escape above.

Tom did his best not to gape. The woman was dressed in a man's suit and tie, though the first few buttons of the collar were undone, and the tie hung loosely around her shoulders. Her hair was cut shockingly short, and she held a cigar in one hand and a glass of absinthe in the other.

"Leona!" Cicero called back enthusiastically. He climbed the escape, and Tom followed, even though it seemed a strange way to arrive at a party. "How are you, darling?"

"Drunk," she replied, holding up her glass. She hugged Cicero clumsily, eying Tom over his shoulder. "You brought a new friend?"

"This is Thomas," Cicero replied. "He tends bar at The Spitting Rooster."

"Erm, hello," Tom said uncertainly.

Leona looked him up and down. "He certainly is large."

"You haven't seen the half of it," Cicero told her with a wink. Tom felt his cheeks heat as Leona let out a whoop of laughter.

"Any idea what sort of surprise Noah has in store for us later?" she asked Cicero.

"None at all." Cicero blew a kiss at her, then grabbed Tom's hand and dragged him into the apartment through the window, which stood open despite the cold. Tom quickly realized why—the room on the other side was packed with people, enough that the heat of their bodies turned the atmosphere to stifling only a few feet from the window.

And what people they were. Tom wasn't sure where to look. Someone had scattered piles of pillows around the floor; two men reclined on one pile, smoking hashish from a hookah and arguing loudly in German. Women wearing men's coats, some with trousers, stood around a piano, where a man played with more enthusiasm than talent. Another woman lounged nearly nude, while her companion sketched her form furiously. The air smelled of alcohol, sweat, and hashish.

Cicero slipped through the crowd with the grace of a cat twining through a forest of legs. Everywhere he went, people called out to him. Clearly he was well-known in the group. Tom received a few curious looks as he hurried along in Cicero's wake.

The man at the piano stopped playing. "Cicero! Have you brought a new friend?"

Tom's blood surged as every eye turned to him. He'd spent the last eight years trying to blend in, and being stared at by so many was disconcerting to say the least.

"This is Thomas," Cicero replied. "He tends bar at the Rooster and is very sweet. So play nice."

Sweet? Cicero thought he was sweet?

"Aw," one of the women pouted. "Where's the fun in that?"

The remark drew a round of laughter. As they crossed the room, the door leading to another room opened and a tall man with sleek black hair stepped in. "Cicero!" exclaimed the newcomer. "My muse has returned to my side!"

Then he pulled Cicero close and kissed him, to the cheers and catcalls of their friends.

Chapter 15

TOM'S LIMBS SEEMED to go numb. Who was this man? And why the devil hadn't Cicero mentioned him before?

A sort of creeping dread settled in his belly. He'd never asked if Cicero had other commitments. He'd assumed a man with a lover wouldn't suck someone else's cock in the back room of a questionable resort, let alone spend the night in his bed. But what had Cicero said, when he spoke of the anarchists he knew, some of whom were probably in this very room? About their beliefs in free love?

Saint Mary, he'd been a fool.

Cicero pushed the other man away. "Noah, I told you before I'd come to your party."

"I know, but I've missed you terribly." Noah all but pouted. "I was starting to think you wouldn't come."

Cicero twined his arm through Tom's. "I've been busy," he purred, glancing up at Tom through thick lashes. "Have you had absinthe before, Thomas?"

At least Cicero had pushed the other man—Noah—away and laid claim to Tom's arm. Maybe Tom had read things wrong, and they weren't lovers after all. Maybe Noah just wanted to be. Or maybe it was just the way these people acted amongst themselves, away from the public eye.

"Nay," he said, resisting the urge to grab Cicero and make for the door. Or the window, whichever got them out of here the quickest.

Things had been so much simpler back at the apartment, when they were alone together.

"Then let's introduce you to the green fairy," Cicero replied with a wicked grin. He led Thomas to the table where a number of bottles of absinthe waited, along with an absinthe fountain filled with ice water, slotted spoons, a bowl of sugar cubes, and several stacks of hexes.

Cicero released Tom's arm to prepare their drinks. He placed a slotted spoon on each glass, then added a sugar cube. The fountain dripped the cold water over the sugar into the absinthe; when it hit the spirits in the glass, the liquor went from poisonous green to a sort of cloudy mint.

"Hex, darling?" Cicero indicated the cheap paper hexes. "They amplify the hallucinogenic affects of the drink. It can be very entertaining."

Tom shook his head quickly. One of the other partygoers tutted loudly. "Your friend needs to relax," he told Cicero.

Cicero gave him an unfriendly look. "And who are you?"

Apparently Tom wasn't the only newcomer in the bunch. "Augustine Van Wyck," he replied, not bothering to hold out his hand to shake. "Our new mayor is my cousin."

"Several times removed, isn't that right, Auggie?" asked Leona, strolling up to refill her drink.

Auggie scowled. "Yes," he muttered.

"I'm abstaining from hexes myself tonight," Cicero said. He handed Tom one of the prepared drinks. *"Mazel tov."*

The stuff tasted like licorice and was utterly vile. Tom nearly spat his back into the glass, only choking it down with an effort. "Mmm," Cicero said, sipping his. "Good, isn't it?"

The evening only went downhill from there. The crowd ebbed and flowed, and soon Cicero had been swallowed into it, drawn into an argument about poetry by some of his friends. Tom wandered for a bit, making an effort to smile and nod whenever someone caught his eye.

He hadn't felt so out of place since his first days on the police force. At least then he'd had some chance of successfully pretending to be something he wasn't. His chances of convincing anyone here that he was a bohemian were about as good as convincing them he was a chair.

All around him, people argued vociferously over styles of painting, or which composer was a true master and which an unqualified hack. Others smoked or ate hashish, while downing large quantities of hexed absinthe. Artists sketched, poets recited, and a knot of naked people were doing things on one of the piles of cushions that caused Tom to look away hastily. Even his experiences on the force and at the Rooster hadn't prepared him for this.

Did Cicero ever join in such...orgies? Would he expect Tom to do the same?

Eventually he managed to find a slightly quieter corner, where he could pretend to sip on his absinthe and simply watch the other party goers. He didn't see either Cicero or Leona. Maybe they'd gone back onto the fire escape.

"So tell me...Thomas, was it?...you met my Cicero at the Rooster?" Noah asked.

Tom started—he hadn't noticed the other man's approach over the noise of the party. How had he let himself get so distracted?

He glanced at Noah, who was only a few inches shorter than him. Did Cicero prefer taller men? Certainly they weren't much alike otherwise. Noah was slender and dark-haired, his suit far more fashionable than anything Tom had ever owned in his life.

And the way he'd grabbed Cicero and kissed him, as though he had the right...

"I tend the bar," Tom replied stiffly. He wanted to add "*and he ain't 'your' Cicero,*" but managed to restrain his tongue. Cicero wouldn't thank him for starting a fight.

Noah arched a perfect brow. "Oh? I thought that duty fell to Mr. Ho."

"Visited before, have you?" Tom asked. "Mr. Ho mixes most of the cocktails. I crank the ice crusher, bring up things from the basement, and pour the beer." Surely that would be enough to satisfy whatever curiosity Noah had about him.

"Hmm." Noah didn't seem impressed. "Tell me, Thomas, do you have witch potential?"

What the hell? Tom looked around, but no one else was paying the slightest attention. They were all captivated by their own dramas, laughing and singing and arguing. Why the devil hadn't Cicero warned Tom about Noah? Told him they were going to a party thrown by... whatever Noah was to Cicero. An ex-lover, or semi-ex-lover, or a not-at-all-ex-lover. Did Cicero mean to carry on with both of them?

Or had Tom just been a distraction? Cicero's version of slumming? A bit of rough in between more sophisticated lovers, brought to the party to entertain the rest and maybe provoke jealousy in Noah?

"Aye," he said, leveling a cool gaze on Noah. "Cicero says I do."

Noah's hands shot out, seizing Tom's lapels. "Don't get any ideas," Noah said in a low voice. "Cicero is my familiar. We're going to bond after the new year. I assume he told you?"

It shouldn't have mattered. It really, truly, shouldn't have made the slightest bit of difference. It wasn't as though Tom had ever considered bonding with a familiar, not with all of the secrets he had no choice but to keep. But it hurt, somehow, that in all the times they'd spoken of witches and familiars, Cicero hadn't shared this bit of information.

Tom had been a damned fool, thinking there was a connection between them that went beyond the physical. That they were friends, at least.

"Ain't none of my business," Tom grated out. "Now, let go of my coat."

Instead of releasing Tom, Noah twisted the lapels, trying to drag Tom down to his level. Tom set his spine, even though the collar cut into the back of his neck. "I know what you're thinking," Noah said, the words nearly a snarl. "You think you're going to use Cicero to get a better job. Become a witch and make money, instead of working in some dive the rest of your life. But he belongs to me."

Tom's hands curled into fists. "Cicero belongs to himself," he replied, fighting to keep his voice level. "Now. Let. Go. Of. My. Coat."

"I fucked him." Noah's glittering eyes took on a sly expression. "Right over there, on those pillows. Over and over. You're just an unwelcome—"

Tom shoved him. Noah's grip came loose, and he fell back into the wall. His outflung hand struck a picture, and it tumbled to the floor with a crash of shattered glass and broken wood.

The party was going wonderfully. Cicero relaxed amidst his friends, replying to their banter, lapping up their attention. Not to say he hadn't gotten plenty of attention over at the Rooster, but that was different. Work, whereas this was purely fun. He flirted outrageously and without consequence with the ladies at the piano, none of them meaning a word of it. The absinthe warmed his belly, and a tension he hadn't even been aware of slid away like water from his coat.

Leona climbed back out the window. It seemed as good a time as any, so Cicero slipped out after her. "Cigarette?" she asked upon spotting him.

He hunched into his coat, silently cursing the biting wind. "Please."

She gave him one from her case, then lit it for him. The tobacco was laced with hashish, and the edges of the world took on a pleasant softness as they smoked together.

Cicero held up his drink for a toast. "To Gerald," he said.

Sorrow flashed across her face, and she clinked her glass against his. "Gerald. I do miss that boy. When I heard what he'd done...I couldn't believe it."

"Neither could I." Cicero took another drag from his cigarette. "His roommate mentioned a friend, and I wondered if you knew each other. Karol Janowski?"

Leona's eyes widened slightly. "Gerald was friends with Janowski?"

"You know him, then?"

"Unfortunately." Leona leaned against the rail, her mouth an angry slash. "He's just the sort of anarchist that gives the whole movement a bad name. Always going on about 'propaganda of the deed,' as though murder is going to solve anything. His kind adds fuel to the fire, so when agents provocateur start something like the Haymarket affair, the police and politicians can use his words to condemn us all." She shook her head savagely. "Nonviolent resistance, Cicero. That's what will change the world. Show the people that the real threat to their safety comes from a corrupt government enslaved to the whims of rich men who would work the rest of us to death for their profits."

"Of course, darling. But Gerald didn't seem the violent type."

"No." She stubbed out her cigarette. "I didn't believe he could do what he did. But if he was in with Janowski...maybe he'd changed."

Perhaps. Or maybe Gerald hadn't agreed with Janowski's methods. If he'd spoken of his fears to Isaac, that would have been important enough for Isaac to turn to the MWP. Even if he hadn't been able to convince Gerald to come with him, Isaac surely meant to keep his meeting with Cicero and tell him whatever he knew.

Someone must have found out. Isaac had been abducted, and Gerald hexed. Not that they had any proof yet a hex had been responsible, but something had happened to him and to Barshtein both.

Had Barshtein known Janowski as well? Killed, as Gerald had been, for getting too deeply involved, then wanting back out?

But involved in what? Did Janowski and his violent anarchists have some plot afoot?

"So Janowski is up to no good?" Cicero had to tread carefully—though it seemed unlikely Leona had anything to do with what was going on, he didn't want to seem too suspicious.

"Probably," she said darkly. "We had a few mutual friends, before I realized just what sort of anarchy he was advocating."

"He's open about his feelings, I take it?"

"Open? He ran a small newspaper out of a falling-down warehouse off Clarkson, near the docks. But it shut down suddenly a while ago. Maybe he couldn't afford the printers ink anymore." She shrugged.

Cicero's heart beat faster. "Do you recall the address?"

Leona frowned slightly. "Why?"

"I just wanted to talk to him about Gerald." Which wasn't entirely a lie. "What Gerald did was such a shock…I'm trying to understand."

"Of course." Leona's expression softened. "Though I don't know if he's still there."

She gave him the address. He needed to talk to Tom, urgently, so they could decide what to do with this new information. Cicero took a step toward the window, just as the sound of breaking glass cut through the chatter of the party.

Cicero slid back into the now-silent apartment and froze at the tableau before him. Noah lay on the floor, the painting in ruins around him, his hands held up to protect himself.

And over him loomed Tom. Fists clenched. Mouth tight. Nostrils flared. Just like all the big, angry men who had loomed over Cicero, before he fled to the MWP.

"Help!" Noah cried.

Old fear tightened Cicero's chest instinctively, but he thrust it aside and shoved his way through the crowd. "What the bloody hell is going on?"

Tom's fists uncurled, and he looked up. "Cicero—"

"He hit me!" Noah exclaimed.

"I didn't!" Tom extended his hand to help Noah up, but Noah scrambled back away from him. Tom let it fall to his side. "I asked you to let go of my coat. You wouldn't, so I pushed you away. I didn't hit you, and I didn't shove you hard enough to bring down the painting. You pulled it down yourself."

He sounded…not exactly calm, but not in a rage. Not like a man who'd just turned violent. Cicero grabbed Noah's arm and pulled him to his feet. At least Noah didn't seem hurt.

"Why would I do that?" Noah demanded.

Tom's blue eyes were arctic. "Maybe the same reason you said the things you did about Cicero."

Wonderful. Just wonderful. Cicero could practically feel the attention of everyone in the room, avidly fixed on them in the hopes of a bit of drama. "Talking about me, Noah?" he asked as lightly as he could. "I hope it was at least the really *good* gossip."

Someone snickered. Tom didn't, and neither did Noah. Instead they glared at each other like a pair of stage villains about to pull out daggers. After a moment, though, Tom shifted his gaze to Cicero. The anger had drained away from his expression, leaving behind an unexpected pool of misery. "I ought to go."

"I think you should," Noah replied. "And don't come back, you bog-trotting mick."

Tom's jaw clenched. He turned his back on Noah and strode toward the door. Cicero swore and started after him.

Noah's hand closed around Cicero's wrist. "Where are you going?"

"I'm going with Tom," Cicero replied, tugging against Noah's hold. "I don't feel like partying any more."

Noah's fingers tightened. "I barely spoke to you tonight. And you haven't seen my surprise yet. You can't leave."

What the devil was wrong with Noah lately? "I don't care about your bloody 'surprise,' and I can leave if I please."

"You're my familiar!"

Cicero felt as though he'd accidentally touched a live wire, an unpleasant sort of shock racing through him. "I never agreed to bond with you," Cicero said coldly. He jerked free. "I'm not your familiar, and I'm bloody well not your pet."

He turned his back on Noah and made for the door and Tom. Leona gestured for his attention, but Cicero ignored her.

"Come along, Thomas," he said, and strode out the door Tom opened for him. It closed behind them with a decisive thump.

CHAPTER 16

THE SUN HAD gone down, and the already cold air turned even icier. Despite the chill and the holiday, people still roamed the street, in groups or alone. Looking for drink, or company, or entertainment, no doubt. Cabs clattered past, the horses blowing great plumes of steam from their nostrils.

Cicero surprised Tom by hailing a cab to take them back to the apartment. "Leona had some interesting things to say," he said once the cab started off.

Tom glanced at him hopefully, but Cicero stared resolutely out his window. At least he was talking, even if it was just about the case.

"What?" Tom asked.

Cicero told him. "And now I don't know what to do," he finished. "Tonight is probably our best chance to break into the tunnels beneath the Rooster. But it might equally be our best chance to do the same at this hideaway of Janowski's."

Tom tried to ignore the ache of worry and concentrate on the task at hand. "Aye. But the tunnels…I know a thing or two about tunnel gangs, and they're likely just a thoroughfare from one place to another, so the gang can move out of sight of the police or anyone else. This address she gave you is close enough to the Rooster that it might even be where the tunnels lead."

Cicero perked up slightly. "Do you think so?"

"I can't know for sure, but it's one possibility. Not to say that the tunnels don't lead anywhere else as well, of course. But if it were up to me, I'd go to this warehouse instead."

"Could they be holding Isaac there?" Cicero asked, not like he thought Tom had the answer, but more as if he hoped it could be true.

"Don't see why not," Tom said anyway.

"Then that's where we'll go."

The cab came to a halt. Cicero paid, and they climbed the stairs to Tom's apartment. "I'm sorry," Tom said when they were safely inside. "I know tonight didn't turn out the way you would have liked."

Cicero shrugged. He pulled off his gloves and coat, tossing them carelessly onto Tom's table. "I don't know what you mean. This is the best information we've gathered so far."

"I meant the party and Noah," Tom said, exasperated. "And you damned well know it."

Cicero didn't answer immediately. Instead he walked to the room's sole window and stared out. "Don't apologize. Tell me, before you butted heads with Noah, did you at least enjoy the party?"

Maybe he ought to lie. Something was obviously bothering Cicero a great deal. "Nay," Tom said heavily. "I'm sorry."

"I said don't apologize." Cicero breathed on the cold glass, then drew an abstract pattern with his finger in the resulting steam. "Perhaps I'm the one who ought to apologize. I took you there because I hoped you'd enjoy it. Because I hoped you'd become friends with my friends."

When was the last time anyone had worried about Tom's opinion? Wanted him to like something because it was important to them, and they hoped to share it with him?

Never, that he could recall.

He swallowed against the unexpected tightness of his throat. "I don't mean the people were a bad lot." Except for Noah, but that went without saying. "It's just...I ain't fancy like them. I don't have much in the way of book learning. I don't know anything about philosophy, or art, or what have you. But I'm glad you had a good time...up until the last bit, anyway."

Cicero's shoulders tightened beneath his suit coat. "Yes, the last bit. What did Noah say about me?"

Tom didn't want to repeat it...but he could hardly refuse. "He warned me off. Said he'd done things with you, and took the trouble to point out the pillows where it happened."

"How crude of him, to kiss and tell," Cicero said lightly. "It's true, you know. We fucked."

Tom hadn't doubted it, but that still didn't make it a pleasant thing to hear. "And are you going to again?" he asked, even if he wasn't sure he wanted to know the answer.

Cicero didn't speak for a long moment. When he did, his tone was oddly muted. "What if I said yes?"

It was for the best, really. Tom had no business getting entangled with Cicero. He'd been stupid to let it get as far as it had. He should just lie, laugh it off, and let them both get on with their lives.

But he couldn't stop thinking of Cicero in his arms last night. Not just when they'd had sex, but after, when Cicero had drifted off to sleep. He'd looked so beautiful, his head on Tom's shoulder, his arm draped loosely over Tom's chest. And so vulnerable, somehow, with his features relaxed and soft. Open.

He didn't want to give that up. No matter how terrible an idea it was. "That depends," Tom said carefully. "What is this between us? Is this like with me and Bill? We toss each other off in the dark and never acknowledge it in the light of day? Or is it something else?"

Cicero glanced back at him. "Like what?"

"Like...I don't know how to say it." Noah would have known, no doubt. Probably any of Cicero's friends at the party would have had the right words. The pretty words. "Like the sort of thing where you break my heart."

Cicero's lips parted, as if in shock. As if he'd never considered the possibility. "I don't want to break your heart."

"Then tell me what you do want." Tom moved closer. "One or the other. If it's just two friends seeing to a need, then there's no obligation. Carry on as you like, and I'll do the same. If it's something else...then I ain't sure my heart can take knowing you're in someone else's bed."

There. It was out, as honest as he could make it.

"I don't want to sleep with Noah anymore," Cicero said, his voice so low Tom had to strain to hear it.

His heart did a little leap in his chest. "Can't see why you did in the first place," he agreed. "What about other people?"

"Or other people. I want to give this...us...a chance."

The relief flooding Tom's veins startled him with its intensity. And it shouldn't have. This was stupid, foolish, insane. He'd spent years avoiding any entanglements, and for damned good reason.

Nothing had changed. Except for Cicero's presence in his life, like a brightly colored bird against a drab winter sky.

There was one other question he had to ask, though. "About Noah...

is it true, then? He's your witch?"

Cicero laughed softly, but there was a slightly wild edge to it. "No, tesoro. You are."

Tom froze.

He'd misheard. Or Cicero was toying with him, playing some silly prank to lighten the mood.

Cicero turned to face him. "Not the reaction I was expecting," he said, folding his arms over his chest.

"You're joking, right?"

"I'm afraid not." Cicero glanced down at the uneven floorboards. "I knew, from the moment I saw you."

Tom's head reeled. He'd never considered something like this might happen. Was it possible? "And you didn't say anything?"

"Oi! You try walking up to a complete stranger and saying 'you're my witch.'" He glared up at Tom. "I didn't know if we'd get along, or if you'd punch me in the face for the way I dress, or what."

"Like Isaac's witch did," Tom said slowly. He felt as though he looked back over the last few days through a new lens, one that brought everything into focus. "No wonder you were so angry at me."

Cicero's glare faltered. "You're not supposed to be so bloody understanding."

Tom arched a brow. "I'm so sorry," he said dryly. "What should I be doing?"

"I don't know." Cicero shrugged awkwardly. "Demanding I bond with you immediately."

"You're confusing me with Noah."

"Then shouting dramatically and waving your hands."

"Now you're confusing me with yourself."

Cicero burst out laughing. "You arse!"

Tom knew what he should do—what he *had* to do. If he'd really been Tom Halloran, it would be one thing. But he wasn't. And if rough-around-the-edges Tom Halloran was a poor match for someone like Cicero, a tunnel rat like Liam O'Connell was even worse.

"Let me make sure I understand," Tom said. "What you mean is our magic is extra compatible, right? If we bond, it would be stronger than if you bonded with someone else."

"That's right."

"But you could bond with someone else."

"Yes." Cicero swallowed. "If I wanted to."

This shouldn't be so hard. "And what do you want?"

"I thought I knew." Cicero's mouth twitched into a rueful smile. "But I'm not so sure anymore."

He shouldn't ask. But he did anyway. "So you ain't decided against me?"

"No." Cicero glanced up and met his gaze. "Not in the least."

"Then maybe…I should think about it too?" Tom asked, because he was apparently a fool who'd lost what little sense he'd had to start with.

Cicero's eyes widened. "Think about it? What's there to think about?"

"The rest of my life, same as you?" Tom said, confused. "What, did you think I'd just drop everything and leap at the chance to become your witch?"

The offended look on Cicero's face told Tom he had, in fact, thought exactly that. Tom burst into laughter. "You did, didn't you!"

"Well, of course!" Cicero's lower lip protruded slightly. Tom had to restrain the urge to kiss it. "Why on earth *wouldn't* you want to be my witch?"

"I never even thought about working for the MWP, for one thing."

Cicero didn't look at all mollified. "So? I told you the tests were wrong, that you have witch potential. Why didn't you start thinking about it then?"

Tom couldn't help but laugh again. "Because not everyone wants to be a witch, or work for the MWP? Maybe I'm content being an unmagical patrolman. Did you consider that, even for a moment?"

"No," Cicero muttered. "Then you don't want to bond with me."

This was it. His chance to agree and refuse the bond. Break Cicero's heart in the process most likely, but that was a small price to pay.

Because he'd never considered doing anything that would lead to the truth coming out. Becoming a detective with the MWP left him too exposed. It was harder to fade into the background, to be unexceptional.

And Cicero was anything but unexceptional. There would be no hiding with him.

But Cicero looked so alone, his face turned to the side, his arms folded tight over his chest. Alone and rejected, and maybe the latter was the fault of his own ego, but what did Tom expect from a cat?

"I never said that." Tom closed the remaining distance between them. When he set his fingers lightly under the other man's chin, Cicero allowed him to gently tip his head back, so Tom could look into his face. "Don't go putting words in my mouth. I said I had to think about it, and

I do. This is a big thing—the rest of my life, and yours, we're talking about. Would you want a witch who wouldn't even take a little while to think over a decision like that?"

"I suppose not," Cicero said grudgingly, although it was clear his pride still stung.

Tom leaned in, not near enough to kiss, but close enough their breath mingled, and Cicero had no choice but to meet his gaze. "There's no other familiar I'd even think about bonding with." He ran his thumb tenderly along Cicero's jaw, feeling the light scratch of stubble. "Understand?"

Cicero's expression relaxed fractionally, and his arms unfolded to slip around Tom's waist. "I suppose."

"So we take a few days. Keep on as we have. Consider our options. Then we'll talk again."

Cicero nodded. "All right." A reluctant smile stole over his features. "You do insist on surprising me, Thomas Halloran. You'd think by now I would have learned not to make any assumptions when it comes to you, tesoro."

"You'd think," Tom agreed. "You've called me 'tesoro' three times now. What's it mean?"

Cicero slid his arms up to drape around Tom's neck. He eased forward, so their thighs pressed together. "It means I like you a great deal. Probably more than is wise."

Tom's ribs felt too restrictive around his heart. "Oh." But he couldn't just leave it at that. "So if we can't be wise, then at least we're fools together."

Cicero laughed. "Quite, darling." He kissed Tom. "It's still too early for our intended skullduggery. What say we spend the time practicing our French?"

Cicero huddled deep within his coat, wishing in vain for a warmer hat. The night had grown colder as the hours plodded on, and the air taken on a crystalline sharpness. At least the temperature blunted the scents of the docks: river water slick with filth, slime-encrusted pilings, and dead fish.

"That it?" Tom asked, nodding to one of the dilapidated buildings lining this particular stretch of wharf.

Cicero glanced up at him, but Tom was nothing but a black shape against the starlit sky. He held a lantern in one hand, but kept it shuttered for the moment, so as not to give them away to any guards.

A little worm of doubt chewed at the edge of Cicero's heart, one that had never been there before. What if he decided he wanted Tom as his witch…and Tom refused him?

Noah certainly hadn't rejected him. He'd been so possessive, as if their bond were already a done thing. Had he given Noah the wrong impression somehow? Made him think Cicero had agreed to bond after New Year's, instead of just making a decision then?

Well, the display had certainly made his decision easier, hadn't it? He certainly wasn't going to bond with Noah now.

"That's the address Leona gave me," Cicero said, forcing his mind onto the task at hand. "It looks deserted."

"Aye, but is it? That's the question." Tom started forward. "And not one we're going to answer from this distance. Time to get up close."

Cicero padded after him, every sense straining for any sign they might not be the only ones in the immediate vicinity. The creak of rope from the ships tied up at dock was accompanied by the whisper of river water against the pilings. The sound of carols came from one of the vessels, the men on board celebrating the holiday together. Otherwise, all was silent.

The building Leona had directed him to had seen better days, probably around the same time George Washington had lived on Cherry Street. A century later, affluence had swept north, leaving behind slums and buildings that looked like a good wind would knock them down. Tom shook his head in disapproval. "They've let the fire hex fade," he murmured. "One spark and the whole dockside will be ablaze."

"You can write them a citation later," Cicero whispered back. "Right now, we need to find some way inside."

They avoided the large doors meant to accept cargo from the wharf and found a smaller door around the side. Tom carefully placed his hand on the latch.

"Hexes," he confirmed. "More than one, I'm thinking."

"What kind?"

He closed his eyes in concentration. "An alarm hex. And one to keep unlocking hexes from working on the latch."

"Impressive," Cicero said. "How on earth did you learn to tell them apart?"

A wary look crossed Tom's face, there and gone so fast Cicero wasn't sure he'd actually seen it in the dimness. "You pick up these things," he said vaguely. "There. Hexes are broken."

Cicero took out one of the unlocking hexes he'd brought from the

MWP, in anticipation of going into the tunnels tonight. Had this hideout been the destination of those traveling unseen to and from the Rooster?

Was Isaac inside even now?

"Unlock," he whispered, and the latch clicked softly open.

Tom drew his revolver from inside his coat. "Ready?"

Cicero nodded, his guts tight with anticipation. Tom eased the door open, wincing when the hinges squealed from rust. They both froze, but there was nothing beyond but silence. Cicero slipped into cat form and around Tom's ankles, into the building.

The door opened onto the main room—a cavernous space once used to store cargo. Now it was dominated by a printing press. Great rolls of paper awaited printing, but the damp had started to warp the fibers. Stacks of completed newspapers waited in bundles, but they too appeared to have been sitting neglected for a long time.

Tom eased up the shutter of his lantern, casting a narrow beam of light. He joined Cicero near the stacked papers. "November 15," he read. "That must be when Janowski decided he had better things to do than be a newspaper man. I wonder what changed his mind?"

Cicero hopped down and padded toward the back of the room. Two doors opened off the warehouse. He went to the leftmost one and sniffed at the crack. Mice, of course, but there was another, more disturbing scent.

He shifted back to human form. "Blood," he whispered as Tom joined him. "It's faint, but I smell blood."

Tom's jaw firmed. "I'll go first."

The door was unlocked and unhexed. Tom stepped in, revolver at the ready. The light from his lantern spilled across a row of tables, surrounded by chairs. Broken nibs scattered across the floor, and squares of blank paper waited on one of the tables. Empty bottles sat near the blank paper, each with a layer of brownish residue on the inside.

"So the anarchists are making hexes for Sloane," Tom said.

"Let's hope he made sure to find good hexmen." Cicero went to the bottles. "A misdrawn hex can have ugly consequences." He picked up one of the bottles and sniffed. "Blood."

Tom paled. "Blood?"

Cicero picked up one of the broken nibs from the floor. The tip was discolored and stank of blood as well.

Which didn't make any sense. Hexes were drawn with ink. And yes, the ink was often specialized in some fashion—made from ground gemstones, or a specific dye or the like. But blood? Cicero had never heard of it being used in hexing.

"This doesn't make sense," he murmured. "Let's see what's in the other room."

As they stepped into the warehouse, Cicero froze. "Did you hear that?"

Tom stilled as well. But there came nothing more, not even the scratch of mice. Then the wind picked up slightly, and the roof creaked above them, as if in protest.

"Just the building," Cicero said in relief.

Tom remained grim. "Let's see that other room, before this place comes down on our heads."

They went to the other door. "Hexed," Tom said.

Cicero's breath caught. So far, they'd found nothing to take back to Ferguson. But surely the anarchists wouldn't have a locked door inside their own hideaway if there was nothing important behind it.

Tom broke the hexes, and Cicero unlocked the door. Taking a deep breath, he pushed it open and stepped inside.

The space was utterly packed with crates, boxes, and barrels. The light from Tom's lantern wavered over them.

HIGH EXPLOSIVES: DANGEROUS was stenciled on the crates. BLASTING CAPS on the boxes. GUNPOWDER on the barrels.

"Saint Mary, Holy Familiar of Christ, preserve us," Tom breathed.

A footstep sounded behind them, and the click of a hammer cocking froze Cicero's blood. "Stay right where you are, and put your hands where we can see them."

CHAPTER 17

TOM TURNED QUICKLY, his revolver leveled. Cicero stood between him and the door, already raising his hands. Two men filled the doorway, one with a pistol and the other a shotgun. Both looked hard-bitten, their mouths twisted in anger, and he didn't question they intended to kill Cicero and him both.

The one with the shotgun pointed it at Tom. "I said hands up! Revolver on the floor, now!"

The world seemed to sharpen to unnatural clarity. The black bore of the gun trained on him. Cicero's coat, bright against the washed out clothing of the anarchists. The smell of gunpowder from the barrels.

The hum of hexes from the boxes and barrels, so many he could feel them vibrating in his teeth. Meant to keep the gunpowder and dynamite from exploding too early, or catching fire from open flames.

"Let's just talk about this," Cicero said, voice shaking.

"Shut your hole," said the one with the pistol. "And you, drop the damn gun, or we'll put a bullet in your face."

Even with the hexes, the anarchists were hesitant to shoot in the direction of the explosives. Magic could only do so much, after all. As soon as they were out of the room, though, it would be another story.

"All right," Tom said. His pulse beat in his throat, and the hexes buzzed in his bones. He'd never tried breaking a hex without touching it, let alone so many at once. "Just hold your fire."

He crouched slowly, then set the gun on the floor. The wood gave him a connection to the hexes, a channel through which he could push his magic, and the vibrations in his teeth intensified.

Now or never.

Black spots danced across his vision, and he nearly pitched forward. "On your feet!" one of the men shouted. "No funny business, or we'll put an end to you this second."

Tom's head spun, but he rose to his feet. The vibrations had fallen silent.

"Now out," said the man with the shotgun. He and his companion stepped farther back into the warehouse.

"Go on," Tom told Cicero.

Cicero glanced at him. His face was white with fear, so pale Tom could make out the beginnings of black stubble along his jaw. Surely he knew just as well as Tom that the explosives behind them were the only thing keeping them alive.

"It'll be all right," Tom said. "I'm right behind you."

The fear eased from Cicero's face, and he nodded. Hands still up, he edged out the door. Tom started after him.

Then, in the doorway, he turned. Before either of the other men could react, he smashed the lantern down onto the floor with all his strength.

Flaming oil splashed everywhere: onto crates and barrels and boxes. The rest of it ran across the wooden boards, making for the huge pile of explosives.

"Fuck!" shouted one of the anarchists.

They both bolted for the side door. Tom grabbed Cicero around the waist, tossed him over one shoulder, and pounded after them.

"Are you insane?" Cicero shouted. He thrashed, but Tom merely tightened his grip and kept running.

They burst out of the warehouse into the cold air. Tom didn't bother looking around for the anarchists, only kept going, stretching his legs to their fullest. The river lay before them, surging in its banks, lapping at the pier he dashed onto. Ignoring Cicero's high-pitched shriek, he leapt from the end of the pier, just as the warehouse exploded behind them.

The river water was so cold it stole Cicero's breath and seized his muscles. For a moment, he was only conscious of darkness and water, of Tom's arm still locked around his waist.

Then light appeared above.

Flaming debris slammed into the water all around them. A hunk of timber twice as large as Cicero plunged toward them, and he squirmed madly, trying to get away before he was crushed or drowned or...

Tom's shoulder shifted beneath his belly, and the water raked his hair forward as Tom began to swim. The timber sank lazily past Cicero's face, bubbles streaming from its heated surface.

Then they were going up, faster and faster, until Cicero's head broke the surface.

He drew in a great gasp of breath as Tom emerged beside him. "You —you—fottuto bastardo! Cazzo!"

"Steady!" Tom seized him by the collar, keeping his head above water. "Don't thrash. Can you swim?"

"Of course I can't bloody swim!"

"Then relax. Trust me. I won't let you drown." Tom slid his arm around Cicero's chest. "There we are. Just stay still. I ain't letting you go."

Cicero managed to relax into his hold. Tom swam for the docks with purposeful strokes. Behind them, the night sky was bright with fire. Alarm bells sounded, and a fire company raced past.

The current had carried them a short distance downstream by the time Tom pulled them shivering back onto dry land. "Are you all right?" he asked.

The cold seemed to have eaten into Cicero's bones, but he nodded. "Other than being soaked, you mean?"

"Aye." Tom slung an arm around Cicero's shoulders. "We need to find somewhere dry and warm, as quick as we can. I'm thinking the nearest precinct house. Can you walk?"

Cicero tucked his hands beneath his arm pits and huddled against Tom's side. "I'm not hurt. Just wet. No thanks to you, madman."

Tom winced. "It was the only thing I could think of at the time. And it worked, didn't it?"

"I suppose." Cicero felt like ice, except for the places Tom touched him. The warm solidity of his arm around Cicero's shoulders, both kept him on his feet and comforted him. That moment, when the anarchists had pointed their guns at them, and Cicero had been certain they'd both end up dead...

Tom had already come up with a plan. And when he promised Cicero it would be all right, despite the guns aimed at their heads, he'd believed Tom with his whole heart.

"You make me feel safe," he whispered. It felt like a revelation. Because large, strong men had never been safe in Cicero's experience.

But Tom was different. Tom used his strength as a shield, not a bludgeon. His hands to protect and uphold, not beat down.

Tom made him feel…well…*loved.* In a way he never had been before.

"I won't let nothing happen to you, cat," Tom said. "Not while I'm still breathing." He nodded at the green lamps which had appeared around the corner. "There's the precinct house. What say we go inside, dry off, and get something warm in you?"

Cicero's teeth had started to chatter, but he still managed, "Not in front of everyone, Thomas. I'm not that sort of fellow."

Tom snorted. "Like hell you ain't."

"Well, not where it would get me arrested." He slid out from under Tom's arm regretfully and straightened his coat. "All right. Let's tell the officer on duty that we just blew up his wharf, shall we?"

It was nearly dawn when Tom reached his neighborhood again. His whole body ached with exhaustion, and he longed for nothing more than to curl up on his bed and sleep for the next three days. The streets were nearly deserted when he descended from the El's platform. The gaslight fought through a low fog, and shadows gathered beneath the spindly trestle. Tired as he was, when one of the shadows moved, Tom's instincts kicked in, bringing his hands up ready to fight.

"I hate this time of year," said a voice rough with whiskey and cigarettes. The dim light touched Horton Phelps's face, revealing a wrinkled map of pain. "Used to love it. Picking out toys for the children —a wooden train for Hal, a doll for Missy. I'd set aside a bit from every job, just to make sure they could have something waiting for them Christmas morning." He stopped a few feet away from Tom. "Until you fucking killed them, Liam O'Connell."

Tom's heart pounded, and he had the absurd desire to run. As though he could leave the past behind. "It was an accident," he said, his voice rough even to his own ears. "Old Mogs knocked over the lamp and set himself on fire too."

"Like I care!" Phelps lunged forward to shout it in Tom's face. Tom started to step back, but Phelps seized him by the collar. "You O'Connells cost my gang the job that would have made us all rich. But that wasn't enough for you. You killed my men. Burned down my home and roasted my family alive, so I can still hear them screaming in my sleep." His eyes narrowed, and a wild look came into them. "You took everything from me. Seems only fair if maybe I take everything from you."

Tom shoved him, hard. Phelps stumbled back, and Tom grabbed him by the collar in turn, pushing him into the maze of the trestle. "You'll keep your mouth shut, if you know what's good for you," he blustered. His mind raced frantically—there had to be some way out of this. He just had to keep Phelps talking long enough to figure out what.

Phelps laughed; it turned into a phlegmatic cough. "I thought you were Mike, when I saw you at the restaurant," he said. "Risen from the grave and come back to haunt me. By why would Mike's ghost be dressed as a copper, eh?" He shook his head. "Too young to be Danny, and I saw his body anyway. So I knew you had to be Liam."

"So you what—followed me?" Tom gave him a hard shake. "Not smart, Phelps, following a copper so you can threaten him."

"I've got nothing to lose, do I?" Phelps's grin was manic, as if he'd taken some cocaine-laced tonic. "But you...I asked around your tenement. Looking for my friend Liam. But they said oh no, that apartment belongs to good old Tom Halloran, local copper and hero of the people." The grin faded. "I lost everything, but you? You gained a new life."

"At the cost of my family's blood," Tom said. "You ain't the only one who lost everything, you goddamned fool."

"Don't you dare. Whatever happened that night, you brought it on yourselves." Phelps's gaze turned haunted. "Your gang...they were like rabid dogs. Worse—rabid familiars. Like they'd been human once, but forgotten how to ever be again."

Tom swallowed thickly, fighting back the memories that threatened to overwhelm him. The smell of blood, Danny's red eyes, the ruin where Ma's face had been before Da tore it off. "What do you want?"

"I want my wife and children back."

Tom's grip loosened. Saint Mary, he was so tired. "I know. I want Da back, and Molly, and Danny, and all the rest. But I can't do that."

"Then what good are you?" Phelps stared at him coldly. "I haven't decided what I want yet. Maybe I should just come to your tenement one night and burn it to the ground. Stand outside and listen to you scream, just like my Hal screamed."

Bile coated the inside of Tom's mouth. "You can't. You'd best believe I make sure every landlord on my beat keeps the fire hexes painted fresh and charged. Ain't none of those buildings burning down." Not like the wharf tonight. At least the final count had only been three old buildings and no lives lost, not half the precinct.

"I could tell the Police Board they've a wanted criminal on the force."

"You could." Tom's heart thudded wildly, but he kept his voice level. Bored, almost. "Then what?"

"Then you rot in Sing Sing for the rest of your life. Illegal hexes, inciting a riot, arson, murder…hell, they might send you to the electric chair."

"They might." Fear iced Tom's veins, but he struggled to keep it from showing on his face. "Maybe it would even be justice served if they did. But you ain't interested in justice, are you, Phelps? If you were, you'd have turned me in the first day you saw me. You want revenge."

Phelps cocked his head. "I suppose I do at that."

"Then what? We meet up someplace quiet, have it out between us?"

"I haven't decided yet. But I will." Phelps took a step back, then another. "Until then…watch your back, copper."

Cicero led the way through the detectives' area to Ferguson's office, his step lighter than it had been in days. True, they hadn't yet found Isaac —but they'd made real progress. Now they knew the anarchists had been making hexes, and it wasn't hard to infer Sloane was involved. The two men from the warehouse had been caught by an alert patrolman who found their behavior suspicious, and transferred to MWP custody. Neither had talked yet, but surely it was only a matter of time before they did.

Even better, after finding the explosives, they had real proof of a serious plot afoot in the city. He and Tom weren't alone in this any more. After last night, they'd have the full weight of the MWP behind them.

Cicero glanced up at Tom, who walked beside him. Even though Tom looked awful—bags under his eyes, his hair unkempt, his shoulders slumped from weariness—warmth filled Cicero's chest.

He paused outside of Ferguson's office. "Thank you," he said with a smile. "I couldn't have done any of this without you."

Tom returned the smile with one of his one. "I could say the same."

Cicero pushed open the door and strolled in. Ferguson and Athene were alone; Athene on her perch, and Ferguson behind his desk. Ferguson appeared almost as exhausted as Tom, and he didn't smile when they entered.

"Close the door," he said.

A little of Cicero's good mood slipped away. Tom shut the door and took off his hat. "Sir, ma'am," he said, nodding to Ferguson and Athene in turn.

"Halloran. Cicero." Ferguson didn't sound any more pleased than he looked. "Sit down."

Cicero perched on the edge of a chair. "No need to thank us for a job well done," he said, not bothering to hide his annoyance. "I suppose you want to discuss the next steps?"

Ferguson rubbed at his face. "Well done, you two. You found and stopped an anarchist plot, that's for certain. You'd be up for a medal, if you hadn't blown up a building and set two others on fire."

"What?" Cicero blinked, hardly able to believe what he was hearing. "Better their warehouse blow up than city hall, or the post office, or whatever target they had in mind!"

Tom didn't seem nearly as surprised. "Aye, sir, but we had no choice. Like I said in the report last night, it was us or them. And if they'd done away with us, those explosives would still be sitting in their warehouse, waiting to be used."

"I'm not disagreeing." Ferguson sat back and folded his hands in front of him on the desk. "It would have been nice if we'd been able to recover the explosives, but I was a detective for fifteen years. I know you do the best you can at the time."

"Then why don't you seem more enthusiastic?" Cicero asked cautiously.

"Because the Police Board, none of whom have ever actually served as police, disagree. I spent three hours in front of the commissioners this morning, explaining why you shouldn't both be fired on the spot."

Cicero felt as though he'd plunged into the river again. "Wh-what?"

"Politics," Tom said flatly. "That's it, ain't it?"

Athene hopped off her perch, shifting on the way down. "Your friend is a sharp one," she told Cicero.

Remembering how he'd argued with her about accepting Tom's help, Cicero felt heat rise to his cheeks. "I don't understand."

"The New Year's Eve celebration is Friday night." Ferguson leaned back in his chair and exchanged a glance with Athene. "Delegates have already started arriving from Chicago, San Francisco, cities all over America. The explosion of a warehouse full of bomb-making materials makes New York look bad. Like we can't control the anarchist element and keep the delegates safe."

"We probably kept them from being blown up!" Cicero exclaimed hotly.

"We know that, Cicero," Athene replied. "The truth is, if this had happened under the supervision of the regular police...the board still wouldn't be happy about the explosion, but they also wouldn't be shutting down the investigation."

Cicero sank back into his chair, feeling as though the world had dropped away from beneath him. "They're…shutting it down?"

"That ain't fair," Tom exclaimed. "And it don't make any sense, neither."

"The Police Board hasn't been friendly toward the MWP since former Chief Cavanaugh tried to assassinate Roosevelt," Ferguson explained. The words sounded oddly distant to Cicero's ears. "They're inclined to take the explosion and fire as more evidence the MWP is… not out of control, precisely, but in need of firm direction from them. And their direction is to keep things quiet until after New Year's."

"But New Year's was circled on Sloane's calendar!" Cicero came to his feet. "The anarchists mean to do something then, surely!"

"There's no direct evidence linking Sloane and the Rooster to the anarchists," Athene said.

"Are you insane? We found hex-making equipment at the hideout, and we heard Sloane say he needed hexes from Janowski!"

"Which doesn't mean Sloane was involved in anything criminal."

Cicero stared at her. None of this made any sense. "So…what? We're just going to let this go? Forget about Sloane? Leave Isaac missing? Ignore the fact we still don't know exactly what happened to Gerald and Barshtein? Don't know what hexes the anarchists were making in their warehouse?"

Ferguson sighed heavily. "Until after the new Police Board is sworn in on the first, yes."

"So no one's gone to question Sloane?" Tom asked.

"That's right," Ferguson said, meeting Tom's gaze squarely.

Tom nodded thoughtfully. "And Sloane and the anarchists got no way of knowing the explosion at the warehouse was anything but an accident? The two men hauled in ain't been allowed contact with the outside world?"

"Precisely."

"So in theory, they don't know what happened. Why did the place go up? Is anyone onto them? They don't have answers. A smart fellow like Sloane ain't going to just run, not unless he's sure the police are on their way. When no official force shows up knocking on his door, he's going to relax."

"So?" Cicero demanded. "What does that matter, if we're not allowed to investigate?"

Tom shrugged. "I ain't MWP. The Police Board might have yelled at Chief Ferguson here, but my captain ain't told me to go back to the beat."

A small smile touched Athene's lips. "I said he was smart."

"I'm afraid informing your captain seems to have slipped my mind," Ferguson said. "And will probably continue to do so for the foreseeable future."

Maybe there was some hope of salvaging this, then. "So Thomas and I go back to the Rooster, and…what? Try to find evidence even the bloody Police Board can't ignore?"

Ferguson sighed heavily. "Unfortunately, Cicero, you are MWP. Halloran is going to have to finish this alone."

The world seemed to narrow in, his vision tightening to focus on Ferguson's face. "Like hell he is," Cicero snarled. "If we had any doubts at all as to how dangerous these people are, last night put paid to them. I'm not letting Thomas walk in there with no one at his back!"

"I'll be fine," Tom said, because of course he did. "Don't worry about me."

"Talk to your friends among the ferals, Cicero," Athene suggested. "I'm sure there's someone—"

"Who can what? Take my place somehow?" Cicero's nails bit into his palms. "Get a job at a moment's notice, play at being a detective? I'm the only choice, and you bloody well know it."

She snapped her teeth together angrily, like the clack of an owl's beak. "There is no choice."

The world seemed to settle around him, much as it had when he'd first laid eyes on Tom in this very office. Old fear made his hands shake, because he remembered what life had been like before the MWP. When he'd been on his own.

But he'd almost let old fears cost him the chance to get to know Tom. And he wasn't alone any more.

"You're right. There isn't." He tore off his familiar's badge and flung it on Ferguson's desk. "I quit."

CHAPTER 18

"**ARE YOU GOING** to be all right?" Tom asked uncertainly.

Cicero sat by the window of Tom's apartment, slumped over the boxes and bags that represented all that he owned in the world. Clothing, mostly, from what little Tom had seen. He hadn't been allowed in the familiar barracks while Cicero packed; that territory was apparently off limits to anyone but the familiars themselves.

"Of course," Cicero said with a careless shrug. "Cats always land on their feet."

Tom couldn't even imagine what Cicero must be feeling now. As for himself, he was damned angry the Police Board couldn't see past their desire to punish the MWP whenever the chance arose. Cavanaugh was serving his time in Sing Sing, wasn't he? What more did they want?

And of course it was people like Cicero who paid the price for their vindictiveness. They ought to be pinning a medal on Cicero, not forcing him to choose between his safety and everyone else's.

At least Tom could help with that. "You can stay here as long as you like," he said. "I won't...you know...expect anything in return."

It drew a shadow of a smile from Cicero. "Now that is disappointing, tesoro."

"Didn't say I'd turn anything down if you offered," Tom pointed out with a return grin. "But I mean it. I can sleep out here, and you can have the bed, if you want."

"I don't." Cicero rose to his feet and stepped closer. He ran his hands down Tom's chest, not seductively, but more as if he just craved the touch. "You don't seem worried about your neighbors gossiping, I must say. A fairy staying with big, strong Thomas Halloran. What will they think?"

Tom shrugged awkwardly. "I look after my neighborhood as best I can. But I don't owe them my entire life. If they want to talk about me, let them. And if it turns nasty…well. I been through worse."

Might still be through worse, if Phelps decided to move against him. Having Cicero here complicated the situation, to say the least. But what other choice did Tom have? He couldn't throw Cicero out on the street, tell him to find someone else to stay with. Not and look himself in the eye ever again.

Besides, the idea of having Cicero around all the time, even temporarily, had a certain appeal. And not just because they'd fall asleep and wake up in the same bed.

Cicero's smile was sad. "So have I," he said, as if reminding himself as well as Tom.

"It was brave, what you did," Tom said, taking Cicero's hands in his. "I mean that. Walking away from the MWP, knowing they won't protect you any more than they protected Isaac…that took real courage."

Cicero's peridot eyes widened in surprise, but he seemed at a loss for words. So Tom just leaned forward and pressed a kiss to his forehead. "I'm proud to know you, cat," he whispered. "Now, we'd best get ready to go to the Rooster for the evening shift."

"You're right." Cicero dabbed at his eyes, careful not to disturb the kohl around them. "The tunnels, do you think?"

"Aye. We've only seen bits and pieces so far—Sloane's office, the warehouse. What we ain't found is what ties them together and makes sense of all the parts." Tom stripped off his coat and exchanged it for the one he habitually wore to the Rooster. "Every instinct I have says we'll find the answer down in the tunnels that link the two."

Cicero took a deep breath and squared his shoulders. "Agreed. It's all up to us now, and to hell with the MWP. We're getting Isaac back and sending Sloane to prison no matter what."

Unfortunately, their plan to sneak into the tunnels was once again scuttled, this time almost as soon as they arrived.

Stepping into the Rooster felt different than it had before. Tension curled beneath Cicero's skin, and it was an effort to wave at the other performers, to smile and nod at Sloane.

At Kearney, who'd hit him with the hex that first day, testing to see if he was truly unbonded.

Then, he'd had the certainty that the MWP would come in force if anyone tried to restrain him. And yes, it had still been dangerous, but it wasn't the same. Because now the only thing he had left to rely on was himself.

And Tom.

If there was anything good about this disaster of a day, it was Tom's absurd attempt at chivalry. He hadn't even suggested bringing in a cat-sized bed, just offered his own, as if there was anywhere else in the apartment he could fit lying down. Other than the floor, presumably, which no doubt he would have taken without complaint if Cicero had agreed to such nonsense.

Probably Tom would have done the same for anyone. But that didn't make it—him—any less special.

Cicero went to the back and readied himself for his first performance. He kept a closer ear out than before, starting at every footstep. Fur and feathers, if Sloane or Kearney saw him so jumpy, they'd start wondering why. He changed into his hoochie coochie outfit, fixed the kohl around his eyes, then applied rouge to his cheeks and lips.

Enough. He had to calm down. Perhaps a drink at the bar would do it. Not to mention it would give him an excuse to talk to Tom, without raising Sloane's ire.

The main room was still empty of customers, and Ho mercifully absent from behind the bar. Not that Cicero disliked the man, but he'd insist on serving Cicero himself.

"Glass of wine, if you please, Thomas," he said, leaning on his elbow on the bar. "And dear God, don't water it. I had to spend Christmas with the relatives, don't you know."

"Horrible," Tom said dryly, with a glance at the fellow pushing a broom around the room. He poured the wine, then pushed it across the bar, lowering his voice as he did so. "I've bad news. Kearney has a guard on the cellar."

"Blast." Cicero took a sip of the wine and glanced around the room. Neither Kearney nor Sloane were anywhere to be seen. "Any idea as to why?"

"I asked Ho what that was about, and he said Kearney claimed some booze was stolen."

"All right, change of plan. We'll just have to fall back on an earlier idea." Cicero didn't like making the suggestion, but he didn't see they had any choice. "I've talked to the other performers, and I have a list of Isaac's regulars. It's possible one of them is with the anarchists, or knows something about his disappearance."

Tom wiped down the bar with a rag, pausing to polish the brass rail. "Possible, but how likely?"

"Do you have a better suggestion?"

Tom's mouth tightened. "Not really."

Cicero took a deep breath. "I'm going to start seeing customers. Drinks at the tables only, if I can get away with it. But if one of the regulars seems to know something, I might have to go behind the curtain."

Out of the corner of his eye, Cicero saw the movement of the rag hitch. Then it resumed. "I'm sorry," he said. "I won't unless I have to."

"I understand." Tom didn't sound happy about it, but then Cicero hadn't expected him to be. Cicero wasn't exactly thrilled himself. "Will you be all right?"

The question was simple, but its unexpectedness brought a lump to Cicero's throat. He'd expected jealousy or posturing, and once again Tom turned everything on its head.

Life with him certainly wouldn't be boring.

Cicero swallowed his wine and set the glass carelessly on the bar. "It's nothing I haven't done before. Wish me luck, darling."

"Luck," Tom murmured as Cicero sauntered away.

By the end of the night, Cicero was acutely grateful that the bar heavily watered the drinks served to the entertainers, or else he'd have been flat on the floor. He talked with any number of men, some of them Isaac's regulars and some not, between performances. They bought him drinks, and he pretended to be deeply interested in everything they had to say, occasionally slipping in a bit of flattery when it seemed needed. He received one or two invitations to go behind the curtain, but begged off, saying he had to get ready for his next performance. Naturally he dangled the possibility that he might say yes another night.

Most of them wanted to talk more than fuck, though. They went on about their problems, their jobs, their lives. Cicero batted his eyes and listened intently, occasionally steering the conversation in a direction that seemed like it might be profitable. But this wasn't Techne—no one came here to talk politics or rant against the state of the world. They came here to relax, to see pretty people do scandalous things, and to feel like there was somewhere in the vastness of the city where they belonged.

Although Cicero could sympathize, it wasn't remotely helpful. When they left that night, he couldn't help but feel time was running out. Perhaps the Police Board was right, and Janowski and Sloane's plans had been completely disrupted by the destruction of the explosives. But the anarchists hadn't given up printing newspapers to draw hexes for no reason.

Then on Tuesday, Karol Janowski came in.

Cicero recognized Janowski from his police photo. He sat at a table midway back in the room, his eyes hooded, his gaze fixed on Cicero. No doubt he'd been there throughout the performance, but the lights of the stage had blinded Cicero to the darkened room.

He swallowed against a sudden lump of fear and forced his hips to sway as he went into the crowd. Sweat still clung to his skin, and he felt all the eyes fixed on him, tracing the slow slide of a bead of perspiration down his belly.

Janowski signaled him to come over.

Was this luck? Or disaster?

Perhaps he could get Janowski talking. This might be exactly the opportunity they most needed.

Cicero sashayed to Janowski's table. Janowski watched his approach, and Cicero read hunger in his gaze. But something else, too. Or maybe the lack of something, as though Cicero was nothing but a stage prop, or a doll, existing only for Janowski to play with.

He'd seen that look plenty of times. Sometimes it was something he could use to his advantage. And sometimes it was a warning to run.

"Hello, handsome," he said as he slid into the seat beside Janowski's. Because *"ciao, bello"* belonged to Tom now, and he couldn't bear to say it even lightly to this man. "I haven't seen you here before." He fanned himself. "Dancing certainly works up a thirst."

Janowski snapped his fingers at one of the servers. "Two whiskeys," he said, without asking what Cicero wanted.

The drinks appeared with alacrity. Cicero sipped on his watered one and leaned closer to Janowski. "So what brings you to the Rooster, love?" he purred. "First time here?"

"No." Janowski's hand slid onto Cicero's knee. Then to his thigh. Cicero gritted his teeth and managed not to pull away. "I'm meeting a friend, later. But in the meantime, I wanted to watch you dance."

This was good, wasn't it? A chance to learn something. He just needed to keep that in mind, despite every instinct screaming at him to pull away. "You came for little old me?"

Janowski's grin showed too many teeth. "I've heard so many interesting things about you." His hand slid higher still.

Fur and feathers. "All true," Cicero said with a flirtatious smile. "But aren't we going to wait for your friend?"

"He has other business to attend to, first." Janowski leaned in. His breath reeked of onions. "Which gives us plenty of time to get better acquainted somewhere more private."

Cicero hesitated. He didn't want to take Janowski up on his offer, but what choice did he have? Maybe with a few more drinks and a quick tug, Janowski would become more talkative about this friend he was meeting. And whether they had any plans for New Year's Eve. "Over there?" Cicero suggested, nodding at one of the alcoves whose curtain was drawn back to show it was empty. "Five dollars, but I assure you, I'm worth it."

Janowski's hand tightened on Cicero's thigh, the pressure bordering on pain. "Upstairs."

Cazzo.

New plan. Janowski made his tail bristle. Nothing on this earth would convince him to let the man fuck him. He had the unpleasant feeling Janowski was the sort who liked pain. Inflicting it, anyway.

But maybe he could still get something useful out of this. "Sure thing, handsome," he said, wriggling provocatively against Janowski's side. "Let's go."

They made for the stairs, Janowski's hand gripping Cicero's arse the whole way. As they passed the bar, Cicero caught Tom's eye. Tom, of course, was staring, although at least he'd managed to keep any look of alarm or jealousy off his face.

"Five minutes," he mouthed at Tom.

Thank God, Tom nodded to indicate he'd gotten the message. What excuse he'd come up with to justify interrupting a customer in one of the upstairs rooms, Cicero frankly didn't care at this point.

The upstairs hallway mirrored the one on the first floor with the dressing rooms, except that here doors opened off either side. Ten in all, just enough to satisfy the arcane requirements of the liquor laws and allow the Rooster to serve alcohol on Sundays. Several doors stood open, and Cicero selected the closest to the stairs.

How could he keep Janowski talking, just long enough to learn something useful? "So what business is it you do, darling?" Cicero asked as they entered the room. There was—naturally—a bed, accompanied by a low table with a jar of oil waiting on top. A washstand and mirror were the only other furniture. "I'll bet it's important. I can tell just by looking at you."

Janowski closed the door firmly. There were no locks, to prevent drunken customers from locking themselves in and refusing to come out. He reached inside his coat, felt around, and took out two hexes.

"Lock," he said, slapping one on the door, followed quickly by the second. "Silence."

Then he turned to face Cicero, an ugly grin on his face. "Now. Let's have some fun, you wop whore."

CHAPTER 19

FIVE MINUTES.

Tom checked his pocket watch, then checked it again. Not much could happen in five minutes, could it? Besides, Cicero meant to keep the fellow talking, not actually get physical with him, or else he wouldn't have asked Tom to intervene.

He needed some reason to interrupt. A cry for help? Or maybe pretend someone had sent down for a bottle of wine, and he got the wrong room?

Oh hell. How was he to find the *right* room?

There was a connection between him and Cicero. Maybe he could use that somehow? Let it tell him which door was the one concealing his familiar?

Well, not his familiar; no one had agreed to that. But the man who could be his familiar.

Time was up. He'd just have to improvise.

He turned to Ho, intending to say he'd just gotten an order for a bottle upstairs, and would take it up real quick. But before he could, Kearney appeared, leaning on the bar.

"Halloran," he said. "Sloane wants a bottle of the scotch. Run down to the cellar and get it, would you?"

Shit. Of all the damned timing. He bit back a curse and forced himself to nod. "Sure thing. I'll be right back."

He hurried to the cellar door, past the guard. "Scotch for the boss," he said as he passed. The fellow just nodded, thank heavens. Tom needed to have this over with as fast as possible so he could get upstairs to Cicero.

What would Cicero do if Tom didn't show up quickly enough? He wouldn't let Janowski actually touch him, would he? The thought of opening the door to find Janowski cock-deep in Cicero quickened Tom's steps down the stairs. Now where the devil was the scotch ...

He didn't see the hex drawn on the brick floor until it was too late. The air suddenly thickened around Tom's legs. Startled, he tried to press forward, then step back, but it was as if an invisible hand held him in place. The sensation spread, pinning his arms and torso as well.

Maybe the hex had been put here to catch someone coming down illicitly, and the guard had just forgotten to warn him? But the hex...

This was the sort of hex the ultra-rich used to guard their priceless jewels, or banks to secure their vaults. Hexes to humanely trap mice might be in the reach of a household with the money to spend, but something large enough to trap a human? That took power and lots of it, which meant an equally large amount of cash.

Sloane was a familiar himself. Was it his magic in the hex? But surely an undertaking like this would have left him flat on his back, drained of magic.

The door opened above him. "Mr. Halloran," Sloane said.

The stairs creaked beneath his feet—and beneath another set of feet as well. Tom managed to turn his head far enough to see Kearney following Sloane.

He hadn't just stumbled into this trap. It had been laid especially for him. And at the same time as Janowski took Cicero up into a room.

Oh Saint Mary. Cicero was in danger.

He could feel the hex humming against his skin. Breaking this would take significantly more effort than an alarm or locking hex.

"Sorry, boss," Tom said, in the vague hope he was wrong and there was some way to salvage the situation. "Mr. Kearney said to come down, and nobody warned me—"

"Save your breath," Sloane interrupted. He walked around the edge of the circle until he faced Tom. Kearney remained at Tom's back, at the bottom of the stairs. "We decided to look into your story. Ask around 11th Street." Sloane regarded him with cold, reptilian eyes. "No one had heard of you, let alone hired you to tend bar."

"You must've talked to the wrong people," Tom said, trying to sound as dumb as he could. He pushed against the hex with his ability, felt the hum grow slightly more muted. But only slightly. "I ain't—"

"Stop." Sloane's teeth clicked together, as if he ate the word. Or wanted to eat Tom. "This hex holds you completely immobile. Which means we can do anything we want to you, and there's nothing you can do but take it."

Tom forced his breathing to remain even. He couldn't just use his hands on this hex, like he normally did. He needed to silence it using every inch of skin it touched.

Sloane's flat eyes flickered to Kearney, then back to Tom. "Joe is very inventive, I assure you. He's hoping you'll continue to play dumb, so he can have a bit of fun. Make no mistake, *you* will not be having fun. Not in the slightest."

The thrum of the hex around him slowed. But not enough.

"I disagree with him on this matter," Sloane went on. "I hope you tell us the truth, so I can put this tedious business behind me. So to start. Did the MWP send you and the cat?"

Cicero. "He don't know anything," Tom said. "We got nothing to do with each other."

Kearney hit him from behind, a sharp blow straight to the kidney. Tom's concentration shattered, and he let out an involuntary cry of pain. He tried to turn, to bring up his arms to defend himself, but the hex still held him tight.

"I'd worry about your own skin," Sloane advised. "That little whore will get what's coming to him. Janowski will see to it."

Blind, red rage washed across Tom's vision. A strangled cry escaped him as he threw everything of himself into breaking the hex, like a strongman pulling a fraying rope. Fury pulsed out from him, transmuted by his ability, and the heartbeat of the hex died beneath its savage onslaught.

The effort should have left him drained, but fear and anger pushed him past anything so minor as exhaustion. Before either of the men could react, he spun on his heel and smashed his fist into Kearney's jaw in a vicious uppercut that snapped his head violently to the side.

Kearney went down like a sack of flour. Tom sprang over him and ran up the stairs. "Joe!" shouted Sloane behind him.

The cellar door swung open as the guard on the other side reacted to Sloane's alarmed shout. Tom grabbed him around the back of the neck and smashed him face-first into the wall. Bone crunched, and blood sprayed from his shattered nose, but Tom didn't waste time waiting to see if he was down for good.

Tom burst into the main room. A line of dancers performed a skit, and he raced across the stage in front of them, taking the shortest route to the stairs on the other side of the room. They shouted at him in outrage, and one of the customers threw a glass at Tom's head. It missed, and he hit the steps.

"Cicero," he called. "Hold on! I'm coming!"

"Just cooperate," Janowski said. He drew a knife from the waistband of his pants and held it loosely at his side. "I'll go easy on you, if you do." An ugly smile warped his mouth. "Well. Easier, at any rate."

The metallic taste of fear filled Cicero's mouth at the sight of the knife. He edged away without conscious decision, until the back of his legs hit the bed.

Tom would arrive any minute now. He'd use their partial bond to find Cicero, and...

Bloody hell. Did he realize he could do that?

"Back off," Cicero said, fighting to keep his voice from trembling.

Janowski laughed. "Don't arch your back at me. I'm not impressed. You were so keen to know who I was meeting later, so I'll tell you. Your boss, Sloane. But he's got another problem to take care of first. I hope that chink bartender has enough ice."

Oh hell. Thomas.

Cicero swallowed. He had to get away from Janowski, had to save Tom. But he wasn't even sure how he was going to save himself.

"You're going to kill me, then?" he asked, and now his voice did shake. Damn it. "Or just talk my ears off?"

"Kill you?" Janowski snorted. "You're too valuable for that. I'm just going to hold you here until Sloane's done downstairs." His eyes glittered in the light of the single gas jet as he took a step closer. "But until then... no one said I couldn't have a little fun. Get on the bed."

Cicero held out his hands to either side. "All right." He slid onto the bed, braced one foot against the footboard—and shoved, hard enough to propel himself over the other side.

He was in cat form before he hit the floor. Janowski swore. Cicero darted beneath the bed, making for the door.

Except he needed to change back into human form to have the hands to open it.

Before he could risk it, Janowski grabbed for him. His fingers brushed Cicero's ears, but failed to get a grip. Cicero changed course, claws scrabbling wildly on the wooden floor, before streaking back beneath the bed.

He crouched, as far back against the wall as he could. He had to get out of here, had to get to Tom. But how?

"Your choice," Janowski said. His knees thumped the floor by the bed, on the side between Cicero and the door. "It goes hard for you, then."

He thrust his arm beneath the bed, stabbing at Cicero with the knife. Cicero darted to the side—and sank his teeth deep into Janowski's hand.

Janowski screamed and jerked, but Cicero didn't let go, adding his claws to the mix. The knife fell free. Janowski wrenched his hand back, and Cicero let go to avoid being dragged from beneath the bed.

Janowski was shouting now, furiously, a string of Polish that sounded none too complimentary to Cicero. "I'm going to gut you," he raged, switching to English. "You fucking wop, I'm—"

The door swung open. Cicero glimpsed Tom's shoes and heard a loud *crack*. Janowski collapsed to the floor, moaning. A leather wallet spilled out of his coat pocket, scattering hexes everywhere.

"Cicero!" Tom cried. "Where—"

Cicero slipped out from under the bed. Shouts and the thud of feet on the stairs came through the open door.

Tom ran to the window, ripped back the drapes, and flung it open. "Not too far down," he said. "Come on!"

Cicero started to follow, but the spilled hexes caught his eye. Even a cursory glance showed they looked nothing like any he'd ever seen before. Were these the hexes Sloane had been waiting on?

He snatched one up in his teeth, leapt over the moaning Janowski, and made for the window. Tom was already half out, so Cicero jumped to his shoulders, sinking his claws into Tom's coat to keep his balance.

As the main floor of the resort was underground, it was only a short drop to the street below. The moment Tom's feet hit the sidewalk, he broke into a run. Shouts rang out from the open window behind them, but Tom only put his head down and raced faster, legs and arms pumping. People on the sidewalk scattered before them.

Eventually, the sounds of pursuit vanished. Tom stumbled to a halt in a narrow alleyway between tenements. Above them, sheets swung ponderously back and forth on washing lines, frozen solid from the cold. Despite the icy temperature, Cicero smelled the sweat on the nape of Tom's neck.

He hopped down, dropped the hex, and shifted back into human form. His arms went around Tom, and he found himself hugged close in return.

"I was so worried about you," Cicero said, at the same moment Tom said, "Christ, I was scared they'd hurt you."

Cicero laughed and hugged him tighter. "Are you all right? What happened?"

Tom rubbed at his lower back, wincing. "Sloane set a trap for me in the cellar. I don't know what happened, but he talked as though he knew we were up to something. He didn't seem entirely sure whether we were there on behalf of the MWP, at least."

"You're hurt?" Cicero's hands fluttered, uncertain what to do.

"Kearney hit me in the kidney while wearing his hexed gloves." Tom straightened, letting his hand fall. "Honestly, I was so scared for you, I didn't even feel it until now. I'll probably piss blood for the next couple of days, but Lord willing, that will be the worst of it."

"Thomas…"

"No permanent damage, cat, I swear. At any rate, they weren't counting on me being a hexbreaker."

"Thank heavens."

Tom rubbed Cicero's bare arms. "You must be freezing in that outfit. Put your fur back on."

The icy air bit through the gauzy trousers as though they weren't even there, and Cicero's toes were numb from the half-frozen slush of garbage carpeting the alley. He'd have to clean them thoroughly when he got back to the apartment. "Not just yet." He bent down and picked up the hex. "Look. Janowski was carrying a wallet full of these."

Tom took it and angled the paper to see it more clearly in the light filtering from the street. His face paled to the color of spoiled milk. "It's the hex," he said numbly. Then he blinked. "I mean, is it? The hex that caused Whistler and Barshtein to go mad?"

"I don't know, but Janowski was bringing them to Sloane." Cicero crossed his arms for warmth. "First thing tomorrow, you need to take them to the Coven." He paused as a fearful thought occurred. "Sloane doesn't know where you—we—live does he?"

"Nay. I lied when he asked—which didn't help matters when he started looking into my story," Tom added glumly.

Cicero snorted. "Oh yes, it would have been much better if he'd been able to ask your neighbors about you. If he'd known for sure you were a copper, he might not have bothered trying to interrogate you."

"Aye, true enough." Tom bit his lip. "The hex that trapped me took power to make. And there were hexes on the door to the room where I found you."

"A silencing hex." Cicero had started to shiver, so he leaned against Tom. Tom wrapped his coat around them both. "And something to hold the door closed, even without a lock."

"Fucker," Tom said savagely. "I ought to have ripped his prick off."

Cicero nuzzled closer. "I'm just glad you arrived when you did."

"I know Sloane is a familiar, and he gave the anarchists money, but doesn't that seem like a lot of powerful magic just tossed around?" Tom's voice was a rumble against the ear Cicero pressed to his chest.

"Yes." What it meant, Cicero didn't know, couldn't guess. "Another thing for you to mention at the Coven tomorrow."

It hurt unexpectedly, that he wouldn't be the one to go in. To take the hex to Dominic and see what he made of it.

Hell, even though he couldn't wait to curl up in bed beside Tom, a part of him felt a pang of regret that he wouldn't be going back to the barracks tonight with the other familiars.

"Come on," Tom said gently. "Get back in cat shape, and I'll carry you the rest of the way home, all right?"

"All right." But Cicero lingered for just another moment. "This hex…it doesn't look like anything else I've ever seen before."

"Nay," Tom said, his voice subdued. "It surely don't."

CHAPTER 20

TOM TRUDGED UP the steps to the apartment the next morning. He'd put on his uniform and gone to the MWP first thing, leaving the hex Cicero had taken from Janowski in Dominic's capable hands.

The hex. He'd been right from the start. There was a connection between the Cherry Street Riots and Barshtein's death after all, even if he couldn't quite yet see how they fit together.

Oh, this hex had been drawn on modern paper, not parchment like the ones hidden in the book. But Tom had recognized the form right off: the brutal, angular runes, linked together in savage figures. The rusty brown ink. The curling, twisted shapes that might have been stylized bears or wolves, fanged and slavering. It might not be identical to the old hexes, but it was damned close.

He'd woken from nightmares every time he drifted into sleep last night, certain he heard screaming. He could almost feel the shape of Danny's wrist in his grasp as they struggled. Hear Molly's voice, high with terror.

"Break it, Liam! Break the hex!"

How many had Janowski carried in his wallet? How many had he already given to Sloane? And what did they intend to do with them on New Year's Eve?

Did it have something to do with the explosives? But if Janowski was still delivering hexes to Sloane, it meant whatever they had planned hadn't been entirely disrupted by the loss of the bomb-making materials.

Saint Mary, they needed answers.

Should he have told Dominic? About the riots, about his past, about all of it?

But if he did, then what would happen to Cicero? If he had a charge to look after those as needed him, then surely Cicero was at the very top of that list, now that he'd walked away from the MWP.

As he drew closer to the apartment, Cicero's voice drifted down from above, through the open stairwell. "I'll be sure to mention your visit, darling, but I don't think it's a good idea if you come inside."

"Don't be like that. Tom and I are old friends," said another voice.

Phelps's voice.

Tom dashed up the last of the stairs, taking them two at a time. At the end of the hall, Cicero stood in the doorway to the apartment, arms folded over his chest. Phelps leaned against the frame, looming over Cicero in an obvious attempt to intimidate. From the expression on Cicero's face, it wasn't working.

Red tinged the corners of Tom's vision. "Get the hell away from him."

Phelps stepped back. Alarm flashed across his face, only to be replaced by a sly grin. "Why Tom. So good to see you."

He had to be careful. If he pushed Phelps too hard, Cicero would discover the truth, that Tom Halloran was nothing but a fraud. And if that happened...

He didn't know precisely what Cicero would do. He might not turn in Tom. He might just leave, go to some other friend. Noah, for example.

"If you want to talk," he said with effort, "then we'll do it. But not in my home."

Phelps's grin grew even more manic, and he glanced at Cicero. "No need. I just came by to let you know I saw someone else from the old days. I passed on your regards, of course."

A cold breath licked Tom's spine. Just what he needed—some other surviving member of Phelps's gang out for revenge.

Eight years. Eight damned years of stability, of building up a new life, and now it was all coming apart around him.

"Thanks," he forced himself to say. "I appreciate it."

"Then I'll be on my way." Phelps tipped his hat to Cicero. "It was nice to meet the missus."

"Fuck you," Cicero replied in a falsely cheerful voice.

Tom moved aside just far enough to let Phelps edge past, then followed him to the stairs to make sure he left. When he was certain

Phelps was gone, he came back to the apartment. Cicero waited in the doorway. "Who was that?"

"Fellow who used to run a gang," Tom said vaguely. They went into the apartment, and Tom shut and locked the door firmly behind them.

"And let me guess—you put him out of business?" Cicero asked.

Tom seized on the story. "Not just me, of course. This was years ago, back when I first started on the force. He served his time, and now he's out."

Cicero's brows drew down into a troubled frown. "Is he dangerous?"

"He ain't done anything yet," Tom said, which was the truth as far as it went. "But if you see him, steer clear." Time to change the subject, before Cicero asked too many more questions. "Rook wanted me to tell you the Coven is boring without you."

"Of course it is." But Cicero didn't smile.

Tom slipped his arms around Cicero's shoulders. The smaller man sighed and leaned into his chest. "I'm sorry," Tom said.

"None of it's your fault," Cicero murmured. "The Police Board can all burn in hell, though, as far as I'm concerned." After a moment, he pulled back a bit. "What did Dominic have to say?"

"That the hex ain't like anything he's ever seen."

Cicero's peridot eyes widened slightly. "I'm surprised, actually. Dominic's forgotten more about hexes than most witches learn in a lifetime. I was sure he'd recognize it, even though we didn't."

"He's going to look it over, along with some other fellow. Dr. Yates?"

"Owen. Yes. He's a hexman with witch potential."

Tom sat down and pulled Cicero onto his lap. "Dominic asked us to wait until they figure out what the hex is for."

Cicero arched a brow. "Even though the investigation is closed?"

"Aye." Tom shrugged. "He said what Ferguson don't know won't hurt the rest of us. I got to say, Rook doesn't really strike me as one for following the rules anyway, so I wasn't much surprised."

"Owen, on the other hand, can be a bit of a stickler." Cicero trailed off. "Well, that's Dominic's problem, not ours."

Tom nodded. "There's nothing for us to do now but wait."

A slow grin crossed Cicero's mouth, and he wriggled closer. "I wouldn't say there's *nothing* to do," he murmured, and reached for the buttons of Tom's uniform.

A sharp knock came on the apartment door the next morning. Tom opened it to find Dominic, Rook and a stranger all crowded into the hallway outside. A few snowflakes clung to their coats, and the smell of wet wool competed with cumin drifting from another apartment.

Dominic held up the hex Tom had given him yesterday. "Can we come in?"

"Of course." Tom hurriedly stepped out of the way. "There ain't much room, I'm afraid."

"And what the devil are you doing here, anyway?" Cicero asked, emerging from the bedroom where he'd been sleeping in cat form.

Rook pushed past Tom. "We've come to disturb your nap, of course." But he pulled Cicero into a hug. "Are you all right?"

Cicero shoved him away. "Well, I would be, if you weren't getting me all wet. At least take off your coat before you start touching people."

"We've come because none of us are supposed to be working on this case," Dominic said. "As far as anyone at the Coven knows, we're simply taking an early lunch. If we just happen to stop by a friend's apartment to discuss hexes, well, there's no injunction against that." He indicated the stranger. "Tom Halloran, this is the hexman I told you about yesterday."

"Dr. Owen Yates," said the other man, shaking Tom's hand. He was of average height, his hair so pale it bordered on white. Silvery eyes blinked up from behind gold-rimmed spectacles. His gaze drifted over the apartment, and a small moue of distaste touched his lips. "Forensic hexman."

"A title he gave himself," Cicero added with a roll of his eyes.

"And with good reason," Dominic said, shooting a quelling look at Cicero. "Owen isn't a witch himself, or at least, he doesn't have a familiar yet. But he's brilliant at developing new hexes."

"Oh. That's good, then," Tom said, feeling a bit out of his depth. "Have a seat, please. I've only got the two chairs, but I don't mind standing."

Owen took one of the chairs at the table, and Dominic the other. Rook flashed into crow form and perched on Dominic's shoulder. Cicero leaned against Tom, as if he belonged there. Dominic frowned, just a little, and glanced at Rook. Rook began to assiduously preen his tail, as if avoiding a silent question.

Yates adjusted his glasses. "What Dominic is trying to say, is that I've been working on new ways of uncovering crime by using hexes to analyze blood stains, more accurately detect poisons, that sort of thing."

Dominic nodded. "And one of his breakthrough ideas is the use of chained hexes."

Tom felt like an idiot, but he had to say, "I don't understand what that means."

"No reason you should, darling," Cicero replied. "Dominic is being obscure. Not intentionally, but he forgets the rest of us don't know the difference between a cosine and the Pythagorean Theorem."

Dominic shot Cicero a vexed look. "Which you could, if you only... oh, very well. Owen, would you care to explain chained hexes?"

Yates practically vibrated with eagerness. "Hexes can be added together to create larger effects," he said in a lecturing tone. "A way for witches to multiply individual power to make something greater than the whole. But what if you in essence took a single hex and split it into its component parts? Parts that were still metaphysically linked to have the full effect when combined?"

Tom's head spun. He'd never imagined he'd need to know this sort of thing, and wasn't entirely sure he could follow it now that he did. "I ain't certain I understand."

"Take one hex, and it does something," Dominic supplied. "Makes you feel good, or fearless, or the like. Take the second in the series...and you turn into a mindless killer."

Tom's heart sank into his shoes. "Like the absinthe hexes Whistler and Barshtein took."

"Exactly like," Yates replied. He held up a copy of one of the absinthe hexes. "What appears to be mere ornamentation is in fact what links them to a different hex. This one." He held up the hex Cicero had taken from Janowski.

"Oh," Tom said. "Hell. So people don't even know they've taken anything dangerous?"

Danny hadn't known, either. Or Da. But they'd at least *thought* they knew. No one had told them it was some harmless hex, like the sort handed out at Noah's party.

"Exactly," Dominic said unhappily.

Yates pushed his gold-rimmed spectacles higher on his nose. "It gets worse."

"Of course it does," Cicero muttered.

Yates shot him an annoyed look. "I don't recognize anything about the first hex in the sequence." He tapped the angular runes. "These look Norse, like something which might have been used in the age of the Vikings."

"'From the fury of the Northmen, oh Lord deliver us,'" Dominic quoted.

Saint Mary, Holy Familiar of Christ. Danny's madness, snapping at his face. Da's teeth, red with Ma's blood.

Yates went on, oblivious to Tom's inner turmoil. "Most of their hexwork has been lost. Burned by idiots who wanted the world to descend into a magicless darkness."

"Not now, Owen," Dominic said. "Focus."

"Yes—forgive me." Yates removed another hex from inside his coat. "Dominic, could you?"

Dominic put his hand on the hex. Tom sensed the slight vibration as the magic settled into place.

"Thank you." Yates held the hex directly above the Viking one. "Reveal," he said in a commanding tone.

A glow spread across the Viking hex. Soon every sharp line, every inked fang, blazed with an angry red light, which faded only slowly.

"That hex," Yates said, "is one of my own creations. It reveals the presence of human blood."

Silence fell over the room. "Then they were using blood for ink," Cicero said, his face going a sickly shade of green.

"Human blood, specifically," Yates said. "Whether witch, familiar, or normal, I haven't yet been able to determine."

"Highly illegal, whoever it belonged to." Dominic shook his head. "But I suppose when you're making hexes to drive people insane, legality is the least of your concerns."

"Cicero said blood ain't used for hexes, though." Tom's voice caught. He could see the hexes from eight years ago, their dark, rusty ink against the aged parchment. "And I ain't never heard of a case…"

"It's claimed that in more primitive times, our ancestors sacrificed people to make hexes," Yates said quietly. "The fear of such magic was used to justify conquest, the burning of thousands of books, and ultimately the Inquisition." He reached for the Viking hex, but didn't touch it. "Supposedly the Aztecs used blood in their magic as well. But all traces were wiped out, the traditions eradicated. Witches and familiars slain without mercy. If you gave a modern hexman a vial of blood, he wouldn't even know where to begin with it. What sort of hexes to use it in."

"So this is old magic," Tom murmured. But of course it was. Molly had said the book was from some medieval monastery. Had some monk gotten his hands on the hexes of attacking Vikings, and…what? Decided to keep them himself?

From the fury of the Northmen, oh Lord deliver us. Maybe he'd intended to fight fire with fire and just never had the chance.

"Very old," Yates confirmed. "And yet, here it is, drawn on inexpensive paper from a mill."

"Even if Sloane was keeping the hexes somewhere at the Rooster, he'd be a fool not to have moved them after we escaped," Cicero said.

Dominic nodded. "And where are they getting all the magic to power the hexes? Not from Sloane himself, or else he'd be flat on his back, not running a resort."

"Isaac." Cicero's skin paled to a sickly shade. "If they force bonded him to a witch and are stripping him of magic…Damn it! If they really do have something planned for New Year's Eve, we're out of time. That's tomorrow night."

"There's still the tunnels," Tom said. "If they have another location, where they're keeping Isaac and maybe the hexes, we might still be able to find it. But that means getting into the tunnels in the first place. Dominic, could you and Rook cause a disturbance of some kind? Distract everyone and pull the guard off the door?"

"That would have to be quite the disturbance," Yates remarked.

Dominic glanced at Rook. "I doubt that will be a problem," he said dryly. "Consider it done." He reached into his coat and took out a revolver and a small, silver disk. "Since you lost your gun at the warehouse, Tom, we thought you might need another."

Tom took it. "Thanks. Is that a hexlight?"

Yates seemed slightly scandalized that Tom didn't recognize it. He might work for the MWP, but Tom was willing to bet he came from old money. "Yes," Dominic said. "Rook insisted we bring it, although I'm not sure why…" He trailed off and seemed to take a second look at Cicero. "Never mind. I'll just leave it here. So, tonight?"

"Aye," Tom said, feeling as though he'd missed something yet again.

Tom saw them to the door. Rook peered back over Dominic's shoulder at him, until the door closed between them. "Saint Mary, I hope this works," he said, turning back to Cicero. "If we don't find anything tonight…I don't know. We'll just have to hope, I suppose."

"Yes." Cicero stood by the table, staring down at the hexlight. Then he straightened his shoulders. "I've been thinking, the last few days."

This sounded serious. "Oh?"

Cicero looked up at him, yellow-green eyes bright. "Yes. I've made up my mind. Thomas Halloran, would you consent to be my witch?"

CHAPTER 21

TOM GAPED AT him, replaying the words in his mind again. "I…are you sure? I mean, this ain't just because of leaving the MWP, is it?"

"Of course it isn't." Cicero padded across the room to him. "It's because of you." He took Tom's hands in his own. "Because in the time we've been together, I've come to realize there's no one else I'd rather bond with." He glanced up uncertainly. "What about you? Have you thought about it?"

If only Cicero knew how much. Mostly, Tom had told himself even considering a bond was insane. Terrifying. Even if he somehow bribed Phelps off, could he keep the truth hidden forever? Would Cicero notice he never got mail from his imaginary family back in Ireland?

Maybe Tom ought to kill them off. Manufacture some tale of disease. Pretend to be grief stricken.

"Aye," he said, curling his fingers around Cicero's. "I have. And I…I want this. Want you."

Cicero's smile was brilliant as the sun coming from behind a cloud. "I knew you couldn't resist," he purred.

"Of course not. Who could resist you?" Tom teased.

"No one with any sense." Cicero kissed him, his lips supple and hungry. He was still grinning when they broke apart.

"So, uh," Tom asked, "how do we go about it?"

"Don't sound so terrified, tesoro," Cicero said with a laugh. "You look like you think it involves hot needles and a flogger."

"Sorry." Tom shook his head. "This is all just new to me."

"I know. But you can trust me." Cicero's hands linked behind Tom's waist, pressing their hips together. "It's a two step process. Fortunately, we've already completed step one."

The devil? "We have?"

"How else do you think you were able to see out of my eyes that night at the Rooster?"

Tom drew in his breath sharply. "And you didn't tell me?"

"Tell you what?" Cicero cocked his head to the side. "It's only one step. And, yes, not one I'd taken before, but it doesn't mean a bond has to be made. I could have gone on and done it with another witch after."

"Hmph. We need to work on your ability to communicate, cat."

Cicero eased out of Tom's arms and went to the table. "The next step is simple. All you have to do is draw magic from me and put it in the hex." He held up the hexlight. "Like this uncharged hexlight Dominic so conveniently left for us."

Tom folded his arms over his chest. "So he knew? Or Rook did?"

"Rook thinks he knows everything," Cicero said with an annoyed grimace. "In this case, he happened to be right. I'm never going to hear the end of it, by the way."

"You poor thing." Tom let his arms fall and crossed the small space to Cicero's side. "So how do I draw magic from you?"

Cicero's full lips smirked. "It's like sex. Just do what comes naturally, darling." His green eyes sparked. "Which, hmm, not a bad idea."

"Sex?"

"Making this first time special." Cicero leaned against him, rubbing his thigh over Tom's. "By which, yes, I mean sex. And magic. And us."

"Well, I surely ain't going to say no to that," Tom said with a grin. He bent to kiss Cicero, sucking on his lower lip, then invading his mouth. Cicero groaned, pressing back against him, his prick hard against Tom's thigh. Tom wrapped his arms tight around the smaller man, lifting him onto the table. Cicero instantly twined his legs around Tom's hips, pressing their erections together through the cloth of their trousers.

"I think," Cicero mumbled between kisses, "that you have on entirely too many clothes."

Tom shucked off his coat, then shoved Cicero's from his shoulders. Cicero's hands worked the buttons of his vest and shirt, then ran across the skin beneath. His fingers tweaked one of Tom's nipples, drawing a gasp from him.

"Bed?" Tom asked.

Cicero picked up the hexlight. "God, yes, please."

They left a trail of clothing behind them. Cicero's skin felt fever-hot against his. Cicero put the hexlight on the nightstand, while Tom fell into the bed. Cicero crawled in on top, rubbing his thigh against Tom's prick, his cock leaving a slick trail against Tom's belly.

"What do you want?" Cicero murmured against his lips. The nipple rings pressed against Tom's chest, spots of unexpected hardness. "Shall I suck you? Let you fuck my arse, while we make magic together?"

Tom's prick ached at the thought. But he had something else in mind. "Would you fuck me?"

Cicero drew back, looking slightly surprised. "Do you want me to?"

"You said you wanted this to be special, and I've been thinking I'd like to try." Tom brushed his hand through Cicero's thick black hair, disarranging its perfection. "Unless you don't care to?"

"Oh, no, I do." Cicero shrugged gracefully. "I like it either way, really." He kissed Tom's lips, then sat back, straddling Tom's thighs. He slowly ran one hand up and down the length of his cock, the hood sliding back and forth seductively as he stroked himself. "This what you want, then?" he teased. "You want me to shove this up your arse and fuck you until you come?"

Tom's mouth went dry, and his prick twitched with excitement. "Aye."

Cicero moved to straddle Tom's chest instead. He dragged the tip across Tom's lips. Tom licked, tasted salt. "Suck it."

Tom opened his mouth obediently. Cicero made a soft, purring sound of pleasure and braced himself against the headboard, letting Tom decide how much to swallow. Tom bobbed his head, taking as much as he could without gagging. He grasped Cicero's buttocks with his hands, squeezing the firm globes, feeling the flex of muscle as Cicero rocked back and forth just a little.

"Mmm." Cicero pulled away. "All right, then. Let's get you nice and ready, shall we?"

Tom nodded mutely. Nervous excitement churned in his belly as Cicero retrieved the oil from the nightstand. Cicero paused before coating his fingers. "Hmm. Get on your hands and knees and put the hexlight on the pillow in front of you."

Tom did as he was told. "Good," Cicero murmured. A moment later, Tom felt something cool and slick drip along his crease. He let out an involuntary yelp.

"Sorry the oil's cold," Cicero said. "Don't worry—I'll warm it up."

Cicero seized Tom's cock in one hand, giving it a couple of slow strokes. Tom groaned in response.

A slick finger circled his arse, rubbing the crinkled flesh slowly. Tom closed his eyes at the sensation, then opened them again as Cicero's finger became more probing. More intrusive.

"How is that?" Cicero murmured.

"A bit strange, but—ah!"

Cicero's finger touched…something, he didn't even know what, but it sent an unexpected shock of pleasure ringing along his nerves. Cicero kept at it, pressing and massaging, and Holy Familiar of Christ, was this what he'd been missing all these years?

"I thought you'd like that." Cicero sounded a bit smug. Well, he had a right to. "Shall I add another finger and open you up a bit?"

"Please?"

It was uncomfortable for the first few moments, but that passed quickly enough. Cicero's other hand was back on his cock, stroking, while he found that elusive spot again. Tom groaned and lowered his head, half afraid he'd come before they'd even properly started. "I want your prick."

"Greedy boy," Cicero teased. His lips kissed the base of Tom's spine again. Then the bed rocked slightly as he shifted position. "I'll go slow, but tell me if it gets to be too much."

Tom nodded. Cicero had certainly seemed to like it when they did it the other way, and—

A gasp escaped him as Cicero pressed in. "Relax," Cicero murmured, which was easy for him to say. "Bear down, if you want—that can make it easier."

It did. Cicero slid in further—and then something relaxed involuntarily. "There we go," Cicero said. "Is this good?"

"Aye," Tom said. "More. Please. More."

Cicero's fingers tightened on his hips as he pushed in. "Fuck, Thomas," he panted. "You feel like heaven." He grunted as he started to thrust with shallow strokes.

Then his cock hit just right, and Tom bucked beneath him. "Oh hell, like that, aye, please."

Cicero laughed, a joyful sound, and did it again. Tom groaned and gasped, rocking back to meet Cicero now. Cicero bent over Tom's back, wrapping one arm around Tom's chest and grasping his prick with the other hand.

Tom became aware he was making a low, animal sound in his throat, but he didn't care. Cicero's cock opened him, invaded him, left him with nowhere to hide. Their bodies moved together like one thing, and Cicero's hand stroked him, a tight tunnel slick with oil.

"Now, Thomas," Cicero growled. "Feel me here with you. Reach for the magic."

And oh God, he could *feel* Cicero, so intensely. His prick inside, his arms around, and something else, something more, twined with Tom deeper than any fucking could reach. Something hot bloomed in his chest, right behind his heart—the vibration of magic, but in him now, not outside.

"Aye," he gasped. "I feel you, I feel—"

"Focus on the hex." Cicero's voice was harsh, strained, as if it took all his will to hold back from coming. "Touch it and feel."

Tom wrapped his fingers around the silver disk. A flat bit of crystal set into one side bit into his palm. On the other side, he could sense the lines of the engraved hex. They almost seemed to form a cage meant to hold something wild.

Cicero cried out sharply, thrusting hard as he climaxed. Tom's body acted as a conduit, magic flowing into the hex, until it was full and vibrating.

"Light!" Tom gasped.

The crystal blazed, blue white light spilling from between his clenched fingers. And Cicero's hand was on his prick, tugging, and it was too much, too much, and he shouted as he came.

Tom let his head drop. His arms felt weak, and he collapsed into the bed. Rolling over, he held up the hexlight.

"We did it," he whispered in wonder.

Cicero chuckled and plucked the glowing light from his hand. "That we did, my witch."

Tom grinned. "Your witch. I like that."

Cicero's eyes softened, and he leaned in to kiss Tom tenderly. "So do I."

Cicero tucked his gloved hands beneath his armpits in an attempt to keep them warm. He and Tom huddled in a doorway within sight of the Rooster's side door, trying to look as inconspicuous as possible. Scarves muffled the lower parts of their faces, and he'd borrowed an old hat from Tom, which hung ridiculously low over his forehead. Not that many people were about in the cold to notice them, but after dancing at the Rooster, he didn't want to take the chance that anyone would recognize him on the street.

Not that they'd likely been looking at his face when he danced. But still.

"Rook and Dominic have been in there half an hour," Tom said, voice muffled by his scarf. "What did they have planned?"

"You'll see."

Tom sighed, but it had an affectionate tone. Even though Cicero faced away from Tom, he sensed his witch's presence. He had the feeling that, if pressed, he'd be able to say exactly where Tom stood, in what attitude. Whether he was happy or sad. How fast his heart beat.

After making love, they'd slept the afternoon away in each other's arms. Eventually, Cicero had slipped out of bed, leaving Tom behind while he shifted into cat form. He made a circuit of the apartment, rubbing his head and sides against everything in reach, making sure it all smelled like him, too.

He glanced at Tom, and the sight of his lover's face made his heart swell with emotion. He'd been so lucky to have found a good man like Tom. If he hadn't walked into Ferguson's office that day…

Perhaps they would have met anyway. Maybe there were such things as fate and fairytale endings.

The sound of muffled cries drifted from the Rooster. Cicero returned his attention to the building, his nostrils flaring automatically as he sorted the wind for scent. Not that he could smell much in this form.

The sounds grew louder—the front door must be open now. People spilled across the intersection with the side street, and colored smoke appeared above the roofline, lit from below by the gas lamps.

"Fire!" Tom gasped. "Blast it—they were supposed to cause a distraction, not burn the place to the ground! And why the devil didn't Sloane keep the anti-fire hexes charged?"

"Don't worry." Cicero grabbed Tom's wrist before he could take off up the street to assist. "There aren't any flames, just colored smoke. It's a sort of firework. Mingzhu's relatives over off Elm make them."

"Mingzhu?"

"She's a carp familiar."

Tom's mouth opened, then closed. "You're joking."

"Not at all." Cicero returned his gaze to the side door, which remained shut. "It's a rare form, and valuable. She and her witch patrol the waterfront, search for bodies in the river, follow river pirates back to their lairs, that sort of thing. She's very beautiful, for a fish. Gold and white."

The side door swung open, and the guard whose nose Tom had broken ran out, bluish smoke trailing after him. In the distance, bells clanged—the fire company was on its way. "Now."

They raced up the street and darted into the side door. A haze of smoke hung in the air, and Tom started to cough. "Rook overdid it— what a surprise," Cicero muttered.

The hall was deserted as they made their way to the cellar door. "Let me go first," Tom cautioned. "In case there's another trap hex."

There wasn't. Sloane appeared to think they wouldn't dare come back. Or be foolish enough to do so, perhaps.

They hurried to the wall with the concealed entrance and hastily shoved boxes aside. The door was locked, of course, so Tom took out an unlocking hex. "Open," he murmured. The door swung open onto darkness. Cold air drifted out, bearing on it the smell of damp brick and slime.

Cicero took out their hexlight and passed it to Tom. He felt something, like a sharp tug behind his breastbone, as Tom drew on his magic to charge it again. "Light," Tom murmured, and the crystal began to glow. Raising it above his head, Tom stepped cautiously into the tunnel. With his other hand, he drew the revolver Dominic had given him. "Which way, do you think?"

Cicero slipped in beside him. To the left the tunnel sloped gently down toward the waterfront. To the right, it headed up. "Left?" he guessed. "The neighborhoods are always worse the nearer you get to the docks. Anarchists aren't generally well to do."

"Good point."

"I'll go ahead in cat form," Cicero said. "I can see better, and if there is anyone else down here at the moment, I'll spot their light long before they spot yours."

Tom didn't look happy. "Be careful."

"I will. Remember, I can call you for help now, any moment I need it."

"Still, be cautious."

"I always am, tesoro."

Cicero shifted and made his way down the tunnel. If he had to guess, it was an old drain, blocked or built over and long forgotten. The brick walls were narrow, and the floor formed a "v" shape, which would make footing treacherous for Tom. The scent of rats sent his whiskers to twitching. For now, he ignored them, even when he caught sight of a tail whisking out of sight into a crack between the bricks. He stalked bigger prey tonight.

An unevenness to the bricks and the scent of fresher mortar caught his attention. He sat on his haunches and studied the tunnel ahead, tail curled neatly around his feet. Tom caught up with him in a few moments.

"Huh," Tom said, inspecting the recent alterations. "An iron door. See how it's set into the ceiling, ready to drop? The lever will be a bit further on. Some of the more organized tunnel gangs use them in case of a raid. Gives everyone a chance to clear out while the police are trying to get through. Most of them ain't as sturdy as this, though."

He sounded worried. Cicero's tail twitched as they continued on, past the door. As Tom had guessed, there was a lever set into the wall another twenty feet or so down the tunnel.

The silence in the tunnels felt unnatural, somehow. They passed evidence that people had been down here: cigarette ends, a bit of newspaper that still stank of the fish it had wrapped, an empty bottle. Probably this was just a pass through between the Rooster, the warehouse, and wherever the anarchists holed up, as Tom had suggested.

Other scents drifted on the air, and Cicero slowed warily. A conglomeration of animals had been through here.

Familiars?

And beneath their living smell came something else. The whiff of blood.

Cicero eased forward, nearly on his belly. The tunnel came into a vault, where other drains joined to form a larger one. Water trickled down some of them, and the bricks were green and slick.

A dead body lay in the center of the room.

Cicero's back arched, and he let out an involuntarily hiss. Tom went pale in the ghostly light, and he approached the body cautiously. Cicero shifted back to human form and joined him.

There was little left of the man. He'd been all but torn to pieces, savage bites showing in his flesh, one arm ripped clean away. As if he'd been set upon by beasts. Only his face remained relatively unscathed.

Phelps.

"That's the man who came to the apartment," Cicero said, his voice shaking even as he spoke. "Why is he here?"

"I don't..." Tom shook his head, clearly bewildered. "What happened to him?"

Cicero took a step back, as if to put distance between himself and whatever had happened. "He was torn apart by animals. Familiars, they must be, because why else would they be down here?" Bile rose in his throat. "Dogs. Reptiles. Cats. I even thought I smelled a hawk."

Tom's blue eyes widened, and his skin turned the color of old cheese. "A hawk?"

"Yes."

Tom stared at Phelps for another moment. Then something seemed to fall into place. "It's a trap," he said. "Run. *Run!*"

CHAPTER 22

CICERO DIDN'T WASTE time arguing, only shifted into cat form and headed back the way they'd come. Tom charged after him, steps echoing loudly off the close walls of the vault. The revolver felt heavy in his hand, and the hexlight flung insane shadows on the rough brick. Behind him came the excited barking of dogs, the bay of a wolf.

The *ki-ki-ki* of a goshawk.

It couldn't be Molly. Molly was dead these last eight years. But she shifted into a goshawk, and had been a part of the gang, and Sloane's hexes were similar, if not the same, to the ones they'd stolen, and—

And what had Phelps said at the apartment? *"I saw someone else from the old days. I passed on your regards, of course."*

Tom had assumed Phelps meant another member of his old gang, but what if he'd referred to Molly? What if Phelps, in the course of threatening her, mentioned the name Tom Halloran? The name that just happened to match that of the bartender who'd been trying to get into the tunnels beneath the Rooster.

Phelps had been mauled to death and left here, his face untouched, for them to find.

There came a loud squeal of unoiled metal against metal. Ahead of them, the iron door began to ratchet down.

"Go!" Tom bellowed. "I'm right behind you!"

Cicero easily passed beneath the lowering door. But Tom was slower, his footing less certain on the sharply slanted floor. The door squealed closer and closer to the ground—

He flung himself onto his side and rolled, praying he wasn't crushed by the heavy iron. Instead, he caromed off of it, just a few inches too wide to fit. He caught a glimpse of Cicero's eyes, the only thing he could make out amidst the black fur and shadows.

Then the door slammed shut between them.

"Thomas!"

Tom scrambled to his feet. He could feel Cicero's fear hammering at the back of his brain, but it was all distraction at the moment. He braced himself, feet firmly on the floor, gun leveled and ready to fire.

Dogs loped up the tunnel in front of him, accompanied by a wolf. An adder clung to the wolf's throat like a necklace, its tongue flicking in and out toward Tom. Their eyes reflected the light he still clutched in his hand. He might be able to shoot one or two, but the rest would fall on him and tear him to pieces. He was going to die here, just as Phelps had died.

At least Cicero had escaped.

There came a footstep behind the familiars. One of them had taken human form to pull the lever, no doubt. Tom squinted into the darkness as the steps approached. The pack parted, and his light fell over features shockingly familiar, even after the passage of years.

Molly.

"Liam?" she asked, and her voice cracked, like ice above a river of sorrow. "Fur and feathers, Phelps wasn't lying. It is you."

Ropes bound Tom to a chair; it creaked whenever he moved, but seemed far too sturdy to be easily broken. Molly and the familiars had taken his gun from his unresisting hand, then herded him back down the tunnels. Eventually, they'd brought him to this damp basement. Marks on the floor showed where furniture had stood until recently, but only a few chairs and a small table remained. High above, a narrow window looked out onto ground level. Its glass had been broken out, and the distant sounds of the predawn city drifted in.

"We have to leave," said one of the familiars. His breath steamed in the bone-chilling cold of the basement. "There's no time for this, Molly. Kill him and be done with it."

"There's time," she replied heavily. "Go on, the rest of you. I'll be along soon enough."

Several of them gave her worried looks, but none objected, merely trooped away up the stairs. Whatever was going on, clearly Molly was in charge.

When they were gone, she slowly crossed the room to stand near Tom. She wore a plain dress, gone gray from a thousand washings, the sort of thing that a factory worker or rag picker would wear. The light of the single lantern revealed silver threads in her red hair and played along lines in her face that hadn't been there the last time they'd seen one another.

"You're alive," he said, lips numb. "Saint Mary, you're alive. I thought…"

"You thought you were the only survivor. So did I." She sat down in the chair opposite him. "You're a copper now, ain't you, Liam?"

There was no point in lying anymore. "Aye."

She shook her head, her expression one of disbelief. "Danny must be rolling in his grave. And your parents…it's a mercy they didn't live to see this."

"I didn't set out to be one!" he exclaimed, although why he felt he had to justify his life to her, he wasn't sure. Maybe because they'd been family, once. "If I'd known you were alive, I would never have done it," he went on, which was nothing but the truth. "I would have found you instead. What happened, Molly?"

She looked away, rubbing at her upper arms as if for warmth. "A familiar feels it, when her witch dies," she said, her voice cracking. "Did you know?"

"Nay." And it had been his hexbreaking that had killed Danny. "I'm sorry, Molly. I didn't think it would hurt him."

"Neither of us did. And it ain't like we had the time to consider. Not in the midst of fire and blood, and your da eating your ma's face."

His gorge rose, but he forced it down. "I killed him, too. Da. All of them as weren't shot by the other gangs or burned up by the fire. They called it a riot, after. No one knew what really happened. Except for us, I guess."

"I know." She glanced back at him. "I went to Chicago. I was a feral now, so I found other ferals, and we banded together. Lived as best we could. Lot of politics happening in that city, after the Haymarket affair. Hard times for a lot of people."

"But you came back to New York."

"A few months ago." Her expression eased slightly, to one more of triumph than sorrow. "Big things are taking place here, and I mean to be a part of them."

"The hexes?" he asked.

"Aye. I went to the old tunnels, searched in all the old stashes. Your da was smart—he put one aside, in a safe place. Thinking he'd sell it later, I'd wager, or else use the design to make more."

"Smart?" Tom wanted to laugh, but from bitterness rather than humor. "He used one of the damned things himself! How fucking smart was that?" He tugged at the ropes. "You know what these hexes do, Molly. You saw it with your own eyes. I had to put down Danny and Da and the rest like a bunch of mad dogs, and you're making more of them? Why would that seem like a good idea?"

She rose to her feet. "Don't you judge me, copper. You've spent years upholding everything that's wrong with society. Just a hired thug with a gun and a nightstick, jumping to do the bidding of rich bastards like Roosevelt who sit sipping champagne in their private clubs. And all the while ferals are enslaved and drained until they die, and no one gives a fucking damn!"

The lantern light glittered in her eyes, and her mouth was a savage red slash against her ivory skin. "Well not me. I ain't going to just stand around and do nothing. There are people who want to reshape the world, boyo. And we ain't going to let a little blood stop us."

His heart pounded. This sounded worse, far worse, than they'd ever guessed. "The anarchists?" he asked.

The wild fury drained from her face, and her mouth twisted contemptuously. "Those fools? Thinking they're going to bring down society with a few bombs, as if the police and the army wouldn't crush them like insects. They might be useful tools, but nothing more. But you...we could have used your help. If you hadn't turned traitor."

She reached into the pocket of her shabby coat and pulled out the gun they'd taken from him earlier. "I had to talk to you, one last time. Just to know for sure. But now we're done."

"Yes, we are," said Cicero from the stairs.

Tom flung all his weight to one side, bringing the chair crashing down—and hopefully making his head less of a target in the process. Heavy boots thudded from above, and a swarm of witches poured into the small basement.

Molly didn't waste time fighting a losing battle. She shifted into goshawk shape and took off. An owl and crow—Athene and Rook—cut through the air to intercept her, but she was far more agile than either of them. In a moment, she'd vanished out the broken window. The other two familiars went after her, but Tom's heart sank. Molly was fast as an arrow—they'd never catch her on the wing.

Cicero knelt by him. "Tom? Tom? Are you all right?" His fingers caressed Tom's face frantically.

"I'm fine," he said. "Just untie me."

"I'm so sorry I left you, but I didn't know what else to do," Cicero said as he set to work on the knots. All around them, the MWP detectives fanned out through the room. Several headed down into the tunnels, while the rest inspected what little there was to see in the basement. "I sent Rook to get reinforcements for a raid and used our bond to track you here."

Tom sat up, rubbing his wrists. Cicero flung himself into Tom's arms. "I was so afraid for you," he whispered against Tom's neck.

Tom closed his eyes. He embraced Cicero, pulling him close. Trying to memorize the feel of Cicero in his arms, the smell of his hair.

Because it was the last time he'd ever hold his lover. His familiar.

Ferguson stood in the midst of the room, tapping his foot impatiently. "Report, Halloran," he ordered.

Tom gently disengaged from Cicero and crossed the room to Ferguson. Taking a deep breath, he squared his shoulders and looked the chief in the eyes.

"My name is Liam O'Connell, and I have a confession to make concerning the Cherry Street Riots."

Tom sat in yet another chair, although this time it was handcuffs and not ropes binding his wrists in front of him. Much like the basement he'd been held in, the interrogation room was a small chamber beneath the Coven, with only a table and a few chairs.

He'd been photographed, and the old picture brought from the rogues gallery to compare. The MWP familiars who had photographed and escorted him were strangers, which was a blessing. He couldn't have stood it if the judging eyes belonged to Dominic or Rook.

The respite had only been temporary, of course. Once he'd been secured, the others had come into the room. Ferguson and Athene. Dominic and Rook. A secretary to take notes.

And Cicero.

He'd hoped—truly hoped—that they wouldn't let Cicero in, since he'd quit the MWP. As it was, Tom stared at his hands, unable to bear to look at his familiar. How could he stand to see the disappointment, the misery, the hurt, and know he was the cause?

"All right," Ferguson said. "You have a confession to make. Confess."

"My name is William O'Connell," he said heavily. "My parents were Michael and Sally O'Connell, of the O'Connell gang. My brother was a witch, Danny O'Connell. Molly—the goshawk—was his familiar."

There came the creak of a chair as Ferguson shifted. "Have you been working with her all along?"

"Nay!" Tom looked up in shock, glimpsed judging, angry faces, and hurriedly dropped his gaze again. "I didn't know she was even alive until tonight. I thought she'd died in the riots with all the others."

"Yes, what about the riots?" Ferguson asked. "I take it there's some connection?"

Tom nodded. "We were a tunnel gang," he said. "For the most part, anyway. We'd steal cargo from the docks, from other river pirates, from wherever we could. I'm a hexbreaker, so the official cargo seals and the like were easy enough to get through. We could open any crate. Then one day, another gang came around, looking to make an alliance in exchange for use of my power."

He talked until his throat was dry. Told them everything: about the Muskrats, and Da stealing the book when Liam sensed the hexes, and Molly figuring out what they were for.

"And your father decided to use them?" Ferguson asked.

It sounded so stupid now. "He thought he knew what they did. He didn't realize." Tom's eyes ached, and he wondered dimly what time it was, and how long it had been since he'd slept in his bed, Cicero curled beside him. "Da challenged the other gangs for control of the waterfront." Tom closed his eyes. "I argued with him, before the fight started."

"Not to use the hexes?"

"Don't be daft. He was my Da, wasn't he? I got mad because I was left out. Da said there weren't enough hexes to go around, so he and Danny and the others would take the ones we had. I was a better fighter than Danny, or so I thought." He laughed, but there was no humor to it. "When you're seventeen, you want to think you're the best at everything, don't you? I was so angry when Da said no." He cleared his throat against the sudden constriction. "I guess he saved my life."

Ferguson made a note. "These hexes didn't depend on taking a second one? Just the single hex?"

"Right." The cuffs around Tom's wrists chimed softly as he shifted his hands. He stilled quickly. "The new ones are different, somehow. They don't look quite the same."

"You knew." Dominic's voice, thick with anger. "The whole time when Owen and I were trying to unlock the secrets of the hexes, you *knew*, and you didn't say anything."

Tom's heart felt like a lump of slag in his chest. "Aye. It seemed like Owen and you had worked it out pretty well. I didn't think..."

"That's obvious."

"Detective Kopecky," Ferguson said. "Allow me to remind you that you weren't supposed to be working on this case at all. The riots, O'Connell."

It took Tom a moment to realize the last was directed at him. He'd been Tom Halloran so long, his proper name seemed like something foreign to his ears. "You can imagine what happened. Everyone who used the hex went insane. Their eyes turned bloody, and they just started attacking everyone around them: friend, enemy, it didn't matter. And not with knives and cudgels—with their nails, their teeth. Like mad dogs." He swallowed, but there was no moisture left in his throat. "Ma and some of the others who didn't fight were watching from the side. The hexed men turned on them, too. Da tore into her face with his teeth."

His voice cracked. The silence in the little room was utter. Not a shift of cloth or even a whisper of breath interrupted it.

"Old Mogs knocked over a lantern, chasing after his sister when she fled into the nearest building to escape him. It was a tenement, and the fire hexes hadn't been kept up. The whole thing was ablaze in minutes, the downstairs at least, so nobody could get out." He swallowed. "People were screaming. Innocent people, women and children, who didn't have nothing to do with our fight. They jumped and died on the street, or else burned to ashes inside. And while it was burning, Danny came after me."

He didn't dare shut his eyes, for fear of seeing his brother's face in the darkness behind them. "I held him off, but it was only a matter of time before he overwhelmed me. Molly started screaming at me to break the hex on him. So I did."

"And?" Ferguson prodded when Tom paused too long.

"He died." A tear slipped down Tom's face, but he didn't bother to wipe it away. No one else was going to cry for the dead of the O'Connell gang, were they? Just Molly and him. "It killed him. *I* killed him." He licked dry lips. "And then I did the same to Da, knowing it would mean his death. And to all the rest who were still alive, men I'd known my whole life."

The chair creaked beneath him as he shifted his weight. "When it was over, they were all dead. Danny, Da. Ma. I figured Molly was dead too, but I didn't have time to look for her body. I grabbed all the hexes I could find, and I ran before the coppers could arrive. And I burned the damn things first chance I got, because they weren't from Saint Mary like we thought. They were straight from the devil himself."

"I see." Ferguson shuffled some papers on the table in front of him. Tom's file, maybe? Or Liam's? "And Thomas Halloran?"

"I didn't kill him, I swear," Tom said. "I know you don't have any reason to believe me, but it's the truth. I'd had my fill of death. After the riots...I didn't have anything. Anyone. Nowhere to live, no job, and nothing but screams and blood in my head every time I closed my eyes. It was winter, and cold as Satan's heart. I was walking on Water Street, just trying to keep warm, when I found him. Not far from a saloon, so if I had to guess, the poor bastard got through Castle Garden and went straight to get a drink to celebrate making it to America. He'd passed out, and after a few hours in the cold with nothing to keep him warm but a threadbare coat...well, he wasn't waking up again. I dug into his pockets, hoping for a few coins. Not like he needed them anymore, right? I found a couple of dollars—and a letter."

"A letter of recommendation," Ferguson supplied. Tom's file, then. "To a precinct captain here, from an Irish constable in Dublin."

"Aye." Tom stared fixedly at his hands. "It was a job, wasn't it? I didn't figure it would last long, just until Halloran's family back in Ireland started wondering why they never heard from him, and wrote to the captain asking if he'd arrived. But that never happened. Maybe they were all dead, or maybe they'd had a falling out, I don't know. So I took a dead man's name, and spent the last eight years pretending I was him and trying to forget the past."

"Until Barshtein's death." Out of the corner of his eye, Tom saw Ferguson lean forward.

"Aye. It reminded me too much of what the hexes did to Danny and the rest. The bloody eyes. The biting and clawing. I didn't want to believe there was a connection, but I had to be sure."

"Why?" Rook asked.

"He was one of mine, wasn't he? Barshtein, I mean. I didn't know him well, but he was on my beat, and that made him my responsibility." Tom shrugged. "Da always said to look after those as needed you. Well, it was too late for Mr. Barshtein, but maybe not too late for everyone else." He closed his eyes, then opened them again. "Besides, if you'd been on Cherry Street that night, seen what I did, you wouldn't have to ask. I couldn't let that happen again. No one could."

"Except, apparently, the familiar Molly," Ferguson said. "What does she have planned?"

"I don't know."

Ferguson's voice rose and took on a hostile edge. "Sloane and Kearny have gone to ground, and there's no trace of Janowski, either. What are they up to, O'Connell?"

"I don't know."

"What are you holding back this time?"

"Nothing!"

"You lying son of a bitch!" Cicero shouted. Tom lifted his head, just in time to see Cicero's hand flying at his face.

The slap stung, and Tom jerked back. "Tell him, maledetto stronzo!" Cicero screamed. "Tell him, you fucking—"

"Stop!" Rook grabbed Cicero by the arms, pulling him away from Tom. Unable to hit him again, Cicero spat into Tom's face.

It was far more painful than the blow.

"Cicero," he managed as spittle trickled down his burning cheek. "I'm sorry. I never meant to hurt you."

Cicero's green eyes burned with rage—but tears dampened his lashes as well. "It was all a lie. Every word you spoke. Everything we had."

Tom felt as though his chest was nothing but a raw, gaping wound. "Nay. Please, don't think that. It was real."

"Get Cicero out of here," Ferguson ordered.

Rook started to steer Cicero to the door. Cicero wrenched free and shook himself off. Then, without so much as a glance back at Tom, he stalked out.

It felt as though all the air and light in the room—in the world—went with him.

"As for you, O'Connell," Ferguson said, "do you have anything else to say?"

Tom felt as though the last hour had hollowed him out and left nothing behind. "Nay. I'm done."

Ferguson rose to his feet and turned to one of the familiars who had escorted Tom earlier. "Take him to the Tombs."

CHAPTER 23

HOURS LATER, CICERO curled up on the pillows in Noah's apartment above Techne, his paws tucked beneath him and his heart full of misery.

He'd stumbled out of the Coven, ignoring Rook's urgent pleas to stay. What would have been the point? He wasn't an MWP familiar anymore. If he hadn't bonded, he could have returned, but a familiar bound to a criminal was of no use to them.

There was nowhere left for him to go. Not the familiar barracks, or the apartment where Tom had made love to him…

No. Where Liam had lied to him.

Perhaps there was one place that might still welcome him, though. Assuming Noah wasn't too angry about their argument on Christmas. If he was, Cicero didn't know what he'd do.

He'd staggered into Techne like a sleepwalker in a nightmare. And thank God, Noah had hurried to him. Taken him upstairs, told him to stay as long as he needed.

Once alone, Cicero took cat form, because it meant he couldn't cry. He'd been humiliated enough; no need to add tears to the mix. But wearing his fur reminded him of yesterday in Tom's apartment, when he'd rubbed his head on everything he could reach. Thinking it was the start of their life together…

But it had been nothing but a lie, from beginning to end.

Why had he ever let himself trust Tom? He should have clung to his first, horrified reaction and not given Tom the chance to worm his way into his heart. But he hadn't. And Tom had spun his lies, convinced Cicero he was a decent man. The way he'd smiled, his kindness, his touch. It had all been so good. *They* had been so good.

Except they hadn't, had they? Because Thomas Halloran was just a fiction. Cicero had never seen anything but a mask, worn by a criminal who had tricked him into bonding.

He'd fooled Cicero into feeling so safe. Safe, with a man who'd grown up in the violent tunnel gangs, who'd been responsible for who knew how many fights, how many beatings, how many robberies.

Safe, with a man who admitted to murdering his own father and brother.

God, was what he'd said true? Had he really seen his father tear off his mother's face? Felt his brother collapse in his arms?

No. No, Cicero could not feel bad for Tom. Liam. He couldn't feel bad for Liam, because the man was nothing if not manipulative. Look how he'd convinced the people of his neighborhood that he cared about them.

Although if he didn't, then why had he been so determined to solve the mystery of Barshtein's death, even when it jeopardized his deception?

He'd rot in the Tombs until Monday, when the judges came back. Served him right.

There wasn't any heat in the jail. Was he cold?

The door opened, and Noah stepped inside. "Cicero?" He shut the door behind him and crossed the room. "I closed the café early. Will you talk to me?"

Cicero shifted back into his human skin. He'd been so angry at Noah's assumptions, his possessiveness. But Noah had, in his own clumsy way, been trying to protect Cicero. And instead of listening to his friend, he'd gone off with Tom.

God, what a fool he'd been.

"Thank you for letting me in," Cicero said, because he didn't know how else to begin. How to start to unravel the hot ball of pain and rage and humiliation knotted in his chest.

"Of course." Noah sat beside him and put his hand to Cicero's shoulder. "Now, tell me what's wrong, so I can help you."

"No one can help me." To his horror, Cicero felt tears threatening to slip free. "I've made a terrible mistake, and now I'm stuck with it for the rest of my life, and I...and I..."

Once the first sob escaped him, he couldn't seem to stop. Noah enfolded him in a warm embrace, stroking Cicero's hair while he choked out the whole sorry story.

When he was done, Noah sighed. "I knew there was something off about him," he said. "I don't want to say I told you so, but..."

"I know; I know." Cicero sat back and wiped his eyes. His hand came away smeared with kohl. He must look a mess. "I should have listened that day, but when you said I was yours, it made me feel...I don't know." He sniffled. "It doesn't matter now."

"Exactly right." Noah caught Cicero's head and tilted it up, so Cicero had no choice but to look at him. "Don't worry. I forgive you."

Cicero let out a half laugh. "How generous of you."

But Noah's serious expression didn't change. "It is," he agreed. "I could be angry at you, bonding with Halloran—O'Connell—instead of me. But we can put it to rights. Very soon, this will all be the past, and we'll be together. I'll have a golden collar made for you. It will look so pretty on your fur."

The words sent a little chill through Cicero, and he drew back. "Not funny, Noah."

"Am I laughing?" Noah caught Cicero's wrist to keep him from pulling away any farther. "You've realized your mistake. Soon you'll be free of Halloran, and once I've taken care of other business, you'll bond with me."

"That isn't how it works." Cicero's pulse beat hard at the base of his throat, because Noah *knew* that. "The bond can't be broken—"

It hit him like a spear sliding between his ribs; a sharp, tearing pain out of nowhere. He screamed involuntarily, and the world turned briefly red. Saint Mary, it hurt—was he dying? Having a heart attack?

"Except by death," Noah finished. "Exactly."

The pain disappeared. The relief was so great it took Cicero a moment to realize something was horribly wrong. Where there had once been a warm spot deep within his chest, only hollow darkness remained.

His bond with Tom was gone.

Tom sat in a cell in the Tombs, his head bowed.

He'd never thought to make the walk into the jail as a prisoner himself. Passing over the Bridge of Sighs to the male prison within the complex. The damp air, made worse by the cold. The creaks as the building slowly subsided into the unstable earth on which it had been built.

The clang of the cell door swinging shut.

"Make sure you lock him in good," one of the familiars had advised the keeper. "He's a hexbreaker, so the only thing holding him is a sturdy lock."

"I know my business," the guard said gruffly. "You fancy lads down at the MWP might have hexes on every damn thing, but here we make do."

They'd left him, then, and he was alone. Or more alone than he had any right to expect. Maybe it was because he'd been a copper, but they'd put him in a cell of his own. He was on the second tier, where they held murderers and those suspected of serious crimes. What sort of charges did they mean to press? Accessory to murder, since he'd concealed what he knew about the hexes?

Or did they mean to have him down for murder thanks to his involvement in the riots?

He shivered, but they'd taken his coat, and only the thinnest of blankets covered the excuse for a mattress. Every breath turned into steam. Maybe he'd freeze here, just as poor Tom Halloran from Ireland had frozen. End up in an unmarked grave in potters field beside the man whose name he'd stolen.

How had he been so stupid? Why?

But he knew the answer, didn't he? He'd wanted Cicero. No, that wasn't right. He'd fallen in love with Cicero, and he'd been so stupid, so *selfish,* as to fool himself into believing it could work. That they could be together as lovers, as familiar and witch.

Tom shoved his hands roughly through his hair, tugging at it until pain prickled his scalp. Cicero hadn't deserved any of this. Hadn't deserved to have his trust betrayed by Tom in the most obscene way, so now he had to spend the rest of his life shackled to a witch rotting in prison. At least until a knife or a cough or something else carried Tom away, as it did so many who found themselves behind the gates of Sing Sing.

It wasn't fair.

Tom had done plenty in his life that he wasn't proud of. Stealing and fighting. Killing his own brother and father, even if it was meant as a mercy. But this was the worst thing he'd ever done by a long shot.

Could his hexbreaker talent be used to sever the magical bond with Cicero?

Tom stilled. It might work. But this was no simple hex. This was something deeper. Older. Primal. The sort of magic humans had used from the start, back when they were shivering around fires in caves, afraid of the predators in the dark.

Well, who was to say hexbreaking wasn't the same? It wasn't something he'd been taught; it had come natural since he was a boy. Just like no one had to teach a familiar to turn into a hawk, or a crow, or a cat. It was something you *were*, not something you learned.

It might not work, but then they'd be no worse off than if he hadn't tried at all. And if he did succeed...

Cicero could get on with his life. Put this behind him. Forget Tom had ever existed. Bond with that prick Noah, if it made him happy.

Tom took a deep breath and closed his eyes. He felt the bond with Cicero, like a spot of warmth tucked just behind his heart. Felt the magic, vibrating like a second pulse.

All he had to do was still it.

It *hurt,* like ripping something out by the roots and taking pieces of his own flesh with it. Distantly, he was aware of tumbling off the bed onto the filthy floor, of his own muffled scream, but all of it was secondary to the pain. But he kept on, pressed on, for Cicero's sake.

And then it was gone.

No more warmth. No more second pulse. Just a hole where something wonderful had been.

Tom curled up where he'd fallen, sobbing into his hands. At least the brick walls of his cell hid him from the other prisoners.

Footsteps rang on the iron gallery, coming to a halt in front of his cell. "Would you look at that? Pathetic."

Blinking, Tom raised his head. Karol Janowski stood outside the cell, alongside one of the unbonded familiars who'd escorted Tom here earlier.

Tom jerked upright. "Keeper!" he called. "Keeper!"

"Yell all you like," Janowski sneered. "They're not coming. They're having a nice can of hot coffee someplace warm, and counting their money while they're at it."

The familiar pulled out an unlocking hex and put it to the door. "Thought we'd come and pay you a little visit," Janowski said. He drew a knife, and Tom saw his hand was bandaged where Cicero had bitten and clawed him. "I have other things to do later, but I owe you for that crack upside the head you gave me."

Tom came to his feet. A quick look around the cell showed nothing he might use as a weapon.

"You're an MWP familiar," Tom said to the other man. A big,

hulking fellow in his human form, but that meant little when it came to his animal shape. "This man here is an anarchist. He was behind the explosives in the warehouse that…exploded."

The familiar snorted derisively. "Tell me something I don't know."

Molly and her gang of familiars. Had they infiltrated the MWP? Christ, he and Cicero had been lucky not to have been caught earlier.

The door swung open, and Janowski and the familiar stepped inside.

Tom whisked the mattress from the bed and shoved it at Janowski, who was in the lead. Janowski swore and batted it away from his face with his knife hand. The blade sliced the ticking, sending straw into his eyes.

Not daring to hesitate, Tom lunged forward and seized Janowski's wrist, digging his fingers hard into the bone in an attempt to force Janowski to drop the knife. If it had just been the two of them, it might have worked, but the familiar had a knife of his own. Pain blazed across Tom's side, forcing him to release Janowski and skip back.

The shouts of the other prisoners seemed oddly distant. The world tightened, became no larger than the cell and the men trying to kill him. A metallic taste filled his mouth.

Tom reached for the blanket on the floor just as Janowski rushed forward. He yanked hard, pulling it from beneath Janowski's feet and sending him crashing into the iron bed. Tom wrapped the blanket around his arm like a shield, flinging it up as the familiar reached him. The impact of the knife jarred his arm, but it sliced only through the outermost layer of cloth. Tom lashed out with one foot, catching the familiar in the knee so he toppled onto the floor.

Then Janowski was on him again, slamming Tom into the wall. Where his knife had gone, Tom didn't know—maybe he'd dropped it when he fell—but he seemed determined to kill Tom with his bare hands. He locked an arm around Tom's throat, strangling him. Tom tried to throw him off, even as black spots appeared in his vision. Saint Mary, he couldn't die like this.

There came the crash of a revolver, painfully loud in the tiny cell. The pressure suddenly vanished from around Tom's neck as Janowski shoved him away. A second shot, and Janowski staggered into the wall beside Tom, blood leaking from the neat hole in his forehead.

Shocked, Tom turned to the cell door, expecting to see one of the keepers. Instead, he found himself looking into Bill Quigley's startled face.

The familiar shifted into a silver tabby. Before Bill could draw a bead on it, it shot past him and down the gallery.

"Damn it—he'll warn Molly," Tom said, rubbing his bruised throat.

Bill entered the cell and grabbed his arm. "What the hell is going on here?"

"They bribed the keepers—came to kill me." Tom let his hand fall. "What are you doing here?"

Bill holstered his revolver. "I came to see you. The report came over from the MWP, claiming Saint Tom had been a tunnel rat all this time. I had to hear for myself if it was true."

One more friendship, sacrificed to his lies. "Aye. I was part of the O'Connell gang, back in the day. Born to it."

Bill frowned slightly, his mustache seeming to droop even more than usual. "But you haven't lived that life for a while now, have you?"

"Not since I joined the force." Tom shrugged. "Don't know as that matters much to anyone."

"Well, it matters to me," Bill said decisively. He clapped Tom on the back. "You're a good man, Tom Halloran, or whatever it is you want to be called. I'll stand by you in front of any judge in the land."

Tom gaped at him for a moment—then shook his hand. "Thanks, Bill. That means...you've no idea."

"Ah, well, don't go all maudlin on me," Bill said. "Now tell me why you've got two fellows as want you dead."

"Hell if I know," Tom said honestly. He crouched by Janowski and began to go through his pockets. "That is, I can see why they'd wish me dead, but not why they'd bother taking the risk to actually put me in the ground. This fellow is an anarchist, mixed up in the plot Cic—the familiar and I were investigating."

"The bit about the exploding warehouse?" Bill grinned. "Aye, I heard about it from some of the fellows from the precinct. That must have been quite the show."

"Aye, it was at that. But the other man was an MWP familiar." Tom launched into a quick—and probably somewhat confused—account of everything that had happened after the warehouse. When he was done, Bill shook his head.

"That's a story and a half. So did these fellows mean to kill you out of revenge, or because they thought you might still be able to disrupt any plans they might have, or for some other reason?"

"I've no idea." Tom closed his eyes for a moment, trying to think. "There's something I'm missing. All right. They came after me, either to keep me quiet or for something related to the case. And if they came after me..." His eyes snapped open, and his heart turned to ice. "They'll go after Cicero as well."

CHAPTER 24

CICERO JERKED MADLY against Noah's grip. "Let me go! You have to let me go!"

Noah let out a growl of frustration and yanked Cicero to him. "Stop that!"

"You don't understand." There was a huge black pit opening beneath Cicero's feet, and he had nothing to hold onto to keep from falling in. "Tom's been hurt. He's in trouble."

Tom was more than in trouble.

"No," he said aloud. "It's not true, it can't be, he's not dead. He's not."

Noah let go of his wrist and gently stroked back a lock of Cicero's hair. "I told you I'd take care of it. You're free now."

No. It wasn't possible. Cicero rose to his feet and backed away. Noah stayed on the pillows, watching him.

"What have you done?" Cicero whispered.

"I heard you bonded with Tom Halloran. Or Liam O'Connell, or whatever his name is."

Dawning horror threatened to steal Cicero's breath. "How do you know about that? There's no way you could, unless…"

Unless Noah had been a part of it all along.

Because of course Noah had known Isaac, and Gerald, and even Sloane. He'd been the one to introduce Isaac to Gerald and suggest he find a job at the Rooster. And all this time, Cicero had known that, but

Noah was his *friend*, so of course he couldn't possibly be involved.

"Barshtein wanted to be a bohemian," Cicero said, through lips that felt numb. "Did he come to Techne?"

"Barshtein?" Noah asked incredulously. "What on earth do you care about *him?* Barshtein was a fool who awoke one morning to find his youth gone and his life banal. He thought he could find what he was lacking on slumming tours, or by visiting cafés." Noah's nostrils flared in distaste. "But he had no artistry of his own. No spark."

"So you...what? Tested the Viking hex on him, to make sure it worked?"

Noah sighed. "Really, darling, you're being insufferable. Barshtein was nothing. Halloran was nothing. We have much greater things to concern ourselves with, you and I."

Something was building in Cicero's chest; a scream like a breaking storm that would shatter everything in its path. "You murdered Tom," he grated out between clenched teeth.

"Well, not personally," Noah said with a shrug. "But if you'd just let me explain—"

The dam broke. Cicero didn't recognize the sound coming out of him—a howl or a roar, a sound of animal rage, everything going red. He flung himself on Noah, and this must be how the victims of the Viking hex felt, because all he longed to do was tear Noah apart with claws and teeth.

Noah cried out in shock. He let go of one wrist, and Cicero took the opportunity to gouge at his eyes. Noah jerked to the side, and Cicero's nails raked his skin instead.

They wrestled madly, sending a table over and scattering the pillows everywhere. Noah ended up on top; he struck Cicero a blow to the side of the head that left his ears ringing. Cicero blinked, dazed, while Noah scrambled to a cabinet, ripped open a drawer, and sent hexes scattering.

"Ungrateful creature," Noah snarled, snatching up one of the hexes.

Cicero gathered his legs beneath him and lunged for the door. What the hex did, he didn't know, but finding out might end with him as dead as Tom.

Noah tackled him before he could reach the door. His body slammed against the floor, chin clipping the wood hard enough to send stars sparkling across his vision. Then he felt the press of the hex's paper against his head.

"Sleep!" Noah commanded.

Weariness washed over Cicero. He fought to stay awake, but the hex was too powerful, and he slumped into darkness.

Tom led the way into the Coven, Bill on his heels.

It had taken some doing to convince Bill that Cicero was in danger. After giving the keepers a good dressing down for letting Janowski in, Bill had demanded use of the jail's phone. A quick call to the Coven had revealed the officer on duty hadn't seen Cicero.

Which meant nothing, given Cicero wasn't officially with the MWP anymore. But surely he would have turned to his friends there for comfort, after Tom's betrayal.

Bill hadn't been entirely happy with the situation, but their friendship counted for something with him. "You've still got a copper's instincts," Bill said as they headed out over the Bridge of Sighs. "And I'm surely not leaving you here so they can try to kill you again. Just don't think about running. I won't gun you down, but you'll feel my nightstick."

Cicero would have made a filthy joke out of Bill's comment. The thought sent another wave of fear through Tom.

They took the 3rd Avenue El from the Tombs to the Coven. The weather was utterly miserable: cold rain mixed in with snow. It seemed to make no dent in the crowds gathering for the New Year's Eve celebration, though. At least Tom and Bill were going away from city hall and not toward it.

The witch on duty looked understandably surprised to see Tom come through the doors. "He's in my custody for the moment," Bill said, ignoring the fact no one higher up had authorized such a transfer. "There's trouble." They hurried past, before the fellow could gather his wits enough to ask any questions.

Cicero's former office seemed the first place to check. The door stood open. A queasy feeling lurked in the back of Tom's throat as they approached. Cicero would be inside—and he'd be horrified to see Tom again. He'd yell recriminations, deserved ones. Demand why Bill couldn't have come alone to make sure he was all right.

Tom would face it. Whatever rage, whatever abuse, Cicero chose to heap on him, he'd take. It would be worth it, knowing he was safe.

Cicero's chair was empty. The wolverine familiar, Greta, sat at her desk. When she saw Tom, her eyes widened—then her lips drew back from her teeth.

"What are you doing here?" A growl trembled in the words, as though she might shift at any second and simply attack.

"Bill Quigley, at your service, ma'am," Bill said, touching the brim of his helmet. "Sorry to bother you, but an attempt was made on Tom's—O'Connell's, that is—life, and we're worried about the safety of the cat familiar Cicero. Is he around?"

Greta's snarl faded. "Not that I know of. He's not one of ours any more."

"I'd hoped he came back?" Tom ventured.

Greta looked at him as though he was an idiot. "And what use does the Metropolitan Witch Police have for a familiar bonded to a criminal?" she asked. "You're the only one who can use his magic. He's just an ordinary man now, so far as the higher ups are concerned."

The full weight of just how bad a mistake he'd made crashed down onto Tom's shoulders. "I ain't, though," he said desperately. "I severed the bond."

Greta scowled. "What?"

"Is there anywhere else Cicero might have gone?" Bill interrupted. "He had other friends here, didn't he?"

"Rook is down in Owen's lab," Greta said slowly. "Owen and Dominic are taking another look at that hex, now that they know more about it." Another pointed glare. "Maybe Cicero went with them."

Tom winced. "Can we find out for certain?"

She slid out of her chair. The top of her head barely reached his chest. "I'll escort you gentlemen. But if Cicero so much as looks at you sideways, you'll be leaving with a lot less flesh attached, O'Connell."

"Fair enough."

They followed her through the tangle of hallways until they reached the lab. Cicero wasn't there, and unsurprisingly, Dominic and Rook were less than happy to see Tom again. Bill explained why they'd come, but Dominic's expression only grew darker and darker as he spoke.

"A familiar attacked you?" he asked.

"Aye. One of those as escorted me. I didn't get his name, but he turned into a gray tabby cat."

"Anselm," Rook said, exchanging a glance with Dominic. "This is bad. If they've agents in the MWP…"

"We have to find Cicero," Tom put in. "If they were after me, they'll be after him."

"Don't play the fool, O'Connell," Dominic snapped. "Your patrolman friend might not know the ways of witches, but Cicero is your familiar. You know exactly where he is."

Bill gave him a sharp look. "Tom…"

"Nay." Tom held up his hands. "It's as I told Greta. Cicero was my familiar. He…he ain't any more."

Mary Magdalene, Holy Familiar of Christ, it hurt to say those words. More than he'd ever imagined.

Rook's brows snapped together in alarm. "What the devil do you mean?"

"I broke the bond." Tom had tried so hard to ignore the hollow ache behind his heart, the cold, lifeless place which had once held the most wonderful thing ever to happen to him. His throat tightened, but he wasn't going to cry in front of the others.

Owen Yates looked up from the hex, which he had been examining with a jeweler's loupe. "Broke the bond?" he repeated. "That isn't possible."

"I'm a hexbreaker." Tom swallowed. "And I never should have lied. Should've gone to prison all those years ago and rotted there. Cicero never deserved getting caught up in all this, so I…set him free."

"Admirable," Dominic said, a bit grudgingly.

Rook's scowl only grew deeper, though. "Cicero would have felt it," he said. "And he'd surely think you'd died."

"He knows I'm a hexbreaker—"

"And we're taught the only way to sever the bond is death." Rook glanced at Greta. "You know Cicero—he wouldn't just calmly say, 'oh well, time to get on with it.' He would have come flying back here looking for help."

"Not really the taciturn sort, our Cicero," Greta agreed. "So why didn't he?"

The possibilities were terrifying. "Greta said he wouldn't be welcome here, since he was bonded to me. Where else might he have gone?"

"Techne," Rook said immediately.

Noah. But hell, if Noah had taken care of Cicero, given him a place to stay, Tom would be grateful.

"That still doesn't explain why we haven't heard from him, if he thought Tom died," Dominic pointed out.

"Can we go to Techne?" Tom asked desperately. "Just to check. That's all."

Dominic hesitated, then nodded. "All right."

"I'm coming with you," Greta said. "Damn cat was a terrible one to share an office with, but I'm worried about him anyway."

"Owen, I'd be grateful if you come as well," Dominic said. "I don't like any of this, and we may yet need your expertise."

"What about this Anselm fellow?" Bill asked. "Don't you need to warn your captain, or chief, or something?"

"We will," Dominic replied firmly. "But if there are more traitors in the ranks…damn. Maybe it's a good thing the Police Board kept the MWP back from the celebrations tonight."

"What do you mean?" Tom asked.

"Most of the MWP is out guarding the Battery, which will be firing off rounds at midnight to bring in the New Year," Greta replied. "But most of the celebrations will take place around city hall. The honor of guarding the mayor and delegates, and controlling the crowds, went to the regular police."

"Damned politics," Dominic muttered. "Come along."

They stopped at the desk of the officer on duty just long enough for Dominic to bark orders for a winged familiar to be sent to Ferguson to apprise him of the situation. Although Techne wasn't far, it seemed forever to Tom before they reached the café's doors.

Only to find them locked.

Dominic rapped loudly. When no answer came, he glanced at Rook.

In an instant, Rook was on the wing, flapping up to the apartment above. He landed on a ledge, cocked an eye to peer through a window—then soared back down to them.

"We need inside," he said, the moment his feet touched the ground. "I didn't see anyone, but it looked like there was a struggle."

Terror laid a hand on Tom's throat, while Dominic wrestled out an unlocking hex and opened the doors. How had he managed to make such a complete mess of things? Even when he'd tried to do right by Cicero by breaking the bond, it had proved a mistake.

Just let Cicero be all right. That was all he asked.

He was the first up the stairs once the door was open. As Rook had said, there had clearly been a struggle in the main room of Noah's apartment. Pillows scattered, a table overturned, a hex discarded near the door…

"Sleeping hex," Dominic said grimly as he examined it. "And a powerful one."

Rook's brown skin had paled to a grayish hue. "Surely Noah wasn't at fault. We…are we even sure Cicero was here?"

Greta took on her wolverine shape, then shifted back to human. "His scent is everywhere. Fresh. I don't know this Noah, but other than our group, there's only traces of one human man."

Tom sank down onto the piano bench, his head in his hands. Something terrible had clearly happened to Cicero. Molly and her familiars were planning God-only-knew what tonight. And the Police Board had made certain the MWP, those most capable of stopping Molly and Sloane, were as far as possible from the political targets at the heart of the consolidation celebration.

Tom couldn't shake the idea they were still missing some critical piece of information. Everything swirled together in his head: Sloane and Molly, Barshtein and Whistler, Viking hexes and bohemians drinking absinthe. New Year's Eve circled in red, and Isaac's broken necklace beneath the cabinet. Anarchists making hexes, and a businessman familiar paying for them.

And Cicero in the middle of it all, searching for Isaac, looking for justice for Whistler.

The Viking hexes had taken Tom's family from him. Was he to lose Cicero to them now?

"We could look in the tunnels again?" Rook suggested, sounding desperate for any idea, no matter how far-fetched. "Maybe they're holding Cicero there?"

Tunnels.

"I mentioned the anarchists to Molly." Tom lowered his hands. "And she sneered. As though she felt nothing for them but contempt."

"You think they were being used?" Dominic asked.

"Aye. Molly wouldn't share all her secrets, not if she looked down on them. If she and those working with her had a secret hideaway, it wasn't the tunnels beneath the Rooster." He took a deep breath, knowing that if he was wrong, they might never find Cicero. "I knew her, once. She'd go back to where it all began. The old tunnels beneath Cherry and Water Streets."

"Where the Cherry Street Riots happened?" asked Bill.

"If you're wrong…" Dominic said.

"It's the best I've got." Tom spread his hands. "I know where all the entrances are. If Cicero is there, we'll find him."

Dominic stared back at him for a long moment. Then he nodded. "All right. Let's go."

CHAPTER 25

CICERO'S EARS TWITCHED. He became aware that he was in cat form, lying on something hard and cold. His head ached, and drowsiness tugged at him. He could just slip back into sleep...

But a familiar smell intruded onto his awareness. A scent he would have known anywhere.

Isaac.

Cicero's eyes snapped open, and he leapt to his feet. Or tried to; the affects of the sleeping hex hadn't entirely left him, and he stumbled groggily into iron bars.

He was in a cage.

Isaac was in the same cage, although it was almost too small for them both. He lay unmoving, except for the heave of his flanks as he breathed. His once beautiful tan coat was matted and filthy, the skin of his paws split and cracked. Ribs protruded against his skin.

A witch had stripped him, spending his magic with no time to recover. Much more, and Isaac would die.

"You're awake," said Noah.

Cicero arched his back, tail bristling and ears flat against his head. Noah stood near the cage, an amused look on his face. Hexlights burned bright, illuminating what seemed to be a chamber where several tunnels came together, much like the one he and Tom had found not far from the Rooster.

Tom.

Noah had killed him. Or, rather, had him killed.

A wave of grief so intense it left him unable to breathe rolled over Cicero. But he had to focus beyond the pain. He'd failed to save Tom, but Isaac was still alive, even if only barely. There had to be some way to escape and save Isaac.

Please, God, at least give him that.

Unlike the tunnel juncture beneath the Rooster, this one was furnished, as though people lived here. There were several tables, a comfortable-looking chair, even a cabinet whose open door revealed shining bottles of liquor and wine. The air smelled faintly of absinthe, cigarettes, and animals. A familiar in wolf form sprawled on a rug, a viper curled up on top of him.

The murmur of voices came from one of the tunnels, accompanied by footsteps. Molly walked in, followed by Sloane and Kearney. "It's time to go, Noah," she said.

"In a bit," he replied, not looking away from Cicero. "Right now, I'm having a moment with my future familiar."

"Why bother?" Sloane asked. "He'll end up like the Yid, eventually. No point in getting too attached."

Nausea choked Cicero. Noah had force-bonded and then stripped Isaac. Why? To make the Viking hexes, the absinthe hexes? But he'd offered to bond with Cicero before Christmas, hadn't he?

What had he said, that day in the back room of Techne? *There are some other things I need to attend to first. I'd want to do something to mark the occasion, after all. Just say yes, and I'll start planning right away."*

He'd never intended for Isaac to survive past tonight.

"You're wrong, Sloane." Noah stepped closer. Cicero growled, but Noah ignored the defiance. "Isaac wasn't much of an artist. And his form…I've never been terribly fond of dogs. Cicero, though…we'll be together for a very long time, I think."

Cicero wished he could change form and scream defiance. But the cage was far too small.

A gray tabby emerged from one of the other tunnels, panting from his run. Cicero's ears perked up. Anselm? Was the MWP coming after all?

Molly crouched down in greeting. "What happened? Is something wrong?"

Oh God. Anselm was one of theirs.

Anselm shifted to human form. He grabbed Molly's arm and murmured to her in a voice so low even Cicero's cat ears couldn't pick out the words. She listened intently, the look on her face becoming more and more grim.

"What is it?" Noah asked.

"Nothing that concerns you, witch," Molly said. She made the designation sound almost like an insult. "You go on ahead. I need to talk to Sloane for a minute."

Noah didn't seem happy, but he nodded. Apparently, as much as he wished otherwise, he wasn't the one in charge. "Hurry. We don't want to be late for the party."

Once he disappeared up one of the tunnels, Molly conferred with Sloane, her voice only a faint murmur. Anselm glanced at Cicero and Isaac, gave an almost guilty wince, and shifted back into cat form. Within moments, he'd vanished back the way he'd come.

Molly and Sloane seemed to reach some agreement, because she departed. Cicero half expected Sloane to come over and torment him, but the other familiar ignored the cage. Instead he settled into a chair not far from the sleeping wolf and began to read a newspaper. Kearney got into the liquor cabinet and poured a whiskey.

"One for me," Sloane ordered without looking up. "And don't drink too much."

Once he felt certain they had no interest in him, Cicero turned his attention to Isaac. He nudged Isaac's enormous muzzle with his head, but there was no response. Clambering onto Isaac's shoulder, he began to wash the mastiff's eyelids, but that got no reaction either.

With nothing else to do, Cicero curled up on top of his friend and tucked his tail over his nose. Isaac might be saved, if Noah took no more magic from him for the next few weeks. But it seemed likely Noah would finish him off this very night.

And Noah wanted Isaac to die, didn't he? So he would be free to bond with Cicero.

Noah wasn't stupid. He had to know Cicero wouldn't submit willingly now. But then, Isaac surely hadn't either. Noah would do whatever it took to break Cicero, force him the way he'd forced Isaac.

Cicero would die first. It was an empty vow—easy to make and hard to keep—but it was all he could do right now. He'd die before he'd bond with the murderous bastard who'd tortured Isaac and killed Tom.

Tom.

Had it hurt? Had it at least been quick?

Cicero huddled even tighter into himself. Why hadn't he gone to the Tombs and talked to Tom? Listened his side of the story?

Why hadn't he paid attention to what he'd already heard?

He'd been so angry. Hurt and betrayed, all the way to the bone. But he *knew* Tom, or the man he'd become.

Liam O'Connell had been born into the gang. He hadn't chosen the life, just tried to do right by his family. He'd lived through a horror that would have broken most men. And when he'd had the chance to make his own decision, what had he done?

No one had forced him to become a copper, even if the opportunity had been all but handed to him. And even if that decision was made in desperation, no one had forced him to spend the next eight years trying his best. Cicero had seen how the people in Tom's neighborhood treated him as a welcome sight, not a reason to run and hide. He'd seen Tom's file, the medals for saving two men from drowning, all of it.

If Tom had been nothing but a manipulative liar, the smart thing to do would have been to thwart any investigation into Barshtein's death, not dig deeper. What had Tom said when Rook had asked him that very question, why he'd risked everything when he didn't have to?

He'd said anyone would have done it. But they wouldn't have. Tom had, because he was kind. Decent.

And yes, Tom had lied, and yes, Cicero had every right to be furious and hurt. But the way he'd lashed out, spitting in Tom's face, screaming at him...

Tom had died thinking Cicero hated him.

There came the sound of wings, cutting through the air. "Hey! Who're you?" Sloane shouted.

Startled, Cicero looked up. Rook circled the room, diving at Sloane's face, then Kearney's. The sound of running steps came from one of the tunnels, and Dominic entered the room. Greta raced past him in wolverine form, her teeth bared and ready to rend.

And behind them, his jaw set and his eyes like steel, came Tom.

The sight of Cicero confined to a cage sent a bolt of raw fury boiling through Tom.

The trip through the tunnels had bordered on surreal. He'd found one of the old entrances with ease, and once he'd stepped into the first tunnel, it had almost been as though he'd never left.

At any moment, he half expected to hear Da laughing, or Ma singing a hymn while she worked. This tunnel was the one they'd fled through after they'd snatched a crate of guns from a government ship, and that drain led to the tenement where they'd lived until he was ten. Every step seemed to take him further from the present, from Tom Halloran, and deeper into the past.

Until he stepped into the vault where the O'Connell gang had once met and plotted, and saw Cicero crammed into a cage with an unconscious dog. The only dream of the future Tom had ever allowed himself, imprisoned amidst the remnants of his own bygone life.

Then the only thing that mattered anymore was what came next.

"MWP! Surrender!" Dominic shouted.

"Police! Hands up!" Bill yelled, brandishing his gun.

Sloane leapt from his chair, sending it flying back. Then, in a swirl of gray smoke, his human form vanished, replaced by that of an enormous crocodile.

Bill's eyes went wide at the sight. He fired, but the bullet missed.

Kearney leapt over Sloane and drove his fist into Bill's stomach. The hexes carved into the leather flared, and Bill went down hard.

There came a wild snarl—Greta and the wolf closed with each other, biting and tearing ferociously. Dominic crouched by the cage, sketching a hex, while Rook taunted the snake, grabbing its tail, fluttering just out of reach, then swooping back to do the same again.

Where was Molly?

Kearney made for Dominic, an ugly look on his face and his gloved hands in fists. He was Sloane's witch, so he'd be able to recharge the hexes between strikes.

Tom stepped between them, his own fists up and ready. "Back off, Kearney, and maybe the judge will go easy on you," he said, hoping he sounded confident.

Kearney only sneered. "You don't know what you're dealing with. And you'll be dead before you find out."

Tom swung a fist of his own. Kearney turned his shoulder, catching the brunt of it. Agony exploded in Tom's side, and he staggered from the amplified force of Kearney's punch. The pain brought tears to his eyes, and through their haze, he glimpsed a shadow angling for his head.

He dropped to the floor, and it passed harmlessly above. Before Kearney could swing again, Tom rammed a shoulder into his legs, sending him to the ground.

Kearney swore, and they both scrambled to their feet. Tom hurled himself at Kearney, grappling with the man, trying to grip his forearms. Sweat ran into his mouth, his and Kearney's alike. He felt the hexes vibrating, and silenced both with a burst of power.

Kearney wrenched one hand free and dropped it to the knife

sheathed at his waist. Tom let go fast, trying to put distance between them.

A gunshot rang out, loud in the confines of the room. Kearney went down, blood spreading across the back of his coat. "Got you," Bill said with satisfaction.

Sloane roared, a sound of pain and anguish that rattled Tom's teeth. His tail swept in a great arc, sending friend and foe alike off their feet.

"Shit!" Bill shouted, and fired again. His shot lodged itself in Sloane's body, but the familiar didn't even seem to feel it.

Bill tried to get out of reach of the snapping jaws, but Sloane followed him, intent on the kill. Praying he wasn't about to find himself in the crocodile's teeth, Tom scooped up the knife that had fallen from Kearney's hand. As Sloane's head whipped to the left, tracking Bill, Tom flung himself on the scaly shoulders.

Sloane arched his head back, but couldn't reach Tom. Tom tightened his legs around Sloane's neck and drove the knife into the base of his skull with all of his strength.

The enormous body convulsed once beneath him…then went still.

The wolf lay unmoving, mauled by Greta's sharp teeth. Her jaws closed on the snake, just behind its head, with a loud crunch. Rook alighted on the ground and resumed human form.

The door to the cage sprang open beneath Dominic's hex. Cicero burst out—and made straight for Tom.

Tom barely had time to react before a human Cicero leapt into his arms. Cicero's legs twined around Tom's waist, sending a spike of pain through him where they pressed against the bruises Kearney had left behind. Then Cicero's lips were on his, and he forgot about everything else.

The kiss was hard and desperate; Tom felt Cicero's teeth through their lips. Then Cicero pulled back, hands cupping Tom's face. Tears streaked the already-smeared kohl around his eyes. "Mio caro," he breathed. "You're alive."

"I am." Over Cicero's shoulder, Tom caught sight of Bill staring at them in shock, his mouth agape.

"Don't stare. It's rude," Greta said, poking Bill on the arm. Bill blinked and turned away.

"How are you not dead?" Cicero stroked Tom's cheek, almost reverently. "The bond broke—I felt it! Noah said he'd sent men to kill you!"

Tom winced. "I'm sorry. I didn't mean to frighten you." He let

Cicero slip to his feet. "Of course I didn't mean to hurt you before, neither, and look what a mess I made of that. I used my hexbreaking to sever the bond."

Cicero's gemstone eyes grew clouded. "You did? But…why?"

"Because you deserve a happy life." Tom carefully brushed a lock of hair from Cicero's forehead, patting it back into place. "You deserve a better witch—a better man—than I'll ever be. After all the pain I caused you, the least I could do was give you that chance."

"I don't want anyone else." Cicero swallowed and blinked rapidly. "I want you, amore. I love you so much."

Tom's heart swelled against his ribs. "Oh God, I love you, too."

"Bond with me again, Thomas. Please?"

"Despite everything?" Tom took his hands carefully and noted his own were shaking. "I should never have lied to you, and I'm sorrier than I can say. I've no right to ask your forgiveness."

"You were a fool," Cicero agreed.

Tom snorted. "Thanks."

"But so was I. Less of one, obviously, but I still lashed out instead of thinking things through." He tightened his grip on Tom's hands. "I wouldn't have been so angry if I didn't love you. But I understand why you kept your secret, and…well. To get to the point, I want to be your familiar again. No matter what comes."

Tom took a deep breath…then nodded. "Aye. Then let's do it."

It was done in a matter of moments—a quick look through Cicero's eyes, then a fast charging of a hexlight. Back in human form, Cicero put his hand to his chest and offered Tom a tearful smile. "Feels better, doesn't it?" he asked.

Tom grinned. "Yeah."

"Your timing is atrocious," Rook said. He poked Cicero in the back. "We've still got a job to do. Was the hawk familiar here? Molly? Any others?"

"Sorry, sorry." Cicero wiped his eyes, then shook himself. When he straightened his back, his expression was somber. "She was. And Anselm! He's—"

"A traitor, yes, we know that part," Rook interrupted. "Who else?"

"Noah's involved. He's the one who kidnapped me. He's the witch who was stripping Isaac to make the Viking hexes. He and Molly left together. He said they were going to a party—I assume something to do with the New Year's Eve celebration. But I don't know what they mean to do there."

Dominic and Yates had maneuvered the mastiff out of the cage. It lifted its massive head—then shifted into a thin man. Dark, overlong hair tumbled into his gaunt face, and his eyes were bruised and sunken. "I know," he said, voice cracking as though he hadn't used it in months. "I know exactly what they intend to do."

CHAPTER 26

CICERO RAN TO Isaac's side. He slipped his arms around Isaac's too-thin form, helping him to sit. "What do you need, darling?" he asked.

"Water, please," Isaac grated.

Rook hurried to the pitcher atop the liquor cabinet, and soon returned with a glass of clean water. He held it to Isaac's lips while he drank.

"Thank you." Isaac leaned heavily back against Cicero, unable to sit up on his own. "I overheard…not everything, but a great deal. They didn't dare speak too freely in front of me, just in case Noah was watching through my eyes, but sometimes they let things slip."

"What do you mean?" Dominic asked. "Isn't Noah part of the scheme?"

Isaac's mouth tightened. "It's easier if I explain from the beginning. I knew Noah from Techne, of course. He helped me get the job at the Rooster after…"

Cicero stroked his hair. "And once you went to work there?"

"After a few weeks, Sloane introduced me to Molly. I guess he thought he knew me well enough to trust me by then." Isaac's attempt at a wry chuckle turned into a racking cough.

Fur and feathers, when Cicero got his hands on Noah, he'd make him sorry he'd ever set foot in New York.

Isaac accepted some more water. When he could speak again, he said, "I thought they were just anarchists, at first. Talking about the rights of workers and women and the lot. But it was more than that. They want to establish a theriarchy."

Owen frowned. "Rule by beasts?"

"Familiars."

Cicero returned to stroking Isaac's hair. "I've always said the world would be better if I were in charge."

"Don't joke, cat," Isaac said. His eyes slipped closed. "I don't know who Molly is working for, but this is big. They want to subjugate everyone who isn't a familiar or witch. And even the witches had best stay in line, because there are always more of them than there are familiars. Sloane and Molly thought I'd be sympathetic to their cause. But it's too extreme. I tried to distance myself. I had to warn someone, so I talked it over with Gerald, tried to convince him to come to the Coven with me. He refused—he didn't want to get involved with the MWP. I was going to try once more to convince him to come with me, the night I was supposed to meet you, Cicero. But someone must have talked—maybe Gerald went to Noah for advice, I don't know. I was getting ready to leave the Rooster and go to Gerald's apartment, when Sloane called me into his office. They were waiting with a hex to force me into animal form." Isaac shuddered in Cicero's arms. "Noah..."

"Shh." Cicero cradled him closer. "It's over now."

"Not so long as Noah has Isaac to draw from," Greta said.

Tom crouched beside them. "I can try to break the bond, if you want."

"Isaac is too weak," Owen objected. "It would kill him."

"And if Noah siphons more magic from him?" Tom challenged. "Won't that kill him anyway? And maybe others as well, depending on what he has planned?"

Isaac reached out and grabbed Tom's hand. "You can break the bond?"

Tom hesitated. "I did before," he said carefully. "Between Cicero and me. I don't know for sure if I can do it with you, but I can try."

"Do it, then." Isaac shook his head when Owen made to protest. "Even if it kills me, it's better than letting Noah use me ever again."

Cicero hugged Isaac more tightly, but it was his decision. Tom crouched in front of them. "I'm going to touch you," he told Isaac. "And...I'm sorry, but this is probably going to hurt."

"I don't care," Isaac said. "But let me finish—just in case it kills me. Noah and Molly were on their way to city hall."

"Cazzo," Cicero swore. "Thousands of people will be there for the consolidation ceremony. Not to mention the new mayor, delegates from every major city, the rest of the crowd from Techne…"

No.

His gaze met Tom's in a moment of perfect, horrified accord. "The modified Viking hexes," Tom said. "What do they do on their own? Before the second part of the hex is taken?"

"They make you feel good. Fearless. Not reckless, necessarily, or aggressive." Isaac swallowed convulsively. "Noah took absinthe hexes with him, when he left with Molly. So I assume he already gave the others out."

"Fur and feathers," Cicero whispered. "Noah's 'surprise' at the Christmas party. He must have given them out there."

Tom's eyes widened. "So if we'd stayed—"

"The bloody case would have been solved then, yes." Cicero ground his teeth together. "My friends from Techne. Noah's using them without their knowledge. The midnight toast will turn them all into homicidal madmen, right in the middle of the crowd."

"Then there's no time to waste." Tom leaned forward and put his hand on Isaac's chest.

Isaac screamed, a horrible, thin sound. His body convulsed once beneath Tom's touch—then went still in Cicero's arms.

"Isaac?" Cicero shook him. "Isaac?" Oh God, if severing the bond had killed him after all…

Isaac's eyelids fluttered slightly, and he moaned.

Relief swamped Cicero, and he kissed his friend's forehead. They weren't out of the woods yet, but at least he'd done this. Saved Isaac.

Greta let out an impatient growl. "We need to go."

"I'll look after Isaac," Owen offered.

The policeman knelt on Isaac's other side. "I'll help. We'll get him to the nearest precinct and use the telephone there to spread the warning." He glanced at Cicero. "Name's Bill Quigley, by the way."

"Cicero. I'm Thomas's familiar." It felt good to say that.

Quigley blushed. "Aye, I gathered."

Owen took Isaac from Cicero. As they made their way to the tunnel entrance, Dominic caught Cicero's elbow. "Here," he said, holding out something that gleamed silver. "Athene gave this to me after you quit. Do you want it back?"

Cicero's familiar's badge lay in Dominic's hand. He reached for it, then hesitated, glancing at Tom.

"Go ahead," Tom said. "You've earned it."

The metal was warm against Cicero's fingers as he pinned it to his vest. "All right. Let's go save my friends."

The sky spat a mixture of rain and snow as Tom raced along Cherry Street, Cicero clinging to his shoulders in cat form. Rook had flown to the Battery to warn Ferguson, leaving Tom, Dominic, Greta, and Cicero to make their way on foot. What they hoped to do, Tom had only the vaguest idea. A significant portion of the regular police were already at city hall and along the route of the procession, attempting to keep the boisterous crowds under control. No one would be able to spread word of the plot to them before midnight—and even if they did, how were they to pick out the bohemians among the crowd?

The entire southern end of Manhattan was pandemonium. Fireworks filled the sky with a mixture of lights and advertisements. A rocket set off from atop the Pulitzer building burst to form *Read the Journal!* in shining gold letters against the clouds. A moment later, a competing rocket exploded nearby, adding the word *Don't* to the beginning of the ad and *Read the Sun instead!* after.

Dominic let out an oath. "Rook just spoke to me. He says Chief Ferguson was never warned about Anselm, or the ongoing plot, or any of it."

Which meant either the officer on duty or—more likely—the familiar entrusted to take the message was a traitor. Which didn't bode well for the MWP…but there was nothing they could do about it now.

"I've told him to fly straight to the mayor," Dominic went on. "But he's all the way down at the Battery, along with the rest of the MWP familiars. I don't know if he'll make it before midnight. Especially with all the damned fireworks going off around him."

"Then it's up to us," Tom said, his heart sinking as he surveyed the scene in front of them.

The seething crowd packed the streets. Men, women, and children all braved the cold to bring in the New Year and the new New York. They blew tin whistles, waved signs, and flung paper streamers into the air. Lines of patrolmen had condensed the gathering as far as possible, until the celebrants were wedged into the streets around city hall like sardines in a can. Easier for the police as they didn't have to stretch as thin, but the wall of bodies would be impossible to get through on foot.

They couldn't make it to city hall in time.

"Look!" Dominic grabbed Tom's arm. "Mounted police."

It was probably their only chance. They fought their way through the crowd, Dominic waving his MWP badge above his head, trying to get the attention of the mounted officers. One of them spotted Dominic, then nudged his compatriot, but they did nothing to clear the way.

Of all the times for the rivalry between forces to come into play, this was surely one of the worst.

"Officer!" Tom bellowed, trying to make himself heard over the crowd, fireworks, and mortar barrage. "Patrolman Tom Halloran, on temporary assignment with the Metropolitan Witch Police!" Not strictly accurate, but at this point one more lie hardly made a difference. "We've uncovered an anarchist plot and need your help!"

The mounted police exchanged uncertain looks. "What, the MWP wants us to lend a hand?" one asked with an arched brow.

Cicero slid from Tom's shoulders, shifting on the way down. The horses ignored him, but the officers startled. "We don't have time for a pissing contest!" Cicero shouted as soon as he was in human form again. "The plot will go off at midnight, and things are going to get very ugly. We need to reach the mayor and have him stop the festivities, or these streets are going to be red with blood."

The mounted police exchanged surprised looks. "All right," one said. "Get up behind, and we'll take you there."

Tom scrambled up behind one of the officers, clinging to the saddle as best he could. The horses surged forward, threatening to trample anyone in their way. Those who didn't move quick enough were subject to the riders' nightsticks, and Tom winced at the crack of bone and cries of pain.

Even so, the press of bodies was simply too thick for them to move with any haste. A large platform had been erected on the steps of city hall, with seating for various delegates. As the clock inched closer to midnight, the mayor-to-be rose and lifted one hand. In the other he held a glass of champagne.

"The time is upon us!" he said, his magically-amplified voice booming out over the crowd. "In less than a minute, Brooklyn, East Bronx, Queens County, and Staten Island will join together with New York City, and we shall stand as one! Ten...nine..."

The crowd took up the chant, voices roaring so loud even the fireworks were momentarily drowned out.

"Eight...seven..."

"Tom!" Cicero leaned over from behind the mounted officer beside him. "Look! On the platform! He was at Noah's Christmas party. Auggie."

The madly colored light from fireworks and streamers shone on the faces of the delegates. And there, not a few feet from the mayor, sat the young man who'd been so eager to brag about being his cousin. Auggie's eyes shone with excitement, and he held a glass of green liquid in one hand and a hex in the other.

They were almost at the city hall steps now. "Mayor Van Wyck!" Tom shouted, but there was no chance of being heard over the thunder of the crowd.

"One!" Mayor Van Wyck held up his glass in a toast. "To the City of Greater New York!"

He drained his glass, as did the rest of the delegates, and Mary only knew how many in the crowd.

And the screaming began.

Tom slid from the horse and shoved his way through the police line to the steps. "Let them through!" the mounted officer yelled, and the police gave way.

Too late. Even from a distance, he saw the whites of Auggie's eyes go scarlet with blood. The glass fell from his hand to shatter on the marble. Froth beaded on his lips—and with an unholy shriek, he launched himself at the mayor.

Van Wyck went down, Auggie's teeth biting madly at his coat, nails tearing at his face. Tom reached the platform, grabbed Auggie's collar, and heaved him off. "Run!" Tom bellowed at the mayor as Auggie twisted and shrieked in his hands. "Barricade yourself in city hall, and don't come out until the MWP tells you it's safe!"

Then he had no more attention to spare. Auggie turned on him, slavering, teeth snapping. Tom shouted and fought to keep him off, keep those teeth from his flesh, even as the maddened young man ripped nails across Tom's face.

It was Danny all over again.

Greta shifted to wolverine form and sank her teeth into Auggie's calf. The young man didn't even blink, as though he felt no pain, felt nothing beyond the need to rend. Tom had to break the hex—but doing so would surely kill Auggie, whose only crime had been trusting Noah.

It had to be done. Just as it had to be done all those years ago, when it had been his brother's maddened face glaring into his.

Auggie suddenly went slack. Startled, Tom let him fall to the platform. Dominic stood there, hex in hand.

"It won't keep him out for long," Dominic said, gesturing to Auggie's prone body. "But at least it will give us a respite."

Cicero clutched Tom's arm and pointed. "God. Look. We have to do something."

The crowd had gone from celebratory to panicked. Screams filled the air, and Tom caught sight of knots of struggling people amidst the press. Those on the edges fled, and the whole mass of humanity began to stampede. Uniformed police laid about them with their nightsticks, but there were too many terrified people, and soon they'd been knocked over or swept away.

"Greta, try to help the regular police if you can," Dominic ordered. She took off down the stairs, and the crowd blocked her from their sight in seconds.

Above, the fireworks continued to go off in tremendous blasts, the pyrotechnicians atop the tall buildings unaware of the disaster unfolding so far below. The sky was choked with streams of colored fire, burning like a host of new suns. Amidst the smoke and the flame, something moved.

"Rook!" shouted Dominic, pointing. "He's coming this way!"

As Rook crossed above the small park opposite city hall, a dark shape arrowed out of the sky and struck him.

Molly.

Dominic screamed, a sound of pain and horror. Rook tumbled from the sky, disappearing into the shadows of the park, and Molly followed him down.

CHAPTER 27

TOM RACED ACROSS the street to the park, dodging the remains of the disintegrating crowd as best he could. His feet slipped in blood, and he leapt over a motionless body. Cicero took cat form and streaked ahead of him, his black fur lost amidst shadows that jumped and shifted with each explosion overhead. The air stank of fear and gun powder, and concussive blasts shook the air as the guns on the Battery added their salute to the new city.

Red, white, and blue paper tape hung from the trees of the park, streaming in the wind. Fire flickered amidst the branches, from lanterns either dropped or thrown by the panicking crowd. Smoke began to drift into the air like an unnatural fog. Sheet music lay crumpled in the park's grass, and a platform similar to the one on the steps of city hall stood not far from the street.

Noah stood in front of the platform, holding something dark in his arms.

"Rook!" Dominic shouted.

"Not another step further." Noah's eyes were narrowed into slits, his lips pulled back from his teeth. Rook's wings flapped weakly, and he tightened his grip on the crow's neck. "Come any closer, and I'll twist his fucking head off."

Tom froze, as did Dominic. Dominic's face was white with fear, and he half-raised a hand, as if to stay Noah. "Please," he said, then fell silent.

Noah ignored him, his gaze fixed on Tom. "How the hell are you still alive? Are you literally too stupid to die? Or was it all a trick—did Cicero only pretend the bond was severed, so he could lead you to the tunnels?" His hand flexed on Rook's neck. "He should have been an actor instead of a dancer."

Tom held up his own hands. "Let Rook go." He was painfully aware of his heart beating in his chest, of Dominic silent and afraid beside him. He couldn't see Cicero, but he could feel his familiar's presence, moving through the shadows.

Stalking.

"If you want a hostage, take me," Tom went on. Keeping Noah's attention fixed on him. "Think about it, Noah. You'd rather have me at your mercy than Rook, surely."

"Tempting. But he's easier to control." Noah took a step back. "I'll just have to take satisfaction from knowing you'll be dead soon enough, along with your treacherous whore of a familiar." His eyes widened suddenly. "Where is—"

A black shape exploded from the branches of the nearest tree, launching itself directly at Noah's head.

Noah instinctively let go of Rook, raising his hands to protect his face. But he was just a moment too slow, and he let out a startled scream as Cicero's claws and teeth sank in.

"Get Rook out of here!" Tom shouted, although he doubted Dominic needed the encouragement. Dominic scooped Rook up, cradling the injured crow to his chest. Then he ran back the way they'd come.

Noah had fallen to the ground; Cicero shifted back to human form and straddled his chest. The fire was drawing nearer, and smoke billowed wildly around them, accompanied by floating ash.

Cicero's fingers locked around Noah's throat, and his yellow-green eyes reflected the flames. "Fottuto bastardo," he snarled into Noah's reddening face, "te ne pentirai—"

"Cicero, stop!" Tom grabbed Cicero's shoulder.

Cicero hissed but released Noah. As Noah heaved in great gasps of air, Tom seized him by the collar and hauled him to his feet. Blood streaked Noah's face, leaking from deep punctures in his forehead, cheek, and chin, and his left eye had swelled shut.

"Please, don't kill me!" Noah cried. He looked utterly terrified, all his sneering bravado gone now that the situation had turned against him.

Tom gave him a hard shake. He wasn't going to kill Noah in cold blood—but Noah obviously didn't know that. "Give me one good reason not to," he growled.

"I know things," Noah babbled, his one good eye rolling wildly. "About the ones who planned all this. The ones who are pulling Molly's strings. I can tell you—"

There came the loud crack of a gunshot. A spray of warm, wet blood struck Tom in the face. Noah went limp, half his head gone.

Tom let out a cry of horror and disgust and let the body fall. "Tom!" Cicero shouted in warning, and Tom wrenched his gaze from the dead man to find himself looking into Molly's eyes.

The flaming streamers sent sparks through the air, and smoke rippled as she passed through it. In her hand, she held a gun, which she lifted and pointed at him. "Such a disappointment, Liam," she said.

Cicero stepped to his side, so they stood shoulder-to-shoulder. "His name is Tom."

Despite the fear gripping him, Tom felt a flash of gratitude. Molly tossed her head, hair streaming like the fire behind her.

"All I see is two traitors," she said. "One to his family, and the other to his kind. Tell me, cat, how long did you have left before the witches pressured you into bonding with one of them? Or was a cozy bed and hot meals enough for you to whore out your magic?"

"At least I'm not a murderer," Cicero replied, his voice steady, though Tom could feel him trembling.

"What are a few deaths in exchange for a new age? The time of the witches is over. *We* are in the ascendant now. Too bad you won't live to see it."

Tom stepped forward, putting himself in front of Cicero. "Molly, don't."

Her aim shifted slightly, the bore pointing right between his eyes. "You should have stayed dead, Liam."

Two shapes burst from the thick smoke and collided with Molly. Cicero shoved Tom, hard, and he stumbled to one knee even as the roar of the gun sounded.

Molly screamed. Two maddened shapes crouched over her—the woman, Leona, her eyes bloody and her suit torn to shreds, accompanied by the man who had been painting the nude model in Noah's apartment. Molly swung her pistol at Leona's head, attempting to use the heavy steel as a bludgeon.

Leona's teeth sank into Molly's arm. Molly shrieked in pain, thrashing wildly, but the two hexed attackers ignored her struggles and pinned her to the ground.

Tom staggered to his feet. He had to go to Molly—had to break the hexes on Leona and her companion, even though it would kill them.

Molly's scream ended in a wet gurgle as the man sank his teeth into her throat.

"Molly," he said dumbly.

She would have killed them—had been responsible for the deaths of innocents tonight, and probably before. She'd let Isaac be tortured because it fit her purposes. And yet he felt oddly hollow.

He'd thought her gone for so many years. Believed he was the only one who remembered Danny, and Da, and Ma, and the rest. She might have been his enemy, but they'd been close, once, and he'd never wanted her dead.

Cicero grabbed Tom's arm, pulling at him. Smoke billowed more thickly around them now, fragments of burning paper tape falling like rain. "It's too late!" he shouted. "We have to get out of here!"

Tom drew breath to answer, but ended up with a lungful of smoke instead. His eyes stung and streamed, and a burning branch fell from a tree, dangerously close to Cicero.

"Aye," he managed to gasp.

Together they ran from the park. Once they were in the free air again, Tom halted, taking gasps of the cold night wind and wiping tears and soot from his face. Cicero was filthy, Noah's blood on his mouth and beneath his nails, his hair disarranged and his skin covered with ash and dirt.

"Are you all right?" Tom asked, when he could speak without coughing.

Cicero nodded. His smoke-reddened eyes went to something over Tom's shoulder, and he stiffened. "We're not out of it yet."

Tom turned to peer down the street. Screams and shouts sounded from all directions, and he saw a man desperately fighting to hold off two victims of the Viking curse. "We have to help him. Help as many as we can."

There came the sound of footsteps behind them. Tom turned quickly, half afraid they were about to be set upon themselves. Ferguson and Yates jogged out of the billowing smoke. Ferguson wore his dress uniform, but it was smeared with blood and filth. "Halloran!" Ferguson barked. "That is, O'Connell. Can you break the hex?"

"I'd rather Halloran, if it's all the same to you, sir," Tom said, though he had no claim to the name. "And aye. I don't see why not."

Cicero's eyes widened. "But they'll die! Tom, they're innocent! They didn't know what Noah gave them. Leona…"

Was probably already dead, given the fiery blaze consuming the park. Tom wanted to pull Cicero into his arms, to shield him from the world. To give him a safe place to mourn.

But there would be a great many more to mourn before this was over.

"A lot more people will die if we don't stop them," Ferguson said. "Come along, you two. We're going to—"

"Breaking the hexes one at a time seems inefficient," Yates interrupted. "More people will be injured in the meantime."

Ferguson frowned. "Do you have a better suggestion, doctor?"

"Two, in fact." Yates turned to Tom. "If you had one of the hexes in hand, do you think you could use its resonance to get a sense of the others? Destroy them all at once, using Cicero's magic to boost your native ability?"

"Devil if I know," Tom said honestly. "I broke a bunch at once in the warehouse, but they were all packed in together. Not spread out like this."

Cicero bristled. "You mean kill them all at once? No. I won't be party to the murder of my friends. Not without at least trying something else first."

"Do you think I wanted to kill my brother?" Tom demanded. "Or my da? He tore off my ma's face!" Tom pressed his hands to his eyes, as if he could blot out the memory. "Your friends ain't been out there drinking tea. They're monsters now, and I'm damned sorry for it."

"I know." Cicero's voice was soft, and he leaned his slender body against Tom's. "But there has to be another way."

"There ain't!"

"There might be, if you'd let me finish," Yates snapped. Startled, Tom dropped his hands. "The original hex, yes, you're no doubt quite right when you say there was nothing else to be done. But when it comes to the chained hex, there might be a way around it. If you were to break only the second part of the chain—the absinthe hex—it might return them to the state they were in before. Any effects of the modified Viking hex would still be active, but they wouldn't be murderous killers."

Could it work? Tom glanced at Cicero's hopeful face. "Then they won't die?"

"In theory." Yates took a hex from his pouch and handed it to Tom. "Here is the absinthe hex. Concentrate on it, on any hexes like it, and break them using the power Cicero gives you."

Tom hesitated. "Would that even work?"

"Of course it will work." Cicero folded his hand over Tom's. "I'm Cicero the cat, and you're my witch. We can do anything."

Tom almost wanted to laugh. "No one ever said you were modest. But this is big. Bigger than any magic we've done yet." He hesitated. "I ain't going to be like Noah, hurting you for your magic."

Cicero's green eyes seemed to glow in the night. The fireworks had at last ceased, and it seemed they stood alone in a small bubble of peace amidst the chaos. "I know." He smiled. "I trust you, Thomas. And you can trust me." His grip tightened gently. "We'll always keep each other safe."

Tom nodded, afraid his voice would break if he spoke aloud. Instead, he focused on the hex in front of him.

It vibrated like a plucked string, or a fast-beating heart. His awareness of it sharpened, and he knew he could break it with ease.

But he needed more.

Magic flowed, like a river of light, like a second heartbeat nestled against his own. His awareness expanded, and he could feel other vibrations against his skin, even though they were nowhere near him. He pushed, farther and farther, found more and more of them...until there were no more to find.

Then he stilled their song.

"It worked!" Yates shouted, almost in his ear.

Shocked, Tom opened eyes he didn't remember closing. At the end of the road, the hex victims had ceased their attack. Instead, they stood clutching each other in shock, eyes wide with terror as their erstwhile prey fled.

"I told you," Cicero said. Then his eyes rolled back in his head, and he collapsed into Tom's arms.

CHAPTER 28

"JUST LOOK AT you," Cicero said from his perch on the edge of their new desk in the detectives' area. "All official with your shiny badge."

Tom glanced up from the silver Witch Police badge he'd been examining. A slow grin spread over his features. "Aye. But I'll miss my big stick."

The smile made Cicero's heart beat faster, just as it always had. "Just be sure you keep the uniform, darling," he said with a wink.

It had been two weeks since the New Year's Eve celebration. The number of dead and wounded had been less than feared. Mainly thanks to Tom and him, of course.

Even so, it had taken a while for the MWP to figure out exactly what to do with Tom. He was a wanted criminal, thanks to his involvement in the Cherry Street Riots...and at the same time, the new mayor meant to pin a medal on him for heroism.

In the end, Ferguson had taken what seemed the simplest course of action. The official story was that Tom Halloran had been the victim of mistaken identity. Liam O'Connell was confirmed dead these last eight years, his picture removed from the rogues gallery, and his files mysteriously gone missing.

As for the violence and mayhem at the celebration, one part of Molly's plan was coming to fruition. She'd meant to pin everything on the anarchists, and, in the absence of anyone else to take the blame, that had indeed happened. An extensive search of the tunnels beneath Cherry and Water Streets had turned up no sign of the other familiars who had worked with her, and no hint of the conspiracy she'd been involved with. As for the traitors within the MWP itself…

Perhaps there had only been two. More likely, others lurked within their ranks. Waiting to strike a blow for their cause.

Theriarchy.

Tom tilted his head slightly. "What's wrong?"

"Just thinking that ruling the world sounded a lot better in my head." Cicero admitted. "If the theriarchists had approached me before I met you…I'd like to think I wouldn't have joined them, of course." He swung his legs idly, heels thumping the side of the desk. "But if Ferguson had tried to force me to make a decision, pick a witch even though I wasn't ready…I don't know."

"Well, there's the problem," Tom said as he arranged notepads, pencils, and a small calendar atop their desk. "You wouldn't be the one in charge. It would be people like Molly."

"You're absolutely right, darling." Cicero slipped off the desk and stretched. "Rule by cats, that's what we really need. My first decree would be for more naps."

"And the second for cream fountains in all public buildings," said Rook.

Cicero sighed dramatically. "So much for the peace and quiet." In truth, though, it was a relief to see Rook back on his feet. Rook's face was thinner, but his brown skin had lost the awful grayish hue it had the first few days, when they'd visited him in the hospital.

Dominic was thinner as well, the lines more deeply graven in his face. "Got your badge, then?" he asked, peering over Tom's shoulder.

"Aye." Tom held it up, but didn't move to pin it on.

"Isaac is due to be released in a few days as well," Rook said. He leaned on a cane as he made his way to the desk he and Dominic shared, not far from Tom and Cicero's. "Now that I'm gone, he'll be lonely. You should go say hello."

"Good idea." Cicero reached for his coat. "It's been a day or two. I'm sure he's languishing from my absence."

They left the Coven, but Tom seemed in no particular hurry to get to the hospital. Cicero wasn't either. He fell in by Tom, walking close enough that their elbows brushed. A mixture of snow and rain drizzled from the sky, much as it had on New Year's Eve. The bleak weather had driven as many people inside as could manage it, and left Mulberry Street less crowded than usual.

"What's wrong?" Cicero asked when they'd gone a few blocks without speaking.

Tom's breath steamed in the freezing air. "I don't know. I suppose... I've spent so much of my life looking over my shoulder, afraid of my past catching up to me. I don't know what to do now that I don't have to worry about it any more."

"How about enjoy your life?" Cicero suggested. "If you need some suggestions on how to accomplish that, by the way, I'll be happy to provide them."

It brought a reluctant grin to Tom's face. "I'm sure you will. Let's wait until we get home tonight, though."

A few days ago, they'd found an apartment in a tenement occupied mainly by other witch and familiar pairs, where no one would so much as glance at them twice. It was small, but it was theirs, and that was the important thing.

Tom took the new badge out of his pocket and turned it slowly over in his hands. "Truth is, I can't help but wonder if I really deserve this."

Cicero sighed. "Of course you do. *We* do. We stopped Molly and Sloane. We broke the Viking hexes without killing the victims. You personally saved the new mayor's life, in case you've forgotten."

"But whoever was behind it all...really behind it, I mean...is still out there." Tom ran his thumb across the face of the badge, as if memorizing the feel of the engravings. "Noah said someone else was behind all of it. Giving the orders and pulling the strings. Other theriarchists, I'd guess."

"You worry too much." Cicero plucked the badge from Tom's hands. "Open your coat."

Tom did so. "There." Cicero pinned the badge to his vest. "Yes, there are still bad people in New York City who don't mean any of us well. I doubt you managed to apprehend every last criminal in your old precinct either. Did you throw in the badge because of that, or did you keep coming in, day after day, walking your beat and making sure you protected those you could?"

Tom's smile came easier now. "You're right."

"Of course I am, amore." Cicero patted Tom's coat closed again. "You've done a lot of good on your own in this city. So, shall we go visit Isaac, then see what good we can do together?"

The warmth in Tom's blue eyes set his heart to soaring. "Aye. Nothing I'd like better."

"Excellent. Then I can stop subjecting myself to this damp sidewalk." Tom's coat made it an easy climb to his shoulder. Cicero draped around the back of his neck, tail curling in front like a narrow black scarf. Tom's chuckle rumbled up through his broad shoulders.

"Love you, cat," he said, scratching Cicero under the chin. Then he put his hands in his pockets, and they headed into the city together.

SHARE YOUR EXPERIENCE

If you enjoyed this book, please consider leaving a review on the site where you purchased it, or on Goodreads.

Thank you for your support of independent authors!

Author's Note

HUGE THANKS TO Kikka for help with Cicero's Italian! Any mistakes herein are solely my own.

The consolidation of New York was a real event, which took place January 1, 1898. In our world, the celebration was a peaceful one.

"Little Egypt" brought belly-dancing into the national consciousness during the 1893 World's Columbian Exhibition in Chicago. After her success, the "hoochie coochie" replaced the can-can as *the* scandalous dance in America (although of course both continued to be performed). Hoping to take advantage of the original's fame, scads of belly dancers calling themselves "Little Egypt" cropped up over the next decade, with varying degrees of talent and success.

Although the beliefs of the anarchists seem very modern, they were in fact espoused by multiple groups throughout the period. Free love, easy divorce, marriage between any consenting couple, equality of the races, and the vote for women were all argued for passionately and openly. These were no secret discussions; many groups had their own newspapers, distributed as widely as they could afford (which often was not very).

On that note, The Spitting Rooster is loosely based on several Bleecker Street resorts of the 1890s which catered specifically to gay men. These functioned not only as brothels, but as a sort of social club. Additionally, although middle and upper class neighborhoods had the space and privacy to retain a division between "respectable" life and "vice," such luxuries were not available in the lower and working class areas. Hence the sight of male prostitutes and "fairies" on the street was simply a part of every day life in places like the Bowery. For more information, I recommend the first chapters of *Gay New York* by George Chauncey as an excellent starting point.

About The Author

Jordan L. Hawk grew up in North Carolina and forgot to ever leave. Childhood tales of mountain ghosts and mysterious creatures gave her a life-long love of things that go bump in the night. When she isn't writing, she brews her own beer and tries to keep her cats from destroying the house. Her best-selling Whyborne & Griffin series (beginning with *Widdershins*) can be found in print, ebook, and audiobook.

If you're interested in receiving Jordan's newsletter and being the first to know when new books are released, plus getting sneak peeks at upcoming novels, please sign up at her website:

http://www.jordanlhawk.com

Made in the USA
Charleston, SC
03 February 2017